TOUGH
CHOICES

TOUGH CHOICES

AN AMISH ROMANCE

STEPPING STONES
BOOK THREE

LINDA BYLER

Good Books

New York, New York

TOUGH
CHOICES

CHAPTER 1

Dawn was heralded by the chirping of birds, accompanied by a lilting warble, then the shrill cawing of the flapping crow on top of the walnut tree beside the small brown house. The first rays of the sun brought out the orange edges of the green leaves on the sugar maple and revealed the frost on the low-lying areas in the pasture.

The oval indentation on the fir tree was filled with the bright-eyed face of a gray squirrel who'd woken to another fresh morning with things to see, places to go. Beside the small barn, Honey stood on all fours evenly, her pleasant eyes half closed. Among the hills and hollows, Amish farmers quickened their step, hoisted stainless steel milkers, spread fresh shavings for the driving horses, sang snatches of the "Lob Lied" to practice song leading for Sunday morning. Housewives drew a Maytag wringer washer of steaming hot water, added Tide, and yanked on the Honda engine's rope, then stood back with satisfaction as the agitator came to life, producing instant soap bubbles.

In the little brown house over on the north ridge, Mary Glick stood in the first sunlight, her dress covering the nightgown underneath, her dark red hair in tendrils of disarray, a *dichly* tied haphazardly, but a cloth covering her head. Otherwise, she would have no power to pray, or so she had been taught. Those first rays through the kitchen window revealed the red veins crosshatched on the whites of her eyes, the tender, swollen lids, the desperate gleam from the depths of her green eyes.

Mary had dozed intermittently, paced the floor, gone from her bed to her recliner and back again, while her visitor from Pennsylvania slept soundly in the guest room.

What was a person to do? How did one go about deciphering the will of God?

Their conversation had been stilted, awkward, after her initial outburst of tears, the story of Bennie Lapp's proposal, the color draining visibly from Steve's face. They'd attempted a conversation, with fits and starts, but every avenue resulted in a dead end. Steve could not believe she'd even entertained the idea of marrying this stranger with eight kids, and was hurt and angry and concerned all at once. Mary defended herself by saying Steve hadn't come to visit when promised, so she'd assumed he'd lost interest. And besides, they'd only ever really been friends.

Now here he was, larger than life, and she suddenly entangled in the life of Bennie Lapp and his eight children. Her stomach rolled; a bitter taste rose in her throat. She longed for her father's presence, a solid form whose words she could follow. Had he actually been right to dispose of all the men in her life, because she was meant to be the wife of a widower in need? Had the Holy Spirit led her father?

She lifted the top of the coffee maker, then sniffed with appreciation. She had to talk to Steve, honestly and openly, since it felt as if all avenues of prayer were not accessible, as if they were closed for construction. God was like that. So far away so much of the time.

She poured the steaming brew, added half-and-half and a dollop of maple syrup, and held the thick mug in both hands as she carried it to the living room window, a wide swath of forested driveway and sloping hill before her, the opposite mountain bathed in the first light of the rising sun, creating a rich tapestry of emerging tints of autumn. She loved this scene, these three low windows revealing the whole Pinedale Valley in New York, the home of her childhood.

Decisions were tough, but she would take her time. She would not allow Steve to persuade her of anything. The first sip of the perfect cup of coffee heartened her resolve, and she squared her shoulders, took a deep breath.

"Good morning, Mary."

She jumped, felt a warm splash of coffee.

"Oh. Yes, good morning to you."

"Have you slept well?"

He was all heavy-lidded eyes, tousled blond hair and white teeth, the embodiment of the one she had carried in her head for so long. But not yet her heart. She met his eyes, his proving, questioning gaze, and thought, *no, no, not yet.*

His eyes fell away, slid down by the force of his disappointment.

"No, not really," she mumbled, suddenly ashamed.

He nodded, then turned abruptly and went to the kitchen, opening cabinet doors as he searched for a mug, pouring coffee. Mary joined him at the kitchen table but kept her eyes averted, chattering rapidly about the weather, the need to feed Honey, the late carrots in the garden, and how her mother used to cover them with straw.

A long, painful silence then.

Steve sighed, set his mug on the tabletop, and courageously opened the subject.

"So, Mary, since last night went so badly, do we want to try again? Or would you rather I'd just leave, go back home, and give you time to think about all of this?"

"I don't know what to say."

"Can you believe I don't either?"

"Will you listen without judgment if I tell you what kept me awake?" she asked, her troubled green eyes fixed on him.

"Sure. I'd be glad to."

So she told him about God, and the great distance between them, and the ever-present voice of her father, and did he think God spoke through her father?

"You see, Steve, if I set you beside Bennie Lapp, I know what my father would say. Bennie is a proven person, *gehorsam*, a good father, a sad widower in need, and it's up to me to practice self-denial."

"So . . . is that your final decision?"

"Not yet. I don't know him the way I know you."

"But you don't approve of much of what I do, or say, or the attitudes I have. We most certainly are not on the same page spiritually."

"Sometimes I don't even know what 'spiritual' means," Mary admitted, a trace of sorrow edging her voice, a hand going to her coffee cup, wrapping around it for comfort.

"To me, it means being close to God. Our spirit is aligned with His, and love rules our daily outlook. Compassion and mercy, steady, fair-minded, esteeming others higher than ourselves. Being spiritual brings a deep sense of peace and the only true happiness we can have."

"I don't have that."

"Surely, Mary, you find bits and pieces here or there."

"I mean, I love my home, and it brings me happiness, but all that other stuff you mention is a mystery to me."

"Still, Mary? After all this time?"

She stiffened. Her face fell and when she met his eyes, a tone of anger sparked in the green irises.

"What am I expected to do? I can't help it if I don't understand the Bible. My father always said we aren't expected to understand it, that if you search for too much knowledge, you might be misled. And I don't want to be led astray."

"But . . ." Steve fumbled for the proper words, fully realizing the danger of evoking that self-defense in her, seeing how she was still ruled by the voice of her father.

"I don't think the Bible itself will mislead anyone, only the attitudes and judgments as you read."

"Could be."

But Mary had lost interest, disliked this conversation, had no longing to search her Bible for anything. She didn't have to agree with him and his monumental opinion of his own relationship with God.

He sensed the dragging of her feet, the shift of attention, so he dropped everything.

"Okay, Mary, we'll make breakfast. I'm starved. And while we do that, you can tell me about Bennie Lapp and the children."

They made sausage gravy, toast, and scrambled eggs with cheese melted through. And pancakes, golden brown, each one the size of a dinner plate, with butter and real New York maple syrup. And a fresh-baked shoofly pie. To wash it down, there was home-canned grape juice and more coffee.

While they cooked, Mary did talk about Bennie Lapp—his kindness, the need for a wife, the nice house, the organized shop.

They sat at the table, bowed their heads in silent prayer, filled their plates, and lifted forks. Mary stopped hers midair.

"It's the children," she burst out. "I don't know if I have it in me to love another man's children. Oh, Steve. You have no idea how I struggle to accept the flashbacks of being a *maud* for my brother's wives. My tired sisters. So many babies, and so much endless work. Do you think to be righteous in the eyes of God, I am expected to marry him?"

Steve helped himself to a generous serving of eggs, topped it with a ladle of sausage gravy, then reached for a piece of toast.

His face was set in a rigid line of concentration.

"I don't know the answer to that, but I know we're up against a tough question, a tough situation, knowing you are still guided by your father's voice in your mind."

"But he was righteous. He knew."

"He knew what?" Steve laid down his fork, lifted weary embattled eyes.

"He knew right from wrong. He was sure in his footsteps, never doubted that the true way to Heaven was through obedience to the *ordnung* (rules) of the Amish church."

Instantly the verse came to Steve's mind. "I am the way, the truth and the light. No man cometh to the father but through me."

But he held his peace.

"You see, Steve. If I am perfectly obedient—I still need to sell the chair, then the blessing will shine down on me—I will be righteous and can enter Heaven when I die."

"So, Jesus didn't necessarily have to die on the cross for you, since you found another way to God?" he asked quietly.

Her eyebrows went down, and she shook her head, puzzled.

"Well, no, not really. Of course, I believe He was on the cross for me, but that's not all it takes."

"What else?"

"*Gehorsamkeit.* Obeying the rules of the church."

"Yes, that is a factor, but only if it's kept in the proper perspective. If you . . ."

Here he gestured toward her loose hair, the wavy auburn-colored tresses he so admired.

"If you wear that large covering and plain navy dress to be seen of men, to tout your own righteousness, you are no better than the Scribes and Pharisees who sewed wide hems on their garments, a sign of deep religion, who stood on the curbs with loud prayers. Jesus did not approve of them. But if you dress plain out of appreciation for what He did for you, that's a whole other story. You must accept Him, and love only Him with your whole heart."

"But how can I love him if I can't see him? How can I know He died for everyone—even me—for sure? We can never know if we qualify, for sure."

Her voice had lowered to a husky whisper, and he heard the tears so close to the surface. He had never loved her more.

"It's called faith, Mary. We go by faith, starting on a journey believing His death on the cross was sufficient. We never qualify as 'good enough.' Never."

"But I've never heard it explained that way before."

"It's true."

"But my father . . ."

"Mary, he's not here anymore."

"Why did you come into my life?" she asked suddenly. "I mean, you complicate everything. It would be so simple to go on believing the words my father spoke. Like a child, we listen, obey, and hope we're okay with God. That's it. What is all this turned-around stuff?"

She paused. He made no move to give her any answers.

"I mean, I wish I would never have met you. Now my life would be simple. Sell my house, give up my own will, live in the required self-denial, and marry Bennie Lapp. There you go. Blessed beyond measure, plenty of provision to enter Heaven's gates."

"So, you would have paid your own way in, then?"

"Well, no, not really. I mean, Jesus was on the cross."

"But not for you, since you paid . . ."

The sound of her chair scraping the wooden floor was deafening, as she rose to her feet, slapped the table with the palm of her hand, and said in a strident voice she wasn't listening to any of his nonsense anymore. Enough was enough. He watched her fill her coffee cup with shaking hands, and asked her to sit back down, quietly.

She did.

"Why did you cry last night when you saw me?" he asked gently.

"Because, I don't know. I had the blues."

"What gave you the blues? Seeing me? Or Bennie Lapp's house?"

For a long moment, nothing was said.

"Honestly, Steve? His house. Him. His children."

He looked deeply into her troubled eyes, but realized it was a rare moment of being completely frank. He put his hand on hers, his thumb tracing her knuckles, sending sparks up her arm.

She took her hand away. She must abstain from his touch. He should know this.

"I love you, Mary."

"No. Don't say it, you don't."

"I do. I would ask you to marry me here, now, in this kitchen, if I knew there was a slight chance of acceptance, but I know you well enough that I wouldn't have a prayer. So now this Bennie Lapp is in the picture, and all I can do is disappear again, and allow your future to unfold as you decide."

"I don't love you, but I don't love Bennie. Or his children." Then, she said very low, "I don't know if I can love anyone."

"Maybe you need to love Jesus, first of all."

"Let's stop having this conversation. It makes me terribly sad and weary."

They washed dishes together, then decided to hitch up Honey and go for a long drive, pack a picnic lunch, and forget about the seriousness of life. There was a time for laughter, a time for lighthearted conversation, and a time for friendship.

She dressed, combed her hair, adjusted her white covering, hoped he would notice how the deep green of her dress brought out the green of her eyes. When he came out of the bathroom, showered, wearing pale blue, the scent of his earthy cologne, her knees were weak with an emotion she could not understand. Not love, and certainly not the forbidden desire, that shameful human emotion that held adulterers in its grip, that caused fornication and broken hearts, the devious ways of the devil. She turned away from him, fully realizing how a single girl must walk uprightly, always watchful, never weakening her resolve.

But seated beside him in the buggy, the scent of him, his closeness, brought the emotion back, even stronger, a force to be reckoned with. Happily unaware, he talked about horses, the weather, the way his mother feared for his safety, breaking those young horses, and she nodded agreement, smiled, and tried to sit as far away from him as possible, which seemed to be not far at all.

"So here we are, Mary. Enjoying each other's company on a beautiful day. What more would we want, right?"

Mary smiled, recognized the light words as an attempt to erase the conversation at the breakfast table.

Down a steep incline, the brakes holding the buggy steadily, Honey picking her way carefully, they came to "Cabin's Run," a winding creek bed cut between banks of towering ferns, lush and green, well-watered during the summer months by the constant flow of moisture at their roots.

"Whoa, that's beautiful," Steve commented, pulling back on the reins. Instantly, Mary was transported back to the hike, the sense of awe, the feeling Steve claimed as the presence of God. She did not want to experience that again, so she told him there was no room to tie Honey.

He looked puzzled, but was agreeable, and they drove on, past more trees, pastureland, a cluster of homes with barking dogs running excitedly inside chain link fences, mailboxes painted lime green and cherry red, with red and blue political signs stuck haphazardly in unmowed grass. Vehicles passed cautiously on narrow roads, the drivers waving with one hand on the wheel, or ignoring them altogether.

At a crossroad, she told him to go left, avoiding Elam King's place. She had no *haslduch* (cape) on, and he was certainly not in the *ordnung* at all, hatless, which no black vest.

They rode together quietly, the swaying of the buggy and the rhythm of steel rims on macadam enough to relax them, each lost in his or her own thoughts. She was glad to have him here, she recognized that, but she must not allow herself the freedom of enjoying his company too much, unsure of what God wanted from her. And now there was Bennie Lapp, the one needing her most. It was the honorable thing to do.

When they found a suitable spot, they unhitched, tied the horse, and spread the buggy blanket on the sweet grass, the scent of summer's end like the close of a chapter. He smiled at her as they sat side by side, and he bumped her shoulder with his.

"Like hiking, only cleaner," he quipped, laughing.

"It was a challenge, and that's saying it nicely," she said, smiling.

"You were so mad sometimes."

He threw his face to the sky and laughed, leaned back on his elbows, and said she was losing a pin in her apron, then proceeded to fix it, his large fingers steady, a pressure on her back until the pin was properly in place. Chills raced up her spine, and she imagined being married to him, asking him to make her *shots āva,* the Dutch term for aligning the belt apron in the middle of her back, the way her mother used to do, her father grasping the black belt of the apron and sliding it a bit to the left or right, leaning back to make sure it was straight. It was a simple thing, but portrayed an honest picture of trust in each other, a comfortable acceptance of receiving help.

And she knew Steve would be someone she could lean on, a strong shoulder, a knowledgeable outlook, an all-around good person. Except for his liberal views of religion.

He didn't call it that, but had the more modern term of "spirituality" which, she supposed, was every man's loose variation of his own interpretation of the Bible.

"Okay, so tell me, about Bennie's place."

Lost in her own thoughts, she blinked, wondered who Bennie was. Then it all came back like a sickening plunge off a cliff.

"I did tell you."

"But how did you feel in his house?"

Mary unwrapped a bologna sandwich, handed it to him, but he shook his head, then said he'd take a glass of lemonade, though.

She handed that over, then pinched a bit of crust from the sandwich and ate it, following with a rind of bologna. Finally, she shrugged.

"I don't really know. Nothing, I guess."

"I bet none of this is easy."

"It isn't."

"I mean, imagine eight children. That's a handful. Especially if you're thrown in all at once. Usually they come one at a time."

"Yeah, well."

"You don't have to, you know. Just tell him no."

Mary was shocked. "I can't do that."

"There are plenty of old . . . I mean, single girls."

"You were going to say old maids."

"I was, actually. But I caught myself."

She slapped his arm, and he caught her hand, held it firmly, said, "Look at me." When she finally relented, he looked at her, really looked in her eyes, and said in a soft tone. "Don't marry him, Mary. It will be too hard. You can't marry someone jut because you think you 'should.'"

"He's giving me a month to think about it."

"Tell him you want six months."

He was still holding her hand. She swallowed, looked at his hand holding hers, the long, brown fingers with the soft, blond hairs on the back of his hand, hers freckled, smaller, fitting perfectly.

She pushed that frightening thought away before it could take root, then drew her hand away, or tried to. His fingers tightened on hers, drawing her gently closer.

She turned her head, raised her eyes to the tops of the trees, watched a pair of squabbling sparrows, said something senseless, her breathing between them.

"What would you say if I asked to kiss you?" he whispered.

"No."

She jerked her hand away, leaped to her feet, and walked away, blindly. She stumbled over a tree root, righted herself, and walked even faster, across the mowed grass, into another bunch of trees, then turned to see if he was following her. She let out a relived whoosh of breath when she saw he remained seated, watching the clouds move across the blue of the sky.

What was this? Not love, certainly not. A companionable time, a friendship, but with an added element, the magnetic pull of one to the other. Every day spent with Steve was a rollercoaster of unnamed emotion, but she would remain on guard.

She walked slowly back. He watched her and thought he couldn't take much more of this. Should he merely extract himself from any further attempt at love, at building a relationship with this lovely woman?

He groaned his prayer for direction, asking the father to give him the wisdom he so sorely needed.

His feet on solid ground now, they made small talk, light banter, and arrived home as twilight crept across the hills and a light frost covered the hollow places. He started a fire in the stove, and she held out her hands to the warmth as it cracked and popped, the orange flames licking greedily at the fresh cut kindling. She felt warmed through and through, and dreaded the thought of Monday morning's arrival.

When he straightened, took her gently in his arms and held her, it was as natural as breathing, and as quiet. When he lifted her chin and found her mouth, she held very still, and felt the beginning of what could only be described as courage, and a certain trust in the future.

The fire in the stove cracked, and Mary sighed, stepped away, and lowered her face, only her forehead lightly touching his holder.

"Steve," she whispered. "I don't understand this, at all, but somehow, it seems alright. Do you think there's a possibility that I don't understand love, perhaps not even myself, that everything is so tainted by wrongdoing because of my upbringing?"

And he whispered very tenderly, telling her she had started to find the truth, and it was okay to absorb small amounts.

Closer and closer, their lives seemed to be directed, both unsure of the outcome, but no longer able to deny the bond that kept strengthening.

She stood on the porch, waved goodbye till the Uber driver was out of sight, the promise of his return in two weeks like a silken scarf around her neck. Whatever this was, she needed to have a length of time to figure it out.

CHAPTER 2

By the end of October, Steve had visited twice, only to be pushed into the worst disappointment of his life, with Mary still reeling from a visit with her siblings. As grapevines will do, they carried news of Bennie Lapp's proposal, which Mary's brothers and sisters immediately took as a clear signal from God that Mary needed to give herself up. She had had enough time cavorting with this shady Steve Riehl from Lancaster.

They spoke in hard, accusing words like hailstones. Mary raised her defense courageously, but they left her no room for doubt. If a widower with eight children needed someone, well then, you gave yourself up, knowing that self-denial was the path to blessing. Her days would be lived knowing she had a great reward in store.

Mary swung between listening with humble acceptance and burning with rebellion. But in the end, she relented, saying she would do as they asked and give Bennie a chance.

She was driven to Bennie's house the second time, where everything was much the same as before. His tall frame was at the door, his long dark hair neatly combed, but unwashed, parted in clumps which allowed the tops of his ears to peek through. But his eyes were kind, welcoming, and full of approval. The children greeted her with curiosity, and there were shy smiles and giggles from the smallest. Sarah was quite reserved, which raised a warning flag for Mary. Bennie seemed to notice too and suggested in his kindly manner that Mary help Sarah make supper, which would give them a chance to get to know each other.

Mary asked for a paring knife to peel the potatoes. Sarah reached in a drawer and held out a vegetable peeler. "Mother always used this," she said, and Mary thought she detected a note of disdain in her voice. She took the unwieldy utensil and hacked away with short, choppy strokes, resulting in half-hacked potato skins, a sliced fingertip, and a strong urge to fling it into the trash. It didn't help when Sarah leaned over the sink and said, "Draw it down more." The last thing she needed was a girl half her age telling her how to peel potatoes. And she smelled, too. No antiperspirant. Poor girl—she likely didn't know better.

So, Sarah peeled potatoes with long strokes, the peeler slipping and sliding over the rough, wet skins, gritted her teeth, and saw a long road ahead of denying the flesh.

She rallied, though, when the boys gave her wide smiles and asked her to come see the house they had made of leftover cabinet lumber.

When Bennie joined them and spoke so kindly to his growing boys—words of approval at the skill they showed—she felt a deep sort of relief wash over her. Here was a man who understood the hearts of young children.

The evening bumped along, with high and low moments, but she collected her courage and told Bennie she had enjoyed it, and yes, he could come visit on Saturday evening.

It was only when reality struck later that she knew she had to write to Steve. She was headed down the path of wisdom and righteousness now, and Steve had to deny his own flesh as well. He had to let go.

She started three different pages, tore them all into pieces, threw them in the trash can, and started yet again.

To say goodbye, that final blow, was like losing her own arm, but it had to be done. The pen dragged across the paper, spelling out her own doom, becoming a wife to someone she did not love.

Her brothers assured her that love would come later, which she included in her letter. She also stated that she must carry out God's will and that she was willing to deny the desires of her heart. She covered that sentence with Wite-Out, then cried great, streaming tears that splashed on the Wite-Out like a hot rain of sorrow. She asked him if he thought love was like a plate of cookies, the many different varieties from which you could pick and choose, and did not Wite-Out that sentence, although the small brush hovered above the page.

The righteousness she knew she had chosen seemed to soften the blow, but the final letter of goodbye was, in the end, an impossibility without secretly hoping she might see him again, if only once, before the wedding actually took place.

They set the date for the end of February, but then Bennie thought perhaps April would be better, with the snowy weather a likely hindrance to the guests from other states. Mary nodded approval, winning his kind smile and gentle look.

Mary made stromboli that night, and Sarah told her outright she didn't care for it, flinging her head in a way that seemed *grosfeelich* (prideful) and disrespectful, as if she loved putting Sarah in her place, which seemed to be a few notches below herself. Bennie frowned at her, his cheeks thinning as he did so. But John and Jesse pronounced it "really *goot*," and Amos nodded, his eyes shining straight into hers, guileless and full of a child's mercy.

When she was alone with Bennie, she was always at ease, his quiet kindness soothing to her battered spirit. Their relationship was a secret, the community surrounding them kept completely in the dark, as is the custom in conservative areas.

By the time the frost killed the late garden vegetables, she had a nice supply of sweet potatoes and a small bin of white potatoes, with canned dill spears, tiny sweet pickles, red beets, and applesauce in the basement. She stood by the shelves and wept, thinking of the futile attempts at feeding a family of ten. This was only a drop in the bucket, a small amount needing to be multiplied like loaves and fishes.

She spread her hands, the long, rounded, smooth fingers, thought of the never-ending workload awaiting them, remembered her mother's chapped, liver-spotted, blue-veined hands. The hands that had reached into a chicken's body and yanked out the viscera, washed tons of soiled clothing in a wringer washer and hung them out to dry, hoed and clawed at the weeds in the garden, changed diapers and baked thousands of loaves of bread. A thankless, ongoing job neither her husband nor her children ever appreciated fully, and certainly never would, with her gone now, buried beneath the soil, from dust to dust.

Ah, but wasn't that the plight of women? Was it a plight, or was it a blessing?

The chair was sold, the last remnant of her earthly desires, and she sat on her kitchen chair and waited for her blessing. She felt nothing except wishing she hadn't sold it. But then she remembered a fancy flower pot still sitting on the porch. Yes, it too, must go, the voice whispered. Her sacrifice was not complete. But the green blinds were in place, she had sold the chair, and given up Steve to serve Bennie and his children. *Isn't this enough, Lord?*

She knew the answer according to Steve. He would say it is never enough. We cannot buy or sacrifice our way to Heaven. But Steve seemed to be on shaky ground, to her way of thinking, whereas Bennie never talked about these things. He was content to go to church and live by what the preacher said, which he seemed to think was straightforward and simple enough, not that they'd had opportunity to discuss such things much during their short friendship.

By the end of November, she'd taken to reading her Bible out of desperation. She pored over the pages in English and in German, trying to quiet the voice of her father in her head so she could concentrate on what the words actually said.

Verse after verse reached out with an accusing finger pointed at her, as she cringed in her chair in fear. "Many are called, few are chosen" was like a sniper's bullets singing through the air as she dodged between them, her hands smashed on top of her covering.

So many threats, such a fearful tirade. Why did people choose to read their Bible for comfort? There was no comfort between these pages for her. She knew she was lacking an element of spiritual understanding, but had no idea how to acquire it, so she began to kneel beside her bed every evening and recite the Lord's Prayer: "*Unser Vater, in dem Himmel,*" she quavered in a broken whisper. "*Geheilichet verde die nama.*" At the end, she always said the same thing: "Help me understand."

She felt certain her words never went through the ceiling, and she often felt silly, but she kept on going, faithfully reciting every evening. When she woke in the morning, her thoughts were sometimes in song. "When the Roll Is Called Up Younger," was one of them, which always scared her horribly, thinking how bold that writer was, saying he'd be there. How did he know he would be there? Another one was "Life's Railway to Heaven." The idea of a train chugging along was more reassuring, thinking how God was the engineer.

Her friendship with Bennie and the children was not a source of joy or comfort, but more of a reminder that we are not here to stay, and life is not made to be a bed of roses. So much about Bennie was kind and good, and she was not repulsed, but there was nothing to look forward to, either.

He was boring. He smiled, let his kind eyes shine into hers, but he had no sense of humor. Life was serious, and even more so since the death of his beloved Anna, and now this serious undertaking of pursuing a second wife.

And she continued to pray in her whispered recital of the Lord's Prayer, the winter months looming ahead like a quiet haven of rest and privacy before she embarked on the journey with Bennie.

STEVE READ HER letter, sighed, then flung it across the room, where his sisters found it an hour later and brought it to their mother like a forbidden gossip magazine.

"Mam, you need to read this. It's a real cut-off job."

His mother delighted in all things humorous, and she burst out laughing, then lifted her eyebrows, saying she shouldn't be reading this. But she couldn't help herself.

After many "Hmms" and "Really?," snorts and chirps, she laid the letter aside and felt the empathy for her son welling up. But she told the girls he might be fortunate, in spite of not realizing that fact now.

Later, she wept copiously in the bathroom, sitting on the edge of the bathtub and using the towel on the rack to dry her eyes. Her son. Her poor son, who would be the best husband in the world with his generosity, his quick wit and sense of humor. He'd waited so long, searching for a special girl, and in spite of her own misgivings, seemed to have found someone he truly loved, even if she had some obvious issues.

She sniffed, looked in the mirror, noticed a smudge on her cheek and wiped it off. Her dentures were bothering her a lot, so she pushed them out of her mouth, examined the top, and found a blueberry seed nestled inside. Frowning, she rinsed the dentures and slipped them back, thinking how one blueberry seed could cause so much discomfort.

And one son's aching heart produced a day's worth of sadness. The girls tried to ease her bad day, saying, "Really, Mam. She's not that much. Kind of fat, and sort of plain."

"And all that red hair is enough to give you the shivers."

"And she's from New York."

Steve's whistling and singing was silent, his voice at the supper table stilled. The girls tried to lighten the mood with their banter about silly happenings at school, but nothing seemed to draw him out of his reverie.

Later, when his mother was tidying the kitchen, he went to the refrigerator and poured a glass of milk, then went to the pantry shelf searching for cookies.

"Didn't bake, Steve. It'll have to be Oreos."

"It's fine, Mam. I love Oreos."

She smiled. That was so like her son, to say he loved them when she knew he much preferred the plump chocolate chip cookies she always made. He had a good heart, had never given them a moment's worry, so it was hard to understand why God chose to take away his loved one.

"Mam, did you read the letter?"

"I'm sorry. The girls found it."

"I figured. What did you think?"

"I honestly don't know what to tell you. She is under a strange law, an iron-fisted influence. We can't tell someone like that what to do. I know her father is gone, but you know what they say, their voices strengthen after they're gone, and I found that true with my own father. Except his words were softer, of course."

Steve held an Oreo between thumb and forefinger, kept it in the cold milk for just the right amount of time before popping it into his mouth, shaking his head as he chewed and swallowed.

"She's so close, Mam. It's almost impossible to bear."

"She obviously doesn't have feelings for this widower."

"Not yet. But she says they'll come after she's married."

His mother snorted, a loud derisive sound she felt perfectly entitled to. When she said nothing, he raised his eyebrows.

"Well," his mother sighed. "We can only hope this is true, for her sake. Only God knows."

In faraway New York, Mary fought her own battles without courage, her days filled with numbing doubt and ever darkening clouds over her head, as if the sun had lost its splendor, the colorful autumn scenery erased by gray hues of depression. Her stomach roiled with bitter acid and nausea complicated her days. Dark circles appeared below her eyes, her summer tan gave way to a pale, sickly complexion dotted with a spattering of freckles, her green eyes dulled. She leafed through the natural remedy catalog, sent for a bottle of enzymes to aid digestion, swapped out white sugar and flour for raw sugar and whole wheat, drank almond milk, and ate raw fruits and vegetables. She was pleased when the number on the bathroom scales was lowered significantly. She lay awake at night, her thoughts a churning whirlpool.

Bennie Lapp asked her to spend a Saturday with the children while he attended the Friesian sale in Ohio, thinking it would be good for the children to spend time with her alone. Her breath quickened, her heartbeat loud in her own ears, the hovering clouds closing in.

But she said yes. Yes, she could do that.

When she arrived, the smudged windows and cluttered counter-tops, the dust on the furniture and muddy floor took her by surprise, sending her heart plummeting. Things had really deteriorated since her prior visit. Sarah came out of the bathroom with bold eyes in her direction, a challenge she could not meet.

"You don't look so good," Sarah observed.

Betty and Lea stared at her from the small table where they sat, playing with their plastic dishes, dolls perched on their laps. Their hair was unwashed and uncombed, the fronts of their dresses splattered with bits of food, stained with yesterday's drinks. A sour smell pervaded the house.

"I'm fine," Sarah managed. "A bit of stomach issues."

"Well, I hope you can help do Saturday work. The house needs a good cleaning and there is laundry to be done. Mommy Lapp was here yesterday, but she didn't do much. She has gout, so her right foot is swollen and sore. Dat says we need a *maud* from now till the wedding, that you can't do it yet."

"I can't?"

"No, he said you have housecleaning jobs and need the money."

"True enough, Sarah. I do."

"I thought so."

Sarah met her eyes. A challenge? A smirk? Dark-haired, dark-eyed, already a womanly figure beneath the loose-fitting dress, a young girl on the cusp of her "rumschpringa" years, a future of dating and marriage before her. Mary could tell she felt superior, that Sarah knew Mary was past the point of being a sought-after young woman and was, instead, an older, jaded one who had to take a widower with children. Many felt the put-down, felt herself being stuffed into a box labeled "Past Her Prime."

She stiffened her shoulders, raised her head, took a steadying breath, and asked Sarah where to begin, which was met with raised eyebrow and a pitying stare.

"If you don't know, then I'd say you were pretty inexperienced."

Mary gritted her teeth. She walked stiffly past the leering girl, flung open cabinet doors as she collected clean rags, noting the absence of furniture polish. She searched the *kesslehaus* (laundry room) walls until she found broom, dustmop, and pan.

Her anger drove her. She was a sizzling volcano of energy, dusting, stripping gray sheets and greasy pillowcases, flinging them on the cement floor by the washer, Sarah watching furtively now.

From the doorway came the announcement that they only did laundry once a month and it wasn't time yet. Mary rode the crest of a crashing wave of rebellion, put down her dust rag, and towered over her.

"If I'm expected to live in this household, I will wash sheets when I choose."

Sarah reared back, visibly shaken. Mary felt good about putting her in her place. For a while, she worked alone, with Sarah slinking around corners, saying nothing.

The downstairs bathroom was repulsive. Grimly, she searched for a jug of bleach, with no success. To break down the wall of Sarah's animosity, she asked for it, and was met with an insolent shrug and a snide remark about bleach being hard on the bathroom floor. She found vinegar and an old container of Comet, opened the window, and proceeded to scrub with a vengeance. A mountain of wet, graying towels produced the horror of a shining copper-colored roach, scurrying furiously for cover. Instantly, Mary smashed it with the toe of her shoe.

She shuddered as she reached for the bathroom tissue, wadded it up, and scooped the revolting mess into the overflowing trashcan.

Her chin set with determination, she didn't stop till the fixtures were gleaming, the shower curtain flapping on the sagging clothesline, the rugs clamped down beside it. She washed windows, scrubbed floors and walls, not stopping until she felt weak from hunger and exhaustion. Her anger was subsiding now, replaced by the need to find middle ground with Sarah.

Leah was asking for food, her sweet lisping voice dispelling most of Mary's bad mood. Mary found Sarah outside, playing with the bevy of cats on the porch.

"Sarah?"

No answer.

"Sarah?"

Still no answer.

Sighing, Mary sat down on the faded bench. "Look, I'm sorry." The form sitting cross-legged on the cold floor gave no hint of having heard a word.

"If we're going to live together, don't you think we should try to get along?"

"Nobody said you're going to live here."

"Except your father."

"What?"

"Your father asked me to marry him."

"No he didn't. I don't believe a word you're saying. He would never do that."

"But . . ."

Her dark eyes blazed up at Sarah, the cats shooed off her skirt as she leaped to her feet, her fists clenched.

"You will never be my mother."

"No. I never will. Your mother died, Sarah. I will be a stepmother, and I'm sure even that is hard for you right now. I'm only hoping in time you'll come to accept me."

There was only the dubious response of cold silence, after which she stepped off the porch and walked away, disappearing behind the row of arborvitae separating the lawn from the shop.

Mary felt the bile rising in her throat, the pain spreading from her side across the top of her stomach. She swallowed, then massaged the roiling area. The oldest boys had accompanied their father, so Annie and Betty watched her hand going across her waist, a puzzled expression on their faces.

Mary stopped, gave them a weak smile, and asked what they would like to eat.

"*Sup* (soup)," Annie said, her dark eyes guileless.

"Alright."

She searched the pantry, making herself move boxes and cans despite being certain there would be a cockroach hiding behind one of them. There were torn bags of rice, oatmeal boxes with holes chewed through. If not roaches, they certainly had a mice problem. She found a tin of canned salmon and decided to make salmon noodle soup. She considered making grilled cheese sandwiches to go with it, but the bread drawer was empty.

Her stomach churned. She found a saucepan, browned butter, opened the can of salmon and upended it, sending a hiss of steam into the air above the stove.

"What stinks?" This from the opening to the living room. Sarah stood watching, a hand on her hip, a shoulder leaning against the doorway.

"Salmon," Mary said, tight as a drum.

"We don't eat salmon."

Eat it or go hungry, she thought, but held her tongue. Instead, she turned, met Sarah's eyes, and said she might like it with noodles and cheese.

"Ew. Sounds gross."

Ignoring her, she mixed up some bread sticks, grimacing as a flurry of moths in the pantry came from torn flour sacks. She imagined the flour thick with small brown bugs, but was unable to locate them, so she finished the bread sticks and popped them into a preheated oven.

"Would you set the table please?" she called over her shoulder, as she broke homemade noodles into the salmon and milk.

"We don't eat salmon," Sarah repeated.

"At least give it a try."

They sat down to faded, scratched Melmac soup bowls and a knife, fork, and spoon thrown haphazardly across them. Besides the soup, Mary placed on the table a box of saltines, a jar of applesauce, and the fragrant breadsticks slick with butter and a sprinkle of parsley and oregano.

Mary bent her head, lifted it after the silent prayer, and ladled soup wordlessly. She herself ate two helpings, plus a few breadsticks, pleased with how it had all turned out.

Sarah refused the soup, but the other children ate it happily, slurping noodles and asking for seconds.

Mary found Sarah's eyes on her, a dark challenge in their depths. Mary rose to meet it, smiling and asking her to give the soup a try.

"We're getting a *maud*," Sarah shot back. "I don't think she'll make this gross stuff."

And hopefully, thought Mary, *she'll get rid of the mice and the roaches. Maybe she'll even want to marry your father and I'll be off the hook.*

But this thought was met by a powerful jolt from her conscience. How was she ever to be a good example to Sarah when she struggled so much with giving up her own will?

CHAPTER 3

BENNIE LAPP LISTENED TO HIS OLDEST DAUGHTER THAT NIGHT, taking into consideration the things she said about Mary. In his kind way, and with the humility and wisdom so pronounced in the ways of one knowing great sorrow, he decided to take things more slowly. Sarah's opinions must be taken into account if the poor girl was expected to accept a new mother so soon after the death of her own.

He did hire a *maud*. He knew they needed help, though he didn't realize quite how badly things had deteriorated in his home. With Sarah's help, they picked Enos Swarey's Rachel, an ex-schoolteacher very close to his own age, a tall, thin, dark-haired woman sporting a formidable nose, small dark eyes behind rimmed spectacles, and a beautiful smile enhanced by a gleaming new set of dentures. She was very thin, her long arms dangling loosely, her large feet like webbed duck feet on stick thin legs.

Bennie Lapp talked and smiled with the affable Rachel, his eldest daughter beaming her approval. But on Sunday afternoon he dressed in his best, washed off his horse, and hitched him to the buggy, preparing to pick up Mary. He knew he had to shoulder Sarah's resentment, but she'd come around, he told himself. She had to, for he had fallen hard for Mary. She intrigued him and now took up most of his thoughts and many of his days.

There was joy everywhere, in the fading, falling leaves, in the scent of ears of corn hanging on brown stalks. He looked forward to helping his brother Ammon, driving the big wooden wagon, the sides fitting neatly on the steel racks, the faithful Belgians plodding through the dry, rustling cornstalks. He imagined Mary, her red hair flaming in autumn sunlight, her coat too snug on her well-endowed frame.

He thought of her eyes, so often dark and troubled. He fancied she'd taken more than one wrong turn in her life and was besieged by the need to be forgiven, the way of the cross perhaps not fully understood. He had known her father well, the large family a true light of obedience to the community. But he'd also been rather strict, he thought. He wondered about Mary's time in Lancaster and looked forward to learning more about her life. He knew at one point some of the community had written her off as a disobedient rebel, but she'd obviously returned wholeheartedly to the fold.

Joy coupled with gratitude made the miles fade away beneath the horses' hooves, and a song rose in his heart. Tonight, they would discuss Sarah, which he felt confident would open the way for a deeper understanding and a new closeness between him and Mary.

She greeted him, a wan smile on her pale, freckled face.

"*Vee bischt* (how are you), Mary?" he asked across the horses' back as he looped the reins expertly through the silver ring.

"*Ich bin goot* (I'm good)," she answered quietly.

And he took her words at face value, failing to notice the diminishing figure, the drawn look of her face.

She offered him coffee, which he took, black and steaming hot. She thought of her father when he slurped it, and she grimaced in spite of herself. He smiled at her. "Very good coffee. What kind do you buy?"

"Folgers. Black Silk."

"Black Silk?" His eyebrows raised, he told her he'd never heard of it. Was she sure? Her heart took a dive, a genuine sickening plunge of despair, when she realized there was something, something in the way his dark eyes darted away from her, then back again, that unsettled her. But the moment was fleeting, and he opened the subject of his eldest daughter's reluctance of their marriage, his kindness cushioning the necessary words.

"She's just being difficult, and I feel ashamed, Mary. I didn't think she would react as strongly. I understand none of this being easy, but I've hired a *maud* to help take care of the house for now."

Mary nodded. "Good thinking. It was hard to be there, doing the work my way, when she clearly had her own ideas of how things should be done. But I'm not perfect either," she added quickly.

"No one is. But Mary, I want to know you better. Tonight, I wish you would tell me everything about yourself. There's something different about you."

Mary's shoulders lifted, held, the walls of her defense in place. She appeared very interested in the pattern of the dishes in front of her, before shaking her head slightly.

"There's not much to tell."

"Did you have an ordinary childhood?" His voice was kind, if a bit nasal, his eyes warm.

"I think so. My father was strict, pretty hard on us, and I guess I rebelled, more than my brothers and sisters."

"Anyone could see that."

"I suppose."

"But you have certainly come a long way."

"Yes, I suppose I have."

"The way of the cross is not easy, and it takes some individuals longer than others to realize the weakness of our own flesh and take on the nature of our Savior, *der Heiland Yesu Grischt* (the Savior Jesus Christ)."

These were the exact same words her father had used, only said in a softer, kinder way. She felt almost as if her father were in the room, reminding her of her disobedience.

Oh God, where are you? Who can help me find the path? With all her heart, she longed for Steve, for the way he made her almost believe in the possibility of redemption. What kept her from him?

"You seem distracted, Mary."

"Oh, yes. I'm sorry."

"Your thoughts were far away."

There was a long, tense stillness. Then, "Mary, I want us to be married as soon as possible, but I don't believe it would be wise to rush Sarah into accepting you as her mother. I think we'd best put the wedding off till later in the summer. That will give her time to get used to the idea of having you around. With the *maud* there, Sarah won't be so burdened with keeping house . . ."

Mary cut him off.

"She's not keeping house."

"Why do you say that, Mary?"

"You live there. Can't you see?" She told him about the state of his house, sparing no details. Once she got going, words tumbled out more quickly than she'd intended. It was as if a floodgate had opened and there was no shutting it back up. She said Sarah was as rude as she was lazy, and if she treated their *maud* the same way she'd treated her, he could count on the *maud* leaving within the week. She could understand that the girl was missing her mother, but she'd also clearly been spoiled. In fact, if he wasn't willing to make Sarah change her behavior, perhaps they shouldn't plan on marriage at all.

With great humility, his head bowed, he absorbed her words, his dark eyes turning from eagerness to a dull sadness. The bit of trouble he'd anticipated was, in fact, a formidable hurdle.

They postponed the wedding, with the promise of taking a bit of time off to improve the situation with Sarah. He told her of his disappointment, how hard the waiting would be. She acknowledged this, even as she felt relief washing over her. More time before the inevitable wedding felt like a tremendous gift. But she felt guilt ride in on the heels of the relief. If marrying Bennie was God's will for her life, why was she so happy to put it off?

Bennie did not take her in his arms, but held her hand so tightly it actually hurt, then released it and walked away. She did not help him hitch his horse to the buggy, but instead stayed in the kitchen, gripping the countertop with both hands. She lifted her face to the ceiling and wondered.

Was it possible God would yet intervene to save her from marrying someone she did not love? Could He bless her life at all if she still chose Steve, or must she dedicate her life to her brothers' and sisters' advice, going against her own heart?

RACHEL SWAREY PADDED around the house on her long flat feet, her great nose and small brown eyes set off by the wondrous smile. She was quiet, well-mannered, and arrived at precisely eight in the morning and went home at eight in the evening. She drove a fat gelding named Marty, the buggy always equipped with a freshly charged battery, the blanket warm and thick, the miles between them filled with the sound of her singing.

She sang hymns and children's school songs, and ribald sailors' songs from the 1800s, the words handed down on her mother's side, her brothers having had a hankering for an accordion played with an old Marine Band harmonica. The results were unforgettable, and Babbie, her mother, often tapped her toes in time to the swirling memories in her head. Rachel was intelligent, with a keen wit, sharp as a saber, coupled with a great love of children.

She was happy to be Bennie Lapp's *maud*, for the children, but had no interest in him at all. Men were all the same, as far as she was concerned. She didn't have any problem with them, but no real interest in them, either.

She sang while cleaning, too, her voice filling the *kesslehaus* above the clatter of the Honda engine.

"Life's evening sun is sinking low.

A few more days, and I must go.

To meet the deeds that I have done.

Where there will be no setting sun."

Bennie came in for his forenoon break, stopped to listen, and marveled. Instantly, Sarah was at his side, her dark eyes boring into his.

"Do you hear this, Dat?"

He nodded. Yes, he was listening, the voice sending chills up his spine. He told Sarah indeed God had bestowed her with a *wunderbahr* talent. But he also noticed her spare frame, her large flapping feet and the absence of soft, womanly curves. Ach, my Mary, he thought, as his daughter's eyes beseeched and the voice at the washing machine trilled on.

Rachel yodeled, too. Her uncles had taught her well, howling glee-fully when she hit the high notes.

When the house was in order and the cooking done, she played games with the children. She loved playing Chinese checkers, will-ingly got down the Sorry game with Amos, Annie, and Betty as cher-ished opponents. She slapped exhilarating high fives to every winner of every board game and brought out a bowl of crackers and one of pretzels, the dark evenings suddenly lighter as she doled out her love to each one separately, the horn of plenty in her heart never withering up or drying away.

She was also in on the community grapevine, her keen ears picking up every word spoken within hearing distance at church, at quiltings, and in local stores. All these juicy tidbits fell on Sarah's eager ears.

Bennie noticed the lighter mood in the evenings as he ate yet another plate of mashed potatoes and hamburger gravy with a side of boiled string beans. He ate chocolate cake with thin vanilla icing scored across it. It wasn't as good as anything Mary had made, but it was fine. The children were happy, the house in decent order. Well, decent enough. He couldn't expect everything. After supper, dishes were washed, and out came the board games, little Leah perched on her thin knees, wav-ing and clapping, her dark eyes shining. Bennie took all things into consideration and appreciated Rachel for the restored well-being of his children, even as he dreamed of Mary, his betrothed.

MARY CLEANED OUT her garden, dragging slimy, frostbitten tomato stalks and zucchini squash plants as big as trees, and dumping them in her garden cart to be wheeled to her compost bin. The wind tore at her skirt, whipping the corners of her headscarf across her face.

She stopped, shook her hands to restore the flow of blood, before giving up and going to the house for a pair of gloves.

She should have tackled this job before today, but Mrs. Smith, the most demanding client of all, had wanted her windows washed inside and out, which meant positioning stepladders among old, clipped yews. It was next to impossible, resulting in long days . . . and a generous tip.

Mrs. Smith and her husband had been high school sweethearts. She went on and on about Robert, his many talents, his pleasant personality, his caring of her, the sacrifices he made when her health was in decline. As Mary washed dozens of windows, she listened to Mrs. Smith's life story with Robert, how they met, where they went on their first date, the burgers so good at the Shake Shack, him driving his father's Buick.

"And you never doubted that you were meant for each other?" Mary asked, unrolling a wad of paper towels, picking up the bottle of Windex, knowing the windows would never be streak free.

"Nope. Not once."

"But how could you be so sure?"

"It was love, Mary. Love trumps everything."

Mary nodded, then changed the subject. English people had it easy. They didn't have to worry about the hundreds of ways you could go wrong, always questioning what God wanted of you, your siblings like vultures ready to pick your bones.

One afternoon they took a break from washing windows, had a cup of tea, and Nona Smith told her everything, starting with where love was. God was love, she said, and marriage was meant to be a picture of God's own joyful, perfect, all-consuming love for His people.

But while she talked, Mary's thoughts tumbled like dry straw in a stiff gale. Surely that wasn't the whole truth. Didn't love mean self-sacrifice, giving oneself up, even suffering? That was far more important than things like joy.

A WEEK LATER, Jessie drove into Mary's driveway and hurried to the door, a worried expression on her face. Her voice faltered a bit as she told Mary she'd gotten a message for her. Aunt Lizzie had been in a terrible accident on the way to visit the daughter who lived in Perry County. A car had cut into their lane, delivering a glancing blow, sending the buggy into the guard rail. She had died in the ambulance on the way to the hospital.

The next forty-eight hours were a blur for Mary. After a few moments of shock, adrenaline put her on autopilot as she asked Jessie to help notify her siblings, arranged a car for all who could go to the funeral, threw clothes in her suitcase, and donned her black suit. Once in the car, she gave herself over to weeping as the trees and mountains rushed by outside her window.

Once in Lancaster, she met up with the girls, their swollen faces purple with weeping. They fell into her arms in turns, saying, "Mary, Mary. Oh, you've come." She did her best to console Suse, then Linda and Ruthann, while steadily crying herself. She should have come for a visit sooner, and now it was too late.

At the funeral, Mary was seated with the girls, having been like a daughter to Lizzie. Mary's siblings sat farther back and viewed Mary through disapproving gazes. It was uncomfortable to see her so close with the Lancaster relatives. It was a reminder of her disobedient years, and certainly a threat to her future. Mary was weak, they reasoned. She needed a firm hand, turning her toward the light. They gawked at fancy cousins, telling each other the end was near. Outwardly, they remained respectful, although they felt themselves far superior.

When Mary suggested she stay to help the cousins sort through Lizzie's things, her siblings gave her grave, searching looks. "Do you really think that's wise, Mary?" her brother asked, and the others backed him up with warning looks. But in the end, Mary stood her ground and her siblings left, telling one another she was an adult, and therefore free to choose.

STEVE HEARD OF Lizzie's death and hired a driver to see if Mary had come. He arrived to find the last of the church friends and neighbors loading the last bench wagon, a light on in the house, and a dark figure coming to answer his tapping on the back door.

Mary!

Tongue-tied, he stood as the door swung open. She stepped back, allowed him to enter, lifting an arm to usher him in.

"Hello, Mary."

"Hi, Steve."

"I was hoping you'd be here."

"Yes. As I was hoping to see you."

"Should I be here?"

She sighed, as if her weariness was complete.

"Yes, you should."

"I'm so sorry about Lizzie. I know she meant a lot to you."

Tears overflowed Mary's eyes again. "She's gone so suddenly, and I didn't come visit, and . . . and everything is wrong, Steve."

She bowed her head and pressed a paper towel snatched off the roll to her face. He guided her to a chair, his hand on her back.

"Sit down and tell me."

The whole story tumbled out in broken starts and unfinished endings, but he pieced together that she did not really want to marry Bennie, that Sarah was an older daughter who didn't like Mary, and that Bennie had postponed the wedding.

"Steve, I was so sure I was doing the right thing, and now, I don't know. And I didn't even get to tell Lizzie any of it. She would have helped me make sense of it all."

"Mary, everything is for a purpose. I can see God's hand in this. You do not want to accept marriage on those terms. Can you imagine if Sarah tries to turn Bennie against you, which inevitably she will?"

"Bennie thinks she'll get better with time."

Steve gave her a dubious look. "Mary, it's clear that you don't want to marry him. Is that even fair to him? Would *you* want to be married to someone who doesn't really love you?"

Mary felt her feet move before she'd given herself permission to move. It was like her body had a mind of her own. She moved swiftly to the front door, hit the latch with the palm of her hand, and ran out the door. She had no idea where she was going, but she felt the old weight on her chest, the sensation of something crawling up her throat, and her body took over, trying to flee from its own discomfort.

Steve was on his feet in a flash. He caught her arm as she was going down the steps, but with a broken cry, she wrenched free, took a few more steps, and then stopped. What, exactly, was the point of running? She began to feel foolish for even bursting out of the house like that. What was wrong with her? She stood in the cold autumnal gale, now feeling angry at Steve, though it wasn't clear why. "Why don't you go home?" she half yelled at him, and then was inexplicably relieved when instead he came to her side, gently hooked his arm through hers, and led her back inside.

They sat back at the table and he could see the fight leaving her body, the sagging of her shoulders, the long intake of breath, the slow release.

"Steve, I'm done. I cannot fight anymore. I don't know what's right or what's wrong and have no idea how to find out. All I know is that I love you, and only you. Even when I'm with Bennie, I'm thinking of you. I can't help it. I'm stripping myself of everything, my pride, what anyone thinks of me, of my father's voice. I'm throwing myself at the foot of something, a mountain maybe, and asking for strength, or maybe mercy. I don't even know, but one way or another I have to stand on my own truth."

He was speechless, his mouth working but without sound.

"I don't know if I can marry Bennie, and who knows if I should marry you, but I'm done. Life is so short, so unpredictable. Aunt Lizzie is gone, just like that, her life cut so short. That could happen to any of us!" She paused, breathing heavily. "These last couple days, I've been realizing maybe I have some idols that I have to let go of—like caring so much about what people think of me. I mean, I was at Lizzie's funeral, crying for her, and at the same time worrying about what my siblings were thinking about me sitting with the 'fancy' cousins. It's ridiculous! I don't even know who I am apart from what people think of me."

"Mary," he managed, but then realized she wasn't done.

"Aunt Lizzie always said we are all different, God made us that way, and that I cannot compare myself with my family. As I stood by her casket, I asked God for a second chance at being real.

"That house in New York? I hope God can forgive that monument to myself, and all my misguided beliefs. *Ach*, Steve, once you begin to shed the scales from your eyes, there's no end to it. I just want a fresh start, a new life. Does God provide that, do you think?"

He discovered a quivering in his chest, in his stomach, and realized he was laughing and crying at the same time, creating a maelstrom of feelings and emotions beyond his control. His prayers had been answered, his God had given grace and understanding, the possibility of his heart's desire.

Quietly, reverently, he said, "Yes, Mary. I believe He does." And she went into his arms, where she stayed for a very long time, and he wept with the sheer force of his deepest feelings.

Where death had been, there was now new life in Mary. But it was only the flowering of one single, white, holy rosebud, and the battles of life were still hers to conquer.

SHE RETURNED TO New York only long enough to pack her things, sell her home, and talk to Bennie Lapp. He felt betrayed, bereft of what He felt was God's will. But it wasn't long before he saw the great mother in Rachel Swarey, and knew the sacrifice would be small on his part. The children came first.

Rachel let out a great whoop of laughter when he asked her, and said why sure, she'd marry him. Why not? She wasn't much to look at, but she'd keep him warm at night, that wouldn't be a problem at all. Secretly, she'd begun to take an interest in him, but had tried not to let her mind go there, given his relationship with Mary. When Sarah heard the news, she lifted a fist and pumped it toward the ceiling, thinking, *Finally! We'll be rid of that big, bossy redhead!*

Mary's siblings unleashed a volley of dire threats, but Mary did not back down. She did her best to let the words roll off her shoulders.

She rented a small house south of Gap, in Lancaster, close to the Maryland line. She met Steve's parents and his siblings and was embraced into the relaxed atmosphere of a loving family, complete with a mother overflowing with love and good humor, who helped her find new coverings that suited her conscience. Mary and Steve's mother sat for hours at the sewing machine and fitted Mary into a nice set of dresses and aprons that she felt comfortable in—somewhere between the plain, drab dress of her New York family and the "fancy" dress of most of the Amish in Lancaster. As they sewed, they talked, and Mary found that this woman was a wellspring of wisdom.

As Mary worked, she marveled that the Bible verses that came from this woman's mouth were a true comfort, and not once to be feared. Yes, she agreed with Mary that she had built monuments of self and created pedestals of fear and had run blindly after the doctrines of men. But she assured her that she was not the only one, and acknowledged that her background had made it tough to know differently. Above all, she pointed Mary to Jesus's love.

And Mary grew in grace. Her face took on an inner glow as she cast her cares on the yoke of Jesus. Scary Bible verses turned into lines of truth, new understanding, a new chance. She even understood the words of Jesus to Nicodemus about being born again. She truly did.

The wind ruffled trees and grasses, flapped loose shutters, and chased clouds across the sky. She thought about how you had no idea where that wind started or where it stopped, but it was absolutely there. She didn't fully comprehend what being saved meant, but she was thirstily drinking the milk of the Word.

And Steve moved through his days in a fog of happiness, sometimes a whirl of joy he had no idea a person could experience.

He found a fixer-upper home close to the house Mary had rented. Mary took one look at the dilapidated building and told him he was crazy. But he laughed and said she couldn't see it through a builder's eye. "Just give yourself up. That's what women do," he said, his eyes twinkling. She hit his forearm and he grabbed her hand, and then she came into his arms gladly, leaned back, and gave him all the love in her green eyes.

CHAPTER 4

THE WEDDING TOOK PLACE ON THE FOURTH OF NOVEMBER ON THE farm of Lizzie's daughter Ruthann and her husband, Dave. The day before there were scattered showers, enough to keep women dashing from house to the shop and back again, carrying bowls and roasters and utensils.

Steve and Mary washed celery from packing crates, stalk after stalk of it, with the *nāva sitza* ("beside sitters," the bridal party). Since Steve didn't have brothers, he chose a close friend and a cousin, while Mary chose two of Aunt Lizzie's granddaughters, Ellen and Rosa, both only fifteen years old and absolutely thrilled to be *nāva sitza*. They carried the washed celery to the aunts and grandmothers, seated at a table with cutting boards and paring knives, who chopped it into small pieces for creamed celery.

Across the room at another table were the *roascht-leid*, whose job it was to butter whole chickens and put them in roasters to send home with workers to be roasted overnight. The chickens would be brought back very early the day of the wedding and snipped into small pieces with kitchen shears, mixed with prepared bread cubes, celery, eggs, butter, broth, fat, and the innards. Then they'd add salt, pepper, and seasoned salt, with the whole team weighing in on how much of each ingredient to add. The *roascht-leid* were highly esteemed, carrying a serious responsibility. *Goota roascht* (good chicken casserole) was extremely important, the crowning glory of the wedding dinner. *Die drumbare leid* were next in importance, the three church couples chosen to peel, cut, and cook the hefty stainless-steel kettles of potatoes, then mash them with plenty of cream cheese, butter, and salt, using handheld battery-operated mixers. Finally, two older, experienced church women were put in charge of cooking large kettles of gravy, fussing and stirring, following old recipes and doing themselves proud.

All the siblings from New York were there. Mary was surprised to see them joking and laughing, seeming to accept Steve. Mary had taken her own way, but they said, "let God be the judge." They'd done their level best to guide and direct her and now it was time to give themselves up. Plus, they had to admit, Mary looked healthier and happier than she ever had before. Who was to say the blessing wasn't there?

Mary chose a vibrant blue dress to go with the neat white cape and apron covering. Her red waves were sprayed into subjection, her brand-new covering fresh and neat. Steve stood beside her, blond, tall, his shoulders wide, his new *mutza* a tad snug across his back.

They greeted arriving guests, Steve quietly beaming. Mary was shy and only a bit nervous, buoyed by her newfound faith and at peace with her decision.

A perfect November day, they all said, a day when God's blessing shone on all of Lancaster County's many weddings.

And when Mary slipped her hand in Steve's and stood in front of the minister, her voice was strong and steady as she produced her "*ya.*" Yes, she would take this man, with her whole heart.

They returned to the two folding chairs facing each other, their eyes downcast, suddenly very shy on this sacred ground. But Mary felt ready and able to embark on this long journey of years with the one whom her heart loved. When she dared look up, he was looking directly at her, with so much gladness in his eyes, she had to give him a quick smile of her own happiness before lowering her eyes to the hands in her lap.

Oh, Steve. My Steve now, after all this time. Through all the trials and sorrows you were there, with patience and wisdom and so much understanding. I am truly blessed among women, and this I know in every recess of my being.

Her wedding day was a swirl of happiness and newfound faith. Steve's steady presence beside her was all she needed as the gifts were opened and recorded in a notebook as an assembly of family and friends sang the hymns of marriage and faith Mary had chosen. The slow German hymns rose to the ceiling, filling the room with a mixture of voices, both low and high, a great swelling sound of praise for this day, for this love, for this couple God had joined together, and no man would put asunder.

The absence of parents was keenly felt, and mentioned in the sermon, discreet tears wiped. But Mary knew her father would not rejoice with the remainder of the wedding party, but with sad eyes would evaluate all the many ways in which the Amish were lowering their standards, weakening the fence through which the wolves would break. As Mary thought of this, she felt a wave of nausea. But quickly, she reminded herself that today was a time to rejoice, a time to love, to feel the love of God.

She genuinely enjoyed the remainder of the day, especially when the delicious evening meal was served, the youth seated as couples, paired with careful planning by Mary and Steve. Songs rose in praise to God, song leaders belting out the traditional German hymns set to English tunes, the youth joining in as they celebrated with the happy couple.

THEY STAYED IN a rented apartment while they renovated their home, an ugly brick rancher that had been built in the sixties with frugality in mind. The bathroom was tiled in a peacock blue, with pink rows along the top, and the tub was an old porcelain green, with a line of rust spreading out below the faucet. The tile floor was chipped and broken. The kitchen was painted butter yellow and had a paper border of purple grapes along the ceiling. The linoleum floor had yellowed with age, a pattern like a road map of New York City.

They found a sturdy hardwood floor beneath filthy carpeting in the living room, which was exciting. But then there was a nest of wasps in the garage, and roaches in the cabinets and the basement, which was almost more than Mary could handle. But the exterminator was very effective, and soon the windows were replaced and the hardwood floor refinished. They spent their days planning, ordering materials, and went to bed at night with their heads filled with dreams. They imagined a new horse barn, landscaping, ancient overgrown shrubs removed, a patio in back, a front porch, a winding flagstone walkway.

And Mary was happy, caught up in the dreams of newlyweds, the promise of love that would only widen and deepen until no winds of adversity could shake it, certainly never uproot it.

She discovered Steve's love of morning devotion, a reading of Scripture, sometimes a daily devotional book. Often, he read portions aloud to Mary as they sat at the breakfast table. Those little devotional books made her uncomfortable. Her father had always warned of these books, which were typically written by the English and could easily mislead the reader into worldly views.

For a while, Mary kept her concerns to herself, but one morning she could contain her fear no longer. "Do you have to read that silly book every morning?" she burst out, anxiety written all over her face.

Steve lifted an eyebrow, but then, wisely, decided just to listen as Mary told him her worries about the daily devotional from *Guidepost* magazine, how it could lead him astray, and wasn't it better just to look to the church leaders for truth? Steve sipped his black coffee and watched the torment come and go, her green eyes like a dark shadow in one moment, alive with hope the next.

Finally, he suggested maybe she wasn't used to hearing about the Bible in the English language, but that these devotions were still based on the Word of God.

"But my father . . ."

Steve felt irritation rising in his chest, but carefully set it aside.

"Yes?"

"My father always said many folks are led away from the narrow road, onto the broad, worldly one after they let go of the German. I think the German language is very important to staying true to the Amish church, and it makes me uncomfortable to hear you read verses of Scripture in English. It seems wrong, somehow."

He took a slow breath, and then replied evenly. "Okay, Mary. If you feel that way, we'll put aside these *Guidepost* devotionals and return to the German *Schrift*."

He said these words softly, with the tenderness required for his struggling wife. And every morning, the German Bible was brought to the table, and he read the familiar verse in his gentle voice. And she crossed her hands in her lap, bowed her head, and absorbed the words often spoken by her father.

As she listened, sometimes she was taken back to New York, back to her days as a child, a questioning school-aged girl, whose limited view of life held her to the belief that blessings awaited doing right, and hellfire waited for those who did wrong. No gray areas, no mercy for any missteps until after punishment had been inflicted.

Yes, she had struggled for years, but had been baptized into the church, and promised to help build the establishment, to stay *gehorsam* (obedient) to the *ordnung* (rules of the church), to keep the devil at bay by her *gehorsamkeit* (obedience).

Somewhere in there, Jesus was a factor, but He still felt far off. Much more accessible, as well as understandable, was the concept of obedience. She still worried about how large her covering was, the width of her hemmed strings, the length of her dress and the size of her *lepply*, the piece of fabric sewn to the back of her dress at the waist. To appear humble, plain, in *die ordnung*, was a way of letting her light shine among the brethren. As a child, it had also been a way to fit in as one of Amos Glick's daughters. She had peace, back then. Didn't she? When had she lost it, gone her own way?

Oh, she'd gone so wrong so many times.

But she was forgiven, had a change of heart, been redeemed by the blood of Christ, right? How could she be sure? According to her father's voice, you couldn't ever be sure. You only hoped you were good enough to be counted with the sheep and not the abominable goats which were led to their fate.

As Steve read the German words in his gentle tone, she felt her stomach rumble and heave, the familiar increase of heartbeats. Her mouth went dry as the breathing rasped in her throat. She fought for control, exhaled long and deep.

Steve's voice stopped. She raised frightened eyes to his.

"Mary, are you alright?"

"Yes, of course."

But her face had gone pale, the freckles like thrown bits of soil. He said nothing, but kept his eyes on her face.

It was so soon after the wedding, so soon after her change of heart when she'd been redeemed, when she'd learned to cast her cares on Jesus, when he felt she had truly accepted Jesus as her Savior.

He whispered, "You don't look good. Are you really okay?"

She shook her head. "It's nothing. I'm fine."

He got up, glancing at the clock. His driver would be here any minute and the horse wasn't fed, so he put a hand on her shoulder, bent to kiss her goodbye, with no response at all.

"Bye, Mary. Have a good day."

He imagined a whispered goodbye, but couldn't be sure.

She felt his absence, felt the cold wind on the barren plains of her soul, doubt like a landscape pockmarked with quicksand. She was afraid to get out of her chair, afraid to leave the kitchen. The sight of used dishes with fried egg on them served as a reminder she had to get up, go to work, take charge of her day. She bowed her head, tried to pray, but could not form sentences in her mind.

Here she was, in a rented apartment in Lancaster County, married to Steve. How was any of this okay in God's eyes when she had once been so sure she was supposed to marry Bennie Lapp? No, she could not think these thoughts. She must control them, but how did one go about doing that?

She took a deep breath, then another, steadied herself, and rose from her chair, her knees like rubber. *Oh God, where are you? Where is your strength?*

By sheer force of will, she gathered the dishes, carried them to the sink and ran water, added dish detergent, and fought despair with every ounce of her being.

THAT NIGHT, SHE turned away from Steve, telling him she was sick from the scent of polyurethane varnish she'd used on the bathroom vanity. It was like ice water dashed in his face, but he allowed her space, lying on his back with his hands clasped behind his head and praying with the fervent words of the troubled.

No, his precious Mary was not alright, and hadn't God shown him she wouldn't be? But how long, how deep and wide were the times of being tested?

Love never failed, he knew, but the heat of the battle brought a sense of discouragement. Was he up to the task? He'd been so sure the battle was over, that she'd been saved from her churning, wearying mind.

He slept fitfully, dreamt long desperate dreams, and in the morning, rose without energy or fortitude to face anything. Mary was still asleep as he let himself out, went to the bathroom and stared at his unshaven, bleary-eyed face. He poked a forefinger against the mirror and told himself to shape up, pick up his courage and face the day.

He put bacon in the oven, stirred a batter for pancakes, made a pot of coffee, and opened the door of the bedroom wide enough to see if she was awake.

She was sound asleep.

He finished the pancakes, shoveled the bacon onto a paper towel-lined plate, poured juice, and fixed a nice tray, before taking it to her, saying, "Mary?"

She opened her eyes, and for a second, devastating anxiety crossed her features, before she smiled, shook her head, and told him he was spoiling her terribly. He arranged pillows behind her back and tucked her thick red hair behind her ear, as he adjusted the tray across another pillow on her lap.

"This is wonderful, Steve. Do you know this is the first time in my life anyone ever brought me breakfast in bed? My favorite, too. Pancakes and bacon."

He watched her butter the pancakes, pour syrup liberally, take a bit, and close her eyes as she enjoyed the taste. Then she lifted her coffee cup to her lips, her green eyes heavy-lidded with sleep.

He loved her with all of his being, and the battle to help her suddenly seemed like nothing at all. He would gladly do whatever it took, gladly exercise every fruit of the Spirit to guide her to a healthy emotional state.

When she finished, he took the tray and set it on the dresser, then turned to find her regarding him with an unfathomable look.

"What is it, Mary?"

"I'm sorry about last night."

She held out her arms, and he went to her, as the birds chirped and twittered their morning songs, heralding the arrival of a cold January day.

LIKE TWO CHILDREN, they slipped and slid through snow and ice, making their way to the unfinished house, and stood shivering as he inserted the key into the lock and burst gratefully into the warmth of the oil furnace-heated house.

"Grateful for electricity, for sure," Steve commented.

"How long before we switch over?" Mary asked, an edge to her voice.

"Maybe a few years."

"*Years?*" Mary's voice carried an edge of shock.

"See how everything goes."

Mary shook her head. The laconic regard to *ordnung* was astounding. He wasn't worried about keeping the rules at all. She should have known this, and had, in fact, suspected it, but not quite like this.

"Solar's expensive."

"Solar?"

"Why sure. Everybody's putting solar panels up."

"Not everybody."

He heard the edge in her voice, realized he was on thin ice.

"Probably not. Plenty of folks stick to the old way. Diesel-powered, compressed air, propane lights . . . but I don't see why that's any better, really. At one point, those methods were all new. We have to progress to some degree. Humanity always does."

She shook her head. "But . . . my father says, said . . . nothing new should be allowed, ever. Stick to the old ways. That's where the blessing lies."

"Well, I suppose that's something to pray about before we make a decision."

She smiled her gratitude.

"In the meantime, let's appreciate this blessed electric-powered heat."

And she did, working side by side with Steve, applying paint and another coat of varnish, then standing back to survey the results of a soft white in the bathroom, a coat of bonding primer allowing them to paint over the hideous tiles. Steve had wanted to replace the tile work, but Mary felt that would be too extravagant. The medicine cabinet was replaced with a framed mirror from Lowe's and the tub replaced with a large white one, which Mary worried was too expensive, though this time she kept the opinion to herself.

The new kitchen was finished in February, before Valentine's Day, a perfect gift. The cabinets were white, with a small pine island in the middle, with white granite countertops, breathtakingly modern and stylish. Mary clapped her hands like a child, her eyes shining with joy and appreciation.

Oh, what fun she had, arranging her things on that beautiful countertop. A white kitchen was a dream come true—so clean, so fresh and new. She put her cookbooks on a wooden rack, arranged the glass canisters with wooden lids. Soon, she'd unpack her dishes and place them on the gleaming new shelves. She had to pinch herself to be sure it was real.

On moving day, Aunt Lizzie's girls came with their husbands in tow, flocking into the house, their enthusiasm building with each room they entered.

"Oh, my goodness!"

"Mercy, but you guys worked!"

"Seriously, this is so cute!"

But the kitchen created the biggest stir. The girls shrieked and squealed and ran their hands along the white granite with appreciation.

Suze turned to her unsuspecting husband and announced that she wanted a kitchen exactly like this right away, thank you.

The only sadness of the day was the absence of Aunt Lizzie who would have been so happy to see Mary with Steve, being settled into her home, looking so excited, so into the moment.

They'd brought fresh cinnamon rolls, a pot of coffee, and a casserole to put in the oven for lunch. The men let in great draughts of cold air as they carried in the furniture, greeting Steve's parents when they arrived later.

Towels and bedsheets were stacked in the handy cabinet in the new white bathroom, mirrors were secured to dressers in the bedroom, and the queen-sized bed was set up and clean sheets and quilts placed on it.

All Steve's hunting and fishing items were put in the basement. The dehumidifier would have to stay. Mary's brow furrowed when she heard it, thinking of the electricity it would take. But she soon forgot about it, caught up in the bustle of having her house established.

The finished result was heartwarming, cozy, and absolutely far beyond anything Mary could have imagined when they first set foot in the derelict hovel. Amid praise from her cousins and her mother-in-law's kind words, Mary was lifted to the pinnacle of happiness, something she did not take for granted. All the anxiety, the doubts and rumbling words of her father, were swept away by the love of her family.

Ruthann said there was no way she could go home and be content, and Linda slapped her arm and said she should be ashamed of herself, look at where she lived.

"I know, but my furnishings aren't as tasteful. This house is so . . . how can I say it? So put together. Just so cozy. You just want to stay here." She flopped on the La-Z-Boy, pulled the lever on the side, and leaned back, before grabbing her covering and tilting it to the top of her head.

"I don't know when they're ever going to invent a recliner for Amish women wearing coverings. Sit on one, and smash, there it goes. It's why I wear my *dichly* at home."

Steve's mother laughed, a sound like rippling water.

"I know what you mean. But those *dichlin* slide around on your head, too. Plus, for those of us with big ears, they are certainly not flattering."

"We need to come up with a better idea for a covering," Linda quipped, tipping Ruthann's until she yelled, saying the thing was pinned to her head, in case she'd forgotten.

So the day ended on a lighthearted note, in spite of missing Aunt Lizzie. Steve's parents wished them farewell and many happy days, his mother telling Mary to be sure to come spend the day whenever she felt lonely. She gave her a warm, sincere hug, promising to return soon with the girls.

The three cousins and their husbands wished them the same and offered a standing invitation to come visit anytime. Church was at Linda's house in two weeks, they reminded her, telling her to mark her calendar. "I know it's not your district, but *please* come," Linda urged.

Mary felt a part of family, circled by a group of individuals who were full of love and generosity, accepting her without question. She was a *kyotee frau*, a woman with a husband, incorporated into a close-knit group of Amish people where newlyweds were honored. A new young couple in the church was a sure sign of the blessing from God.

Steve put his arm around Mary's waist as they turned to go inside, and she took a deep breath and went into his arms, tired and smiling from the inside out.

As the stars were obliterated by gathering storm clouds, they slept peacefully that night, waking to a gray, windy morning, the furnace in the basement purring below them.

And God in His wisdom looked down from Heaven and knew the storm clouds were on the horizon for them as well, but His love was great. His strength would be sufficient through the darkest times when even the smallest bit of starlight was erased by the common trials of mankind.

CHAPTER 5

ON SATURDAY MORNING, THEY LINGERED OVER THEIR COFFEE. Mary planned to unpack the last of the wedding gifts that were still in boxes, and Steve planned to spend the day in the basement, building shelves to organize his equipment. The gray skies outside didn't bother them, as the overhead lighting brightened the kitchen.

"You look tired, Mary. Did you sleep okay?" Steve asked, placing the tip of his finger on her eyelid.

"I slept well. Could it be we just had moving day?" she quipped. Steve laughed, that wonderful carefree sound she loved, like a schoolboy.

"I love you, Mary," he said, still smiling.

"I love you, too, Steve. Forever."

The look that passed between them was one no one could capture in a photograph, one meant only for each other and the third part of a marriage, God.

He went whistling and singing snatches of song into the basement where he surveyed the mess, and wondered why he hung on to so much of it. But he grinned wryly to himself and set to work.

Mary washed the few dishes, then sat cross-legged on the floor, unwrapping the three cheese graters and staring at them. What did one do with three cheese graters? In New York she would take them to weddings, marked with her initials, and women would use them to make *graut*, or pepper slaw. But here in Lancaster they had evolved to some battery-operated device that worked like a food processor, whacking the veggies into tiny bits with a minimal amount of effort. It wasn't as good as the more loosely grated cabbage, and Mary thought lovingly of the camaraderie of the young women making *graut*, each one with her own *hovvla*, arms moving the quartered head of cabbage across the grater. Steve would say change was good, of course, and maybe he was right, but there were things about the old ways that she missed.

Next, she unpacked a set of wooden spoons and thirteen spatulas. She spread them out and smiled to herself. White, yellow, aqua, purple, blue. Take your pick. She chose the white Pampered Chef ones and put the rest in a plastic container for storage.

She held up a wall plaque with the word "Gather" in cursive black writing on white, with a black frame. She held it up, frowned, put it back in the box. Dollar General, for sure. She felt guilty, then, but she did not want it on her wall. There was a set of Rubbermaid bowls, with lids, a welcome respite from Tupperware. She liked the handy, inexpensive little bowls to take a fruit salad or soft cheese to church. If they got lost in the shuffle, it was no big deal, compared to pricey Tupperware containers.

There was a blue Pioneer Woman teakettle. She held it up, turned it over, but could not bring herself to like it. It was just so bright blue, not her style at all. She grimaced, replaced it, then thought of her mother's kitchen with the dusty wood range, the stained, greasy teakettle on the back with its peculiar hum, summer or winter. The feed store calendars, with each page torn off put to good use. Her mother wrote letters on the back and sent them to her sisters, usually running out of space and writing between the red and black numbers on the opposite side. The old rusted cheese grater and cracked spatulas.

She shook off the guilt, telling herself she was a new generation. She lifted a glass candle, popped the lid, and sniffed, tilted it to read the manufacturers label, nodded, and put it back in the box. Another cheap candle with an overwhelming scent.

When she looked up, she could see swirling bits of snow outside, and it made her heart glad. She had always loved snow, had always felt a happy anticipation when the clouds gathered in winter and the landscape became cold and still, just before the tiny, icy bits of snow started flying through the air. Snow for Valentine's Day. It was perfect. They planned to go out for supper, to a small restaurant specializing in Italian food, a place Steve said she would love. She was looking forward to it and hoped the snow wouldn't keep them from going. She felt a sense of security, with Steve still whistling in the basement, knowing the decision would be on his shoulders, allowing her the role of follower for the first time in her adult years. What a blessing this institute called marriage really was, she thought happily.

She picked up the cutest little wood-framed plaque, with the words in cross stitch: "The best things in life are not things." It looked perfect propped on her hutch. She stepped back, wondered what should accompany it. A crock? An urn? She had an old egg gathering basket somewhere.

The snow came down thick and fast now, the pine trees across the road already coated lightly, the cars creeping by. For a moment, it seemed like her past was a story she had read rather than her actual life. This beautiful home was so unlike the frugal way she grew up. It had been such a spare existence. She thought of the cabbage on buttered homemade bread that she'd bring to school as a child. Sometimes onion. Never meat or cheese. She'd eat alone, trying to avoid the sneers of the other students, but inevitably one of them would mention the stinky cabbage and onions, which often led to more teasing from the boys. Either she ate the cabbage and onion or went hungry, so she ate the crumbly bread with butter and pretended she didn't hear.

The first time she told her mother, she was firmly reprimanded, saying she should be glad to be mocked, that Jesus Christus was, too. That was terribly confusing. For one thing, she couldn't imagine Jesus eating cabbage and onions. As she got older, she realized her mother meant that Jesus was mocked before dying on the cross, but it still wasn't clear why that should make her happy that kids said her lunch stank. Still, for a long time, cabbage and onion reminded her of Jesus on the cross.

Standing in her own kitchen, Mary felt a shot of remorse, then a stab of rebellion, a need to avenge herself, a tangle of emotions she could never unravel. Who did she think she was, really, living it up in Lancaster, so far from her roots. She turned away from the window, caught her reflection in the mirror, and thought *Ugh. Fat, homely, crazy red hair*. A wave of self-loathing was like the scent of rotting carcass.

She tried to recover the pleasure she had previously felt in their new home, but the lowering clouds had settled, and Steve found her curled up on the recliner, a soft woolen throw covering her entire body, even her head, the half-unpacked boxes strewn across the floor.

"You okay, Mary?" he asked, touching her shoulder.

"A bit of a headache."

"The weather. Pressure system."

A mumbled reply.

Steve lowered himself into the opposite chair and turned his head to watch the snow. He opened his mouth to speak, then thought better of it and closed his eyes. Was this to be his life, then? It was so hard to watch her draw into herself, to a place he could not follow, might never know.

There would be no lunch unless he got it himself, so he wandered to the kitchen, opened the refrigerator door, scanned the shelves, and closed it again. He found Ritz crackers and ate half a sleeve before finding peanut butter, then polished off the rest. He watched the snow and decided he'd better call off the Valentine's Day thing. Too risky after dark.

He went back down the stairs, glancing at the covered form on the recliner, but told himself if it really was a headache, he should leave her alone to rest. But when he finished up at three and there was still no sounds from upstairs, he felt uneasy and went to check on her. He pulled back the blanket and found her unmoving, her eyes open and red rimmed.

"Mary."

Quickly, she threw the blanket off, turned her body, and sat up, lowering the footrest. She seemed disoriented, mumbling, rubbing her eyes.

"I don't know. Guess I fell asleep. Couldn't find the onions."

Suddenly her eyes opened wide, alarm spreading over her face. Genuinely frightened, she reached out and clutched his arm. "I don't know what happened. I was not sleeping. I was awake, but I was a little girl."

Steve felt her fear, but told her she must have been sleeping, really. Dreams were very real sometimes.

But she shook her head, then tried to laugh it off, producing a maniacal giggle that chilled him. She told him brightly that they likely wouldn't go out for supper, so she'd make soft pretzels with cheese sauce, how was that?

And he put aside his misgivings and told her it would be the best. While she mixed the yeast dough, he sat on a barstool and watched, the two of them talking easily about mundane subjects. He convinced himself it hadn't been anything but a harmless dream.

She shaped the long ropes in the shape of a heart and wrote "I love you" with ranch dressing. All felt right again in his world.

THEY GOT UP early on Sunday morning, two weeks later, dressed carefully in their Sunday best, climbed into their spotless buggy with the polished harness on the gleaming horse, and made their way to John and Linda's for church. Mary wore her black suit, since she was still in mourning for Aunt Lizzie, having been less than a year since her death. Steve was proud of how striking she looked in the dark dress, proud to be her husband as they drove behind a row of teams heading to the cluster of buildings along Route 274.

"They built a shop since I was here," Mary commented.

"Good thing. I hope they won't have services in that basement."

"How do you know what their basement is like?" she asked.

"This is my home church district."

"Are you serious?"

"Yep."

"Why didn't you tell me? So, you know everybody?"

"Pretty much."

But Mary was so warmly received that she didn't feel like an outsider for long. It was good to see Steve's mother and sisters, and Mary found it easy to smile and speak when she was spoken to. She sat with Suze, Ruthann, and Linda, as a relative who would help prepare lunch at the appropriate time. Relatives of the host had a special job. All the homemade bread brought to church by friends had to be sliced, replaced in the plastic bags, and placed on a side table with the cheese, pies, peanut butter spread, and other lunch items. And that was just the start of their busy afternoon. These women were the *chvishtot*, the relatives who would sit on chairs placed on the outskirts of the congregation, ready to get to work as soon as the service was over. Mary felt proud to be part of the *chvishtot*, that special group of women in charge of preparing lunch.

The main sermon was preached by a fiery minister intent on stirring up a true wave of repentance among the sinners who sat in rows on the benches, lighting fires of guilt and remorse underneath them. His strident, fast-spoken words contained not a trace of humility and barely a smidgen of grace. Faces lowered, shoulders slumped with discouragement. Rebels snorted inwardly.

But Mary froze in real fear. She was paralyzed. Her twisted handkerchief was frozen in clawed fingers, as if she clung to a life-saving rope attached to a floating device, the cold seas around her heaving in great sucking swells.

Every sentence from the minister's mouth was a death knell, an order to be thrown in the lake of fire where she would burn in all eternity. She trembled visibly. Her mind raced, dashed down one avenue then another, desperately seeking a sense of peace amid this hailstorm of words. Finally, she gave up, left her chair, and walked back to the house, where she found the bathroom and locked the door. She shook like a leaf. She breathed like a winded horse, her ribcage heaving. *Oh God, where are you? I'm going to lose my mind. Where is help when I need it?*

Every harsh word roiled her mind, upset her stomach, and accelerated her breathing. A knock on the door brought her back to her senses, and she ran water quickly, as if to wash her hands, then opened the door and pushed past a gaggle of school-aged girls.

A nursing mother looked up from her seat on the couch. She smiled, looked away. Mary went to the sink, opened the spigot, and filled a glass with lukewarm water, forcing herself to drink it. Suddenly weary, she turned to sit on a kitchen chair, knowing she could not return to that sermon.

A quiet voice reached her. "Are you alright?"

Mary turned to find the nursing mother looking at her, her brown eyes alight, keen with curiosity.

"Uh, no. Yes. I mean, I'm fine."

"Of course. I just thought you looked a bit rattled."

"Well, maybe."

Mary paused, looked around to make sure everything was safe, before asking, "Who is the minister preaching?"

"Is it Chonny? Chonny Lapp, I believe."

"I'm new in the area."

"Yes. You're Shtephy Riel ihr Steve's wife. Mary, is it?"

"Yes."

"I see. I heard you moved. I'm Sadie Fisher. Jonas Fisher sie Sadie. I am a midwife, sort of a doctor in the area."

"Midwife? Really? That's interesting."

"Well. That is as it may be, but you looked unwell when you came out of the bathroom."

"I can't . . . I guess I . . . It's hard to hear such preaching."

Sadie nodded, her eyes looking suddenly sad.

"Yes, I wish it were otherwise, but we'll always have that kind among us, Lord knows. It takes a firm foundation to accept that kind of preaching with grace. He is sincere, though, and also a man chosen by God to carry out His work."

"You think he is?"

"Well, yes."

But their eyes met, and they both knew the thoughts of the other, without a word being spoken.

"I have a weakness," Mary began, and suddenly felt comfortable telling Sadie a bit about her life.

Sadie watched her face, sensing the anxiety.

"*Heit iss Soondag* (Today is Sunday)," she said quietly, after Mary stopped. "But come visit me."

The phrase "Today is Sunday" was a catch-all to stop all business talk or transaction. "Today is the Lord's day, and we must keep it holy" was the unspoken message.

She told Mary where she lived, just before Ruthann swung through the door, a crying toddler perched on her hip, a pacifier with a torn nipple angling from a fastener.

"Hush. Jason Michael. Now you hush right this minute and I mean it. Uh, what will I do? One pacifier and he bit a hole in it. I'll be fit to be tied till it's time to go home. Hush, Jason."

Sadie lifted her baby over one shoulder, carefully arranging a burp cloth, then began a soft rhythmic patting.

Jason bit on the pacifier and set up a cacophony of fresh wails. Ruthann lifted her face to the ceiling and pretended to pull out her hair. Mary got to her feet, surprised to feel the room spin and tilt. She caught the back of a chair, then made her way uncomfortably to the hutch and opened drawers, looking for an extra pacifier.

"He's not going to take another one, I guarantee it. You may as well save your energy."

Jason's howls rose as Ruthann applied a handful of Kleenex to his nose, swiping.

"Here," Mary offered. "Try this."

"He's not going to take it. Here, Jason, *Gook mol da tootie.*"

Jason turned his face away, then peered at the proffered pacifier, reached out, and put it in his mouth. He blinked, then smiled, before resuming a desperate working on the new pacifier.

"Oh, praise the Lord. Can't believe it. Well, Mary, you saved the day. Somebody should go out and give Chonny Lapp a pacifier. I have never."

Sadie and Mary tried to look stern and displeased with that unabashed disrespect, but neither could hide their smiles.

"I tell you, if it's that hard to get to Heaven, I may as well give up right now. Jason, *komm*, let's get your diaper changed."

Oh, to have such a foundation, thought Mary, to come right out and say what you thought.

The remainder of the day was a whirl of preparing tables, washing dishes, and preparing the tables the second time, until everyone in the congregation was fed. Then the women sat gratefully, but not for any length of time, not if you were related to the one who hosted services. Soon, it was back into the house to prepare the evening meal of chicken potpie, baked beans, and a salad for relatives and friends.

Linda tasted the casserole she had prepared ahead, wrinkled her nose, and said, "This needs something."

"Here," Ruthann shouldered her way forward. "Give me a spoon." She tasted, nodded, and said she needed chicken base, that Better than Bouillon stuff.

"I'm not buying that stuff. It's sinfully expensive. Like five dollars for a weeny jar."

"Well then, your potpie will be gross."

"*Ach* come on, Ruthann. Suze, Mary, taste it."

They all agreed, it needed chicken base, though Mary assured her it was quite good.

There were children underfoot, always. Running, laughing, yelling, making an unbelievable mess through the house. Mary watched them go, thought of her new white kitchen cupboards, the pine floors, all the potted plants, and cringed.

Would a flock of unsupervised children scratch her floors, bang her cupboards, upset her plants? Steve was planning a shed in which church services would be held, so they could take their turns the following year.

Every newlywed couple was given a year's grace before hosting services, which gave them time to build the additional space to do so, if needed. Sometimes they didn't have the financial means to do this, so a kind neighbor would host services twice. To be Amish meant you upheld and respected tradition, were steeped in it like a fine tea. "This is the way the forefathers did things, it is a precious heritage, and thus we will follow willingly."

Besides, hosting services was a special event, creating a certain excitement. The house was thoroughly cleaned, no window left unwashed. In summer, flower beds and gardens were mulched, every last weed plucked, the whole place spruced up and prepared for a congregation used to seeing everything at its best. If the woman of the house had a new baby or a house full of small children, sisters and a mother would arrive the day before with the sole purpose of cleaning the place from top to bottom. It was simply a part of life, to give of themselves in time of need. It was just how things were done.

ON THE WAY home, tucked beneath a warm fleece buggy robe, Mary listened to the wet plunking of the horse's hooves, watched the piles of snow go by, noticed the flock of starlings quarreling along the eaves of a heifer barn. Steve was quiet, seemingly lost in thought, his profile stern.

She put a hand on his knee. "A penny for your thoughts."

He grinned at her. "A penny doesn't get very far these days."

"Come on."

"I noticed you left the service early."

She recoiled, shrank into herself. She wanted to be perfect for him, wanted to be everything he thought she was, so she said lightly, "Ladies need the restroom at times."

"That long? I was getting worried."

"I was talking to a new friend, Jonas Fisher's wife, Sadie."

He nodded, "Okay."

The horse plodded uphill, the naked trees on either side standing like sentinels, ushering them toward home. A crow rose ahead of them, startled away from his roadkill, flapping and cawing his indignation.

Then Steve asked, "The sermon had nothing to do with it?"

"Uh, no. No. He was quite interesting, if a bit harsh."

"And that didn't bother you?"

How could she tell him how it affected her? He would think her unstable, emotionally crippled, a backslider in the faith, which was what she was. He had not bargained for a wife he needed to worry about all the time.

"No, not really."

And so he let it go, but was left with a certain uneasiness, a foreboding of his world being off kilter by a few degrees. The darkness of her afternoon on the recliner, the strange dream and weird laugh accosted his thoughts, bringing a sense of despair. Was his own faith strong enough to keep the both of them on solid ground? He prayed for wisdom in how to best help her.

He loved her deeply and knew he'd always be there for her. Whatever he couldn't do, he'd have to leave in God's hands.

CHAPTER 6

WHEN SPRING ARRIVED THAT YEAR, MARY'S BATTLE INTENSIFIED. Her father's warnings echoed in her ear, burning through her mind until she clutched the sides of her head in agony, her eyes squeezed shut as she willed a shred of peace to enter her soul. When she realized she was with child, the days crept by with alternating bouts of vomiting along with the debilitating mental anguish. Every day was an insurmountable challenge, every hour she stayed on guard, carefully preserving the picture of herself that she presented to Steve.

He remained her loyal helper, giving his life the way Christ gave His for the church. Together, they tilled, mulched, fertilized, and planted a large garden. Mary smiled as they worked, desperate to hide her struggles from Steve. But by the sixth month of her pregnancy, she crumbled. She stopped speaking to Steve almost entirely and stayed cocooned in her house, leaving dishes unwashed, laundry in piles all over the house, the beautiful garden grown up in weeds.

Steve contacted the midwife, Sadie Fisher, who did her best to help. She supplied Mary with an arsenal of holistic medicine and herbal pills, and even showed her gentle yoga poses to quiet her mind. While Sadie was there, Mary felt marginally better, but she sank back into her depression as soon as she left.

Steve's mother came to do laundry. She noticed the yellowed covering and unwashed hair, as well as the alarming number of store-bought snack cakes and cookies she consumed with coffee heavily laced with hazelnut creamer. Her heart clanged with real fear as she watched Mary wipe her mouth with the back of her hand before waddling to the couch where she sat, legs splayed to accommodate her girth.

Mary laughed, a strange brittle sound. "Finally, I can eat what I want. No dieting for my little one."

Becky replied with grace, "*Ach* yes, Mary. We certainly enjoy our food when we're in the family way, don't we?"

Steve watched as his beloved wife changed into a person he barely recognized. She refused to go to church, then stayed home and binged—a whole can of ravioli, a full pint of Moose Tracks ice cream, a can of cola—before sinking into bed, exhausted but unable to sleep.

Steve knew something was terribly amiss. He begged her to see a doctor, begged her to go for help, but never forced her. He felt there was nothing he could do until she was willing.

With communication at a standstill, she took to sleeping in the guest room. She felt herself an obese monster, one who would be revolting. She was too ashamed to be close to her handsome husband and his honed physique. She was gross, unworthy, a huge overblown elephant, she told herself repeatedly.

Word of her condition reached the ears of her siblings in New York, who promptly loaded up a van and came to express their concern on a hot August morning.

It was on a Saturday, with Steve in the garden with the cultivator, finding rotting tomatoes and worm-infested corn, his spirits at a new low, his heart bearing the pain of his disappointment.

Mary was in the kitchen, furtively stuffing potato chips into her mouth and washing them down with iced coffee as perspiration beaded her upper lip. She watched Steve pushing the cultivator and felt a pang of horrible guilt, like the edge of a sword, but ate two more chips to assuage the self-loathing that accompanied the guilt.

What was this? A van filled with Amish people.

She swallowed and wiped her mouth, releasing a shower of salt and grease, then crumbled the potato chip bag and stuck it in the bread drawer.

Oh no. Abner, Jonas, their wives, a herd of little ones.

She looked around, a hand to her throat, her mind dashing here and there, searching for an escape route. Why had they come without warning? To catch her in this state of neglect. To rub her nose in the mess she'd made of her life, marrying the wrong person, the one without the blessing.

She swallowed, felt the bile rise in her throat.

Steve looked up and reached into his pocket for a handkerchief, wiping his forehead, then walked between the rows of lima beans to greet them, breathing a prayer things might go smoothly.

Mary's mouth was set in a grim line. Here they were, poking around for another excuse to knock her down. *Well, go ahead, guys. Here I am, everything you expected—a mentally ill, obese woman living in a filthy home. You were right—I missed the blessing. I hope you're happy.*

But as she opened the door, some kind of muscle memory kicked in and she put on a smile, extended a hand in greeting, and spoke to the children, exclaiming how they'd grown. For the first time in many weeks, she looked directly into Steve's eyes, smiled, and said warmly, "You are working too hard, Steve. A good thing we have company."

She moved slowly, but she showed off her house, asking them to excuse the "lived-in look." She laughed convincingly, then got out a plastic tote of books and toys for the children. She cooked a delicious noon meal of lasagna and put together a fresh spinach salad. She poured meadow tea over ice and kept up a lively account of her life with Steve.

After dishes were washed and put away, they retired to the back porch, which was unfinished, but had comfortable chairs with a view of the backyard and garden, the stately oak tree and surrounding pines.

"So," Mary asked innocently, "what made you decide to come visit?"

Abner cleared his throat. "Mary, we'd heard you weren't well, and since we knew how you can be unstable in your mind, we came to have a talk out of love and concern for your welfare here in Lancaster."

Jonas nodded assent. There were sharp gazes from the sisters-in-law. Mary lifted her chin, her small eyes beady, cunning as a ferret.

"And what have you found?" she asked sweetly.

"It seems it was only rumors, for which we are glad."

Steve watched Mary, saw the lowering of eyelids, the righteous tilt of her mouth. His own thoughts churned, divided between honesty and helping Mary with this charade. To blow her cover might have devasting repercussions, so he stayed silent.

"Yes, I'm glad, too. As you can see, I have gained weight, but with good reason. And it has been a bit of a struggle keeping up with the housework while I'm in the family way. But Steve is all I have ever wanted in a husband, so you must never fear for my well-being."

"Of course. And it does seem as if Bennie Lapp and Rachel are quite a pair, for which we are grateful, although we think you would have found a blessing in that union as well."

"That may be," Mary said sweetly, "but I much prefer Steve."

He could not meet her eyes, filled as they were with a strange light.

The remainder of their visit was occupied with ordinary subjects, the children running in and out of the house, laughter, the weather in New York, the women quietly inquiring about her pregnancy, her midwife, her expectations of motherhood. And Mary had all the right answers, the appropriate smiles at the correct times.

They were sent away with smiles and waves. Mary and Steve stood outside as the van disappeared down the drive, turning right, the line of trees obliterating it from their view. Steve turned to Mary, bright hope on his face, thinking this visit might have been the boost she needed. But he was crestfallen when she turned on her heel without a word and went into the house.

He followed her, found her splayed on the recliner.

"Mary, please talk to me. Seeing you like that today—it made me miss you even more. I miss the sound of your voice, your touch."

"There is nothing to say."

"But there is, Mary. You are not yourself. I don't know how you pulled it together for your family today, but they were right to be worried about you. *I'm* worried about you."

"Why would I be myself? Why? I'm nothing but a . . ."

She stopped, bit her lower lip.

Gently, he reached out to touch her knee.

She struck at him, viciously. "Get away from me."

At that moment, he wanted to walk out, walk away and never return. He realized he was married to a kind of emotional con artist, a miserable woman who could turn into a happy caricature of herself when the need arose. He had been so sure, so confident of his ability to help her to a new life in Christ, to set her feet on solid ground and keep her safe from the fear and anxiety she wrestled with.

How did one go about this? Was prayer sufficient? Or should he insist she get help? How?

He left the room, his mind tumbling with thoughts, his face crumbling as tears coursed down his tanned cheeks. He'd done all he knew—been kind, gentle, picking up the pieces after her.

She no longer got up in the morning, but lay in bed till who knew when. He ate Wheaties for breakfast, alone, packed his own lunch, and often ate Wheaties again for supper, or sometimes a can of soup. He bought groceries, cleaned the house as best he could, never complained, never told his family.

He had to go on, he reasoned. Perhaps it was just the hormones from pregnancy and soon she'd be better. He set his hopes on the birth of their child. He tried to picture her caring for their baby, getting her mind off herself, proving to be the competent girl he married.

Lord, you have to take charge. I don't know how. I thought I had it all together, felt capable, ready to do your work, but I have no idea what I'm doing.

MARY'S SITUATION CONTINUED to spiral out of control. Her over-wrought nerves coupled with the deluge of unprescribed pills and potions were too much for her fragile mind. Now that she was well into the third trimester, she was also weighed down with the guilt of knowing she did not want this baby.

She had no reason to believe this child would have a chance at living a normal life, not with a mother like herself. Every movement, every light tap inside of her, served as a sounding bell, her child expressing its dislike of her. She was a gruesome whale, an unfit mother, and she could not see her way through, could not confide in one single soul. She could have told Aunt Lizzie, but she was dead.

Steve made an effort to speak about the baby, to get her interested in buying a crib, some clothes, perhaps fixing up the guest room as a nursery, but she turned her face away, refused to acknowledge his voice.

Steve's parents came and spoke their alarm quietly to their son, who was clearly distraught. Church ladies sat in stern, silent groups, watching Steve come to church by himself, whispered rumors after he left. Ministers arrived, kindly men who offered help. There were places of rest for someone like Mary.

Steve summoned her, told her the ministers wanted to speak to her, perhaps find her help. She was a mound of flesh now, unspeakably tortured, only a shadow of the real Mary remaining, and she only turned her head long enough to snarl her refusal at him.

He told the group of men there was nothing he could do, she wouldn't agree to help, so they laid their hands on his shoulders, offered their support, and told him they would pray without ceasing. Steve bent his head and cried so that his whole frame shook. The ministers cried with him, wished him God's blessing, and left him with a little more peace, a sense of being upheld by strong arms.

By her ninth month, Mary no longer wanted to live. She spent her hours contemplating the ways in which she might end her life.

She could feel the distaste her unborn child had for her, could decipher Steve's utter disgust, felt her own body ballooning like a foreign thing. Gluttony. She was caught in one of the unforgivable sins, but there wasn't much to be done. She slid down the slippery slope of wretchedness, one sin piled on top of another, her life a thing of dejection and fear.

Steve pleaded with her, begged her to seek help, cried and reached out in great tenderness, and assured her of his love, which only escalated the feelings of self-hatred. But now, she just wanted to die, wanted a way out of this constant, life-draining battle of keeping her mind intact. It was like walking up a glass mountain, like climbing a water-fall, or a tree with no branches. Her mental strength was ebbing, her days made up of dense fog. The only thing to hold onto was the taste of food in her mouth.

Mary opened the cupboard door in the bathroom, looked at the blue and white bottle of Advil, shook it. Yes, there were plenty. Her mind took on a new clarity, a sharp vision of how this could be done, but she replaced the bottle with shaking hands, thought, *no, no.*

What else, then?

She could no longer fit into any of her dresses or aprons, so she looked down at the cotton housecoat she wore, the stains of food and drink, her feet mammoth below the hem. Her ankles were swollen to twice their size, her toes like small clubs.

She peered at her face, a pale, sickly mound of flesh protruding from scraggly red hair, having seen no shampoo for weeks. Her lips were thick, swollen, grotesque.

Steve would be glad to have her gone.

And so she found a new purpose in the bottle of Advil, a thing to occupy her weakening mind, her tormented thoughts. She decided to write a note to Steve, who deserved to know what she was planning, but abandoned it after she realized she could be responsible for a life other than her own, that of her unborn child.

She had no feelings for it, had no idea how she'd get through the ordeal of caring for it. She did not want Steve to know, so she kept it to herself, and he knew his pleading only made things worse.

It was on a Friday afternoon that she developed a severe headache, so bad she thought perhaps she was having a stroke or an aneurysm. She got down the Advil bottle and calculated her weight, the amount she might need. For a long moment she held the bottle, then counted out four. She looked at the swollen palm, the bizarre pudginess of her fingers, and counted out four more.

Two thousand milligrams. Four thousand?

Suddenly her marriage, Steve in all his perfection, the impending birth, the days and nights keeping her sanity with the added burden of caring for a helpless infant screaming out its needs when she didn't know what to do, was a crushing weight, one she could not fight.

She shook the bottle of Advil, shook again. With a deliberate plodding gait, she went to the kitchen, got down the thirty-two-ounce tumbler. She opened the top, filled it half full, then went back to the guest room, taking the Advil bottle with her.

She had to make things right with God, somehow, knowing He was the only one who would witness the swallowing of these pills.

She couldn't gather a remnant of her thoughts, only a shred to tell Him she was too tired to fight anymore.

Sitting on the edge of the bed, she looked down at her swollen feet, the huge knees below the stained housecoat. She looked around the pale walls of the guest room, the thin curtains hanging limp, and swallowed too many of them, knowing or not knowing she'd finally find rest from the battle she was definitely losing.

STEVE CAME THROUGH the door, bone weary after a day spent laying a complicated patio wall for an extremely finnicky customer, his spirits at an all-time low. He didn't expect to see Mary, so when the house was quiet, he found nothing amiss, set his lunch on the counter, and opened a cabinet door for a glass, then to the refrigerator for some of the lemonade his mother had brought.

He drank it down, sighed, thought he'd look for Mary in the guest room, where she often lay in the afternoon. The door was ajar, so he pushed it open, saw the large form in the pink housecoat, the sheets rumpled, the quilt sagging to the floor. He took notice of the pink glass, then turned to leave, figured she was asleep. He was walking down the hall when it registered in his brain: the blue and white bottle of Advil. A sickening thud of his heart, and her name rose on his lips.

He was beside her bed, calling her, pleading, a hand to her forehead. Her big wrist, his thumb searching for a pulse, his breath coming in gasps. He tried the inside of her elbow.

Was it a weak flutter, or his imagination?

He called her name over and over, then left the room, burst through the back door and to his office, dialed 911, said "Hurry, hurry!"

Back in the guest room, he realized it might be too late, but asked God to spare her, to please let her live. He had failed her, was failing her now, as she lay between life and death.

He went to the front window, vaguely aware he was crying yet again.

The sound of a wailing siren was music, heavenly God-sent music to his straining ears. Chills raced up and down his spine as two men clad in navy blue dashed up to the house.

MARY'S EYELIDS FLUTTERED, closed again. A deep sigh escaped her, and she slept. Steve lay on a recliner by her side, the room at Lancaster General clothed in semidarkness, the flashing lights on the monitor at the head of her bedside coupled with small beeps of sound the only disturbance. Soft-soled nurse's shoes whispered along the hallway, and there were distant voices, the clattering of wheels.

He was not yet asleep, his mind unable to fully grasp all that had occurred in twenty-four hours. Mary had been delivered of a daughter by Caesarean section, an emergency, then sedated since her mental state was unable to face her situation. Trained medical professionals would supply information as they saw fit, and Steve could do nothing but give himself to their expertise.

He could not sleep, thinking of his beautiful daughter. She was so perfect, with a thatch of hair sure to be as red as Mary's. The pills Mary had consumed meant the baby had to be cared for in the NICU unit, but she would be fine, they assured him. He had been allowed to hold her, and the love he felt, and the intense desire to protect her, was almost overwhelming. He had been so worried about Mary throughout the pregnancy that he had found it hard to feel much happy anticipation about the coming baby. But that first time holding her, the reality of being a father hit with so much joy and gratitude that tears leaked out of the corners of his eyes as he cradled her in his strong arms.

Mary would recover too. But he knew there was a long road ahead, albeit paved with hope.

As he lay awake, he thought over the last year of his life, the burden of Mary's mental anguish so much heavier than he could have thought possible. Oh, he thought he had it down to a science. She would call on him to have her questions answered, and he'd be ready to supply all her needs with his vast store of spiritual wisdom. What a farce. He felt a deep sense of humility, a sense of being a speck, a mere bacterium in the vast space of the earth, and God a holy, great, and glorious being far above anything he could count. God was so much bigger than anything else, especially himself, poor wretched mortal that he was.

He felt a renewed vigor for life, a possibility of happiness restored. He could see his daughter, perhaps her siblings accompanying her, walking to school, an aging Mary waving from the porch, he with his own mason company in their new shop.

Oh Mary, wake up, wake up, we need a name for her. But for now, he would be patient, abide by the doctor's orders.

He was awake at six, his hand on her shoulder as she slept. The IV bag was almost empty, and he jumped when a shrill beep sounded through the darkened room. Her eyelids fluttered. She turned her face, moaned.

A nurse hurried in, turned on the light, brought a fresh bag to hang on the pole. The nurse turned to Steve and wished him a good morning, which he returned.

"When will she be allowed to wake up?" he asked, feeling hopelessly inadequate.

"The doctor will be in around eight. He should have an answer for you."

He ate his breakfast in the cafeteria, brought his coffee to her room, then asked to see his daughter, but had to wait till ten.

No, Mary wouldn't be able to breastfeed, but he had agreed to allow his daughter to receive donated milk through a donor bank.

The doctor gave him an honest evaluation in as few words as possible. The fluid buildup, the ravenous appetite, her depression and ongoing mental issues would be addressed after enough time had elapsed, but for now, she'd remain under sedation. He suggested he prepare for the possibility that the baby would need to be in someone else's care for some time. He said typically in these cases, the mother didn't want her child.

And Steve's heart broke again. Would he lose both Mary and his daughter?

CHAPTER 7

When Mary did awaken, it was slowly, by degrees, as if she could only sip of the cup of reality a little at a time. She winced as she tried to shift position and a nurse quickly explained that she'd had a caesarean section. Tears slowly appeared on Mary's lashes.

"Would you like to see your daughter?" the nurse asked kindly. "She's doing really well. I checked with the NICU nurse and she said we could bring her to you."

Mary just shook her head. Her disinterest was a dagger in Steve's heart.

"Mary, she's perfect. She has your hair! Just wait until you see her." He was practically begging her to care.

Mary allowed Steve to hold her hand but would not make eye contact. "I'm so tired," she whispered, and fell asleep again.

Steve's parents came, and his mother said she had honestly never seen a sweeter, more perfect baby. But then, it was her first grand-daughter. Steve was grateful to have someone share his joy. They passed the baby back and forth, exclaiming over her hair, her tiny toes, her bright eyes. But eventually, the weight of his situation settled back on his shoulders. Haltingly, his voice catching in his throat, he asked his parents if they'd be able to keep the baby for a while.

His mother responded with tears in her eyes. "Of course. *Ach*, Steve. Yes, of course. It will be a joy for the girls as well."

ONE MONTH LATER, on the day Mary came home, the winds of winter were making a decided entrance, but Steve had a new wood stove in the basement and a nice stack of wood in the shop. The house was cleaned and there were fresh flowers on the table. It had taken time, but the doctors had reached a diagnosis and found the combination of medicine that was right for her. She had severe depression and bipolar disorder and was told she would have to be on pills for the rest of her life. "Don't mess around," the kind doctor ordered. "You need these meds, and don't let anyone—even yourself—convince you otherwise."

Mary cried when the doctors praised her strength and courage, telling her it was remarkable that she had lived a normal life as long as she had without the help of medicine. An amazing feat.

She would see a counselor every week, as would Steve, and she'd check in with the doctor again in three months.

Her doctor explained about how a healthy brain functioned with the right balance of norepinephrine, serotonin, and dopamine, and how people with bipolar disorder needed medicine to maintain that balance. Without medicine, no amount of willpower could prevent a depressive or manic episode.

Mary listened, rapt. All her insecurity, her fear and anxiety, her lows and maudlin highs were finally explained. It wasn't her fault. All her life, she'd thought her lack of peace was from her disobedience, from being too strong-willed for her family and yet somehow not strong-willed enough to control her moods.

She felt like she'd been carrying around a weighty backpack that had crippled her posture, and now, with this new information and the help of medicine, she could extend her shoulders, slide it off, and let it fall to the ground. She tried out her new freedom in tiny steps, but each one turned in the right direction.

To be free of crippling guilt was too much to take in immediately, but the medicine supplied a steady stream of the necessary ingredient to live a normal life.

THEY NAMED HER Margaret. Margaret Mary. Mary didn't mind there was no one named Margaret in the Amish church, here in Lancaster or in New York. She'd always loved the name from *Little Women*. Besides, she looked like a Margaret.

Steve called her "Margarine," then changed it to "Blue Bonnet," till Mary made him stop. She had missed out on the first six weeks of her life, a fact that now caused a deep ache in her heart. Steve's mom had offered to bring Margaret to the hospital to visit, but it really wasn't until she got home that Mary suddenly longed for her daughter. It was like something just clicked, and she was ready. Steve felt his prayers answered and shed tears of deep gratitude as he and his parents set a day for his daughter to come home.

The baby had grown to eleven pounds when they brought her dressed in pink with the softest white blanket, and Mary held her in her arms and gazed into the tiny face for the longest time, before lifting soft eyes shining with unshed tears.

"She's perfect. I don't deserve her."

Margaret looked at her with wide open eyes, as blue-green as her own, as if to say, "Where have you been, Mom?" And Mary laughed and cried, then sat down weakly. She didn't think she could ever stop staring at her beautiful daughter.

Steve's family stayed for the day doing laundry, helping with the wood, and talking about Mary's illness.

"What is so freeing, though, is the idea that mental illness is a disease, like cancer or heart disease. For years, I blamed myself, was positive it was just a result of my own sinfulness. I only wish I had listened to Steve sooner when he asked me to see a doctor."

She looked at Steve with so much love that his mother's throat ached. Steve merely sat in his chair and smiled, returning the look of love. "I'm just so grateful you're both okay," he said, his eyes watering again.

His parents went home in profound gratitude and renewed faith that God would always provide, one way or another.

Steve and Mary took little Margaret to church and showed her off good and proper. They went out of services at the necessary time when the deacon announced the amount of their hospital bill. They discussed the discount they would likely be able to get from Lancaster General and then voted to pay monthly installments until the entire amount was paid off.

To be provided for by the giving of alms was a matter of profound gratitude, and after services Mary felt humbled at the genuine smiles of love and caring. To be a part of a loving group of people concerned about each other's welfare was something they never wanted to take lightly, and didn't.

Every morning Mary and Steve read their devotionals, prayed together, and sang a hymn of worship they felt from the heart, and Mary never once imagined the English pages of spiritual guidance to be misleading. She asked Steve if he thought her father might have been diagnosed with this same disorder, and after a brief contemplation, said it could very well be the case.

"But we'll never know, right?" she answered, lifting a baby bottle to squint at the ounce markups on the side.

"No. We don't have to. He's gone now, and grace is sufficient for him, as well as for us."

"Absolutely. Your turn or mine?"

"Mine," Steve answered, reaching happily for Margaret to feed her.

It was a winter of gratitude and joy, and of being awake at night. Baby Margaret lay between them in the cold of night, and Mary and Steve were often both too amazed by the hand of God, the love and care over them, to actually relax and drift off to sleep while Margaret slept.

Mary kept her appointments, talked to a professional counselor, and began to understand her disease more and more. She began to learn to live in the moment, to appreciate each hour more fully.

STEVE BUILT HIS shop, took out a frightening loan at Susquehanna Bank, and started up "Precise Masonry."

When Margaret was two and a half, Mary gave birth to another little girl, this one delivered at the birthing center by a certified midwife after a long, strenuous labor, but a successful one.

They named her Rebecca Ellen, a namesake for his mother, Becky, who beamed and smiled. Rebecca had a fuzz of blond hair, blue eyes, and a strawberry birthmark beside her belly button they both loved to tickle and to blow kisses on. They loved their little Becky as much as any parents could, and reflected on how precious, how uncomplicated, her arrival had been.

More time passed, and they raised the roof of the brick rancher and added an upstairs after the birth of their son, Logan Grant. A fancy name, the in-laws stated, but without reprimand. Logan Riehl had a nice ring to it, and *ach*, it was time for a few new names. Not everyone could be named Amos or Davie or Dannie. Didn't the postal service say they had fifteen David Stoltzfuses on one route?

Logan was all of nine pounds nine ounces, with the same mop of red hair as Margaret had, and Mary's features. He was content, sleeping in his battery-operated swing, his eyes watching any kind of movement from only a few days old.

On Margaret's first day of school, Mary stood on the porch holding Logan with Becky clinging to her skirts, waving goodbye, her chest exploding with pride at her role as a mother, while tears ran down her cheeks. Here was her firstborn, the darling girl who had no mother the first six weeks of her life, leaving her.

Dear God, go with her. Forgive me all my weaknesses and help me to be a better, more patient mother.

Margaret was a handful, no doubt. She was a strong six-year-old, tall, well-built, and a runner like an antelope. Extremely competitive, she did not always play fair with children her age, and wasn't always gentle with her younger brother and sister.

When she came home at lunchtime, she waved five papers, stapled at one corner, and Mary duly exclaimed over them and admired the alphabet she'd traced and the way she'd colored in the cat illustration.

Margaret's eyes narrowed. "Mom, Chonnie said I have a funny name."

"Your name is different, but it's a nice one."

"I don't want to be called Margaret anymore. It's a dumb name."

"Oh now, come on, Margaret."

"I don't like it."

"Okay, so what would you like to be called?"

"Rosie."

"Oh. Well, we'll ask Daddy when he comes home."

When Steve came through the door that afternoon, Margaret threw herself at him.

"Daddy, you have to listen to me."

He hunkered down, grasped her shoulders in his callused hands, and listened to her explain how Chonnie disliked her name, and how she needed to change it to Rosie.

"Chonnie who?"

She shrugged. "I don't know. Just Chonnie. I guess."

"Margaret is at least as nice as Chonnie. His real name is John. Or Johnny."

That seemed to do the trick, and Margaret dropped the subject, went to play house with Becky, and forgot about it.

Mary told Steve how much she'd felt like a real mother, waving at Margaret, holding Logan. Steve smiled, put an arm around her shoulder, and said she wasn't getting any younger—forty was fast approaching and they should have one more.

Life was so good, so full of endless possibilities. Just to sit at the sewing machine, humming a nameless tune, not worrying, was a priceless gift, an undeserved blessing. When Logan cried and Becky needed attention, it was a privilege to care for them. She'd asked Steve if he was sure she wasn't drugged, like a sick animal, or a horse that was crazy, or something, and he asked if she wanted to go back to her former life.

She would instantly remember and become grateful for every moment of happiness, every instance she experienced joy.

These days, she felt so ordinary, like her friends, the other mothers in church who had their ups and downs, exchanged recipes and cape patterns, gave unsolicited advice on everything from viruses to essential oils.

She loved her social life, the outings with friends, going for coffee or out for lunch, a wake of little children behind them.

They even spent a weekend in New York when her sister had church at their house, something Mary would not have done before her diagnosis, afraid of everything, guilty about Bennie Lapp and cringing beneath her father's words.

After services, she asked the name of the very young minister, his voice strident, but mellow, reminding her of Jesus.

"Oh, that's Eli Allgyer's Elam. He had leukemia as a child. You must remember, you were his teacher. Didn't you spend time with him in the hospital?" Lydia asked.

"Why yes, I did! Oh, my goodness."

So, this boy had been spared from death for this purpose, to spread the gospel, to give comfort to the needy, to make known the power and riches of His Kingdom. God had a reason and a purpose for everything. Mary had not found her own purpose until she'd hit rock bottom and found a true diagnosis, and now life as it was meant to be was given to her through grace, and grace alone.

A thousand hallelujahs welled up in her soul, and she had to turn away from Lydia to hide the mounting emotion.

She wished she could remember Elam's mother, but she seemed a blurry figure. She did remember the kitchen, the soft glow of their orderly house, the beige window blinds. How amazing were God's ways, really. Had that kitchen glowed for her alone, a light to her soul, whispering of her own disease and healing?

At any rate, it seemed as if God was everywhere, through everything, and every Christian could only worship with a thousand hallelujahs.

On the way home, as the vehicles' headlights shone along the curving mountain road of New York, Mary marveled at the peace, the lasting calm of her thoughts. She reached over to kiss Logan's cheek in his car seat, patted Becky's knee, and thanked God she was allowed to be a mother to her children. She giggled quietly to herself, thinking about her brother Abner's rumbles, so like her father. "Aren't you concerned about their souls?" he'd asked. "Margaret . . . Logan . . . such strange names. They leave a bad taste on my tongue." Years ago, this would have been branded into her, the pain and injustice of such a remark, but now, she merely appreciated the conservative way, and respected his love of tradition. But these children were hers, not his, and it was none of his business what they named their children.

And she fell sleep soon after they hit the interstate, her chin resting comfortably on her chest.

WHEN MARGARET WAS in third grade, Becky started first grade, a thin, winsome child with thick blond hair and a tendency to mispronounce her Rs. Margaret was fiercely protective of her and wouldn't allow anyone to mistreat or annoy her if she could help it.

They had to go with a school van, a distance of a little over three miles, a constant chafing at Margaret's well-being. She hated riding the van if everyone else scootered, and what was three miles? She could easy scooter that.

Mary explained patiently, telling her Becky was too small, and no, it wasn't safe on winding back roads with dogs, strangers who could lure them into their cars, accidents going downhill. The answer was no.

She was appalled when Margaret stamped her foot, balled her fists, lifted her face to the ceiling, and howled.

"Margaret. Stop this instant," Mary said firmly.

In answer, Margaret stuck out her tongue, crossed her eyes, and flapped her hands above her ears, which Mary caught out of the corner of her eye.

"Come here," she said, very low, but firmly. Margaret flounced away, lifting her skirts above her knees.

Like a flash, Mary reached out and caught her by the shoulder, spun her around, and lowered her face within inches of hers.

"You will not make a face at your mother. Neither will you scooter to school. We said no, and we mean it. Now go to your room and stay there till I call you for supper."

Margaret stared back at her mother, a flattened look in her eyes, like a horse with its ears laid back, a look that told her, "Don't mess with me." And Mary felt a cold draft, even when there was no chill in the room.

She confided in Steve, who shook his head, saying he always figured she'd be a handful, seeing how determined she was, but that, too, could be used in a positive way. She just needed a hand to guide her in the proper direction.

Mary bit her lower lip and told him Margaret took every ounce of patience she possessed.

Steve smiled, "And this is only third grade."

WHEN MARY WAS thirty-nine years old, a dark-haired son was born on a stormy night when thunder and lightning seemed to rip the sky apart. The midwife was as calm as possible with the electricity blinking twice, then leaving them in darkness.

They named him Christopher Riehl, but took some time to decide the middle name. Christopher was a long name in itself, so they considered just using the first letter of Mary's maiden name, an old tradition. Christopher G. Riehl. G for Glick.

"Christopher George?" Steve lit up, looking down on the perfect face with eyes like a half-moon, blond hair like a tiny thatch of wheat.

Mary smiled. Christopher George it would be. And Steve looked deeply into his wife's eyes, conveying so much love, she knew she had obtained the long sought-after blessing without effort of any kind, only an opening of her heart, receiving the Holy Spirit.

CHRIS PROVED TO be a content newborn who slept the day away, cuddled by his sisters. Logan was unhappy at the prospect of sharing his mother with anyone else, but Mary felt perfectly capable, dividing her time between both boys as the seasons came and went.

Margaret was in eighth grade now, a young lady of fourteen, pushing uncomfortably against any boundary set for her. She was undoubtedly turning into a beauty, with hair neither red nor blond, but a rare, true strawberry blond, with large blue eyes fringed by black-tipped red lashes, as unusual as her name. She created her own world of drama, her outgoing personality and sense of leadership coupled with a raucous sense of humor, a group of adoring friends surrounding her.

In January of eighth grade, her last year of schooling, she informed her mother she had a boyfriend.

Mary was breaking up ground beef in a sizzling pan, so she didn't quite hear and asked her to repeat what she'd just said.

"I like someone."

Mary left the wooden spoon in the skillet, turned slowly to meet her daughter's gaze, clear and unperturbed.

"You like someone? You mean, like as in a special guy?" she asked slowly, measuring her words.

"Yeah. He's cute. Jonathan. You know. John King's Jonathan."

Mary's eyes narrowed. "In your grade?"

"Yeah. He likes me, too. We're dating."

"Dating?" Mary turned her back, resumed breaking up the ground beef, buying time as she whispered a quick prayer for guidance.

"I mean, basically. Everybody knows he likes me and I like him."

"Hm. Be careful, Margaret. I'm sure this kind of puppy love is not allowed in school."

"See, there you go again. Negative. Everything I do or say you turn into something bad. What's wrong with liking someone?"

"Nothing, but you are very young."

"Not so young. I bet you had a boyfriend in eighth grade."

"Oh my, no. Life was very different growing up in New York."

"Yeah, I know. You told me all that stuff. But plain people are allowed to have romance in their lives. How else would they get married?"

"Not at fourteen, we didn't."

Mary broke the seal on a jar of her homemade spaghetti sauce, poured it over the ground beef, lifted the lid of the boiling lasagna.

"Well, I do. It makes school less boring. I can't stand Lydia Mae."

"Come on, Margaret. She's a good teacher and you know it."

"She's so predictable. Penmanship every morning, then arithmetic, then drilling the first graders with flash cards. She never changes a thing."

"Children thrive on repetition. Knowing what to expect brings a sense of security."

"Hm. Really? Well, I, for one, do not thrive on boring."

Mary watched her leave the kitchen, no doubt to hole up in her room. At fourteen, she showed none of Mary's substantial build, but remained slim, her figure already blossoming into young womanhood, aware of her own looks and the effect she had on those around her.

Never satisfied with her clothes, her room, her shoes, always demanding new things, Margaret was a handful. She would need to obtain a job after vocational class, being finished with school at fifteen, the way of all young Amish girls. There was no doubt in Mary's mind that she would excel at any form of work, the way she flew through all her duties at home.

Their home had become quite a showplace, with Steve's masonry business booming. Over the years they'd added a stone patio with a firepit, an outdoor cooking area, and many pieces of fine lawn furniture. They'd done another addition to the house, and the vinyl siding and red brick had been replaced by stone and board and batten siding. Landscapers groomed the many shrubs and trees, and Mary's love of gardening and flowerbeds showed across the property.

Blessed, Mary thought. *I am blessed.* The turmoil of former years faded as time went on, a dim memory occasionally welling up, causing a certain dark sadness, but like a well-balanced object, righting itself in time.

But she was worried about Margaret.

Well, she reasoned, life was not meant to be a bed of roses, a smooth easy road without sorrow or challenges. She recognized the challenge taking seed in her oldest daughter, the one who had always been difficult. Rebecca was hardly able to be compared, an unassuming twelve-year-old with blond hair, a soft, porcelain complexion and her own green eyes, a quiet child who followed Margaret, worshipping the ground she walked on. Which, Mary was quick to realize, was a double responsibility, knowing Rebecca would copy anything Margaret attempted.

So she sat and shared her concerns with Steve, the one she knew would always lend an ear. And he assured her that Margaret inheriting her mother's strong will was not a bad thing. "We'll just keep guiding and loving her," he said, without a hint of worry.

Mary drank in his confidence, deciding there was nothing to fear.

CHAPTER 8

IT ALL STARTED WHEN MARGARET DEMANDED AN ALLOWANCE, SAYing her friend Sarah received ten dollars a week for cleaning flower beds and pulling corn stalks. "I need a pair of Nikes like Betty Sue has," she said. "And I know you won't buy them, so I'll just earn the money."

Mary felt an irritation, a stab of anger at the demanding tone, as if she, Mary, owed her something. In fact, the whole world Margaret inhabited owed her something. Everything.

She calmed herself, silently counted to ten, then looked at her oldest daughter with a level stare, the petulance of Margaret's mouth and challenge in her eyes like a dagger.

"In our home, everyone is expected to pitch in," she replied calmly. "Helping out is just part of life."

"You and Dat are so hopelessly old-fashioned," Margaret countered. "All the other kids my age get an allowance. It teaches kids how to handle money. Anyway, when I'm sixteen I'm going to do exactly what I want."

Up went Mary's eyebrows, "And when did you decide this?"

"What? The allowance or doing what I want?"

"Both."

"I don't know. I need stuff that you and Dat won't buy for me. I've worn exactly the same pair of shoes all year long. You should see Betty's Nikes. They're amazing."

Margaret drew out the "amazing" into a long hopeful whine.

Mary was folding towels, didn't yet know what she'd make for dinner, hadn't slept much the night before due to Logan's strep throat, and was not in the mood for Margaret's selfishness, or the derisive tone she used to belittle her parents.

"Margaret, why do you have to put your father and me down? Why can't you simply ask for a new pair of shoes?"

"Cause I wouldn't get them."

"You didn't ask."

"See, there you go. Being all negative."

"But you didn't."

She folded a towel in half, then again, tucked it under her chin and brought the sides in to form a neat rectangle, then expertly flipped it on the pile. How many stacks of towels had she folded in sixteen years? How many meals had she cooked and how often had she cleaned those rooms?

But she loved it. Every chore was a labor of love, a duty she counted a blessing. She had found her calling, which was simply being a wife and mother, a deeply fulfilling role and an honor.

Mary and Steve's love had multiplied, settled into something deeper, an almost spiritual sense of owning a mysterious bond that stayed, even after upsetting disagreements. It was marriage, in all its blessed forms, and for this, she was eternally grateful.

Their life together was far more than she deserved, and she often marveled at Steve's courage and strength through the difficult years, the times when many men would have given up. That kind of love was rare, it was sustaining, a gift from God.

Where would she be without this love?

It seemed as if the veil of fog had been lifted, and she could see clearly, understand life as a believer is meant to understand. She saw that every trial, every sadness, is meant to produce fruit, and this constant rotation was like a large wheel, the turning of time, the ebb and flow of the tide of life.

But here was Margaret, a problem to be faced.

"I didn't ask, because you always say no. Dat does too."

"I don't think so. What about the dress fabric we bought?"

"I didn't want what you made me get."

"Margaret, stop. You know very well that bright red you wanted was too flashy."

"I didn't think it was."

Mary sighed, took up the stack of clean towels, and stacked them in the bathroom closet. On her return, she looked at the clock.

"Margaret, would you run to the basement for a jar of canned chicken breast? It's too late to make much for supper and Dat will be home soon."

"Why do you call him Dat? He's not your father."

Mary chose to stay quiet, knowing any answer would only fuel the fires of her daughter's argumentative mood. Margaret got up and went to the counter to eat a slice of leftover pizza, eyeing her mother as she ate.

Mary looked at the clock. "Margaret, please. I need the chicken."

She finished the pizza, deliberately slowly, then made her way to the basement stairway, calling back over her shoulder, "Ten bucks, Mom."

The door opened, letting in a rush of cold air, just the kind of weather Mary loved. She smiled at Rebecca and Chris, who were building a snow fort in the backyard, their faces red with the cold, their gloves dripping wet. Christopher's beanie was pulled low, so that he needed to raise his face to peer out from under the brim.

"We built a fort, Mom!" he shouted.

"I did, Chris, but you helped a lot. His boots are packed with snow."

"Okay, good job, Chris. But you need to go to the laundry room, on the rug. You're both dripping melted snow." Rebecca ushered Chris ahead of her, obeying immediately, with no questions asked.

The basement door finally opened, and Margaret appeared, carrying the required item.

"Make enchiladas, Mom."

"I don't have flour tortillas. I was going to make chicken spaghetti."

"I love that, too."

Mary glanced at Margaret, surprised by the agreeable words. "Would you make the salad?"

"If I can get the shoes."

"We'll see."

The supper table was something Mary always looked forward to, her favorite time of day. Steve was there, telling them about his day, asking about theirs, teasing the boys, listening to Rebecca, who always waited to speak till everyone else had their share of time.

The chicken spaghetti was steaming hot and gooey with melting cheese and sauteed peppers and onions, the salad crisp and delicious.

Mary apologized for the quick supper, saying she'd returned late from taking Logan to the doctor, and yes, he had strep throat again. Steve said there was no need to apologize, that everything was just right.

There was a lull in the conversation, and Margaret asked her father for the coveted sneakers.

Steve chewed a mouthful of dessert and asked if her sneakers were worn out.

"No, but they are, like, six months old," she said, and went on to describe Betty's new sneakers, which made Steve raise his eyebrows.

Mary lifted a forkful of apple cake with caramel frosting, waiting on Steve's answer.

"So, these pink Nikes are something the other girls are wearing?"

"Dat, they're not pink."

"I thought you said they were."

"Just the laces. And a bit on the sole with the white. And I think maybe the swoosh."

"Swoosh?"

Margaret made an impatient noise. "You don't know the Nike emblem?"

"I'm just teasing. Of course I know."

"Not funny, Dat." But she was smiling, casting her father a look of appreciation.

And Steve smiled back, a genuine look of humorous approval, to which Margaret responded with a softening of her attitude.

"Well, Margaret, Mom and I will have to think about it."

"Don't get Mom involved. She always says no."

Mary felt the barb enter her spirit, and it hurt, but she said nothing. She forced a smile and scraped up the remainder of the cake with the side of her fork.

"Margaret, don't speak about your mother like that, okay? You know it's not the truth, and words like that can hurt."

Mary blinked, swallowed against the forming lump in her throat.

"Well, I might be hurt if you don't let me get the shoes."

"We'll see. But remember, there is so much more to life than our own selfish wants. Things are not what make us happy."

This scenario was repeated over and over as Margaret grew into her fifteenth year. She was constantly seeking to keep her status as a leader, harboring a deep-seated fear of falling into second place. Her whole world revolved around herself, and her sister and two brothers were merely background props for her own stage.

Margaret went to sleepovers, to volleyball games and birthday parties, had a wide circle of friends and a new boyfriend in her head every few months. Dating and "running around" started at sixteen, so before that, any kind of attraction to boys was strictly put on hold, which certainly did not keep Margaret from talking about it.

Dissatisfied with the way Mary sewed her dresses, the colors, and the length of the sleeves, she taught herself how to change patterns, and did all of her own sewing. Mary kept a watchful eye, but realized soon enough that criticism or correction only widened the ever-growing chasm between them.

Margaret hated her market job, couldn't get along with her boss, claimed she was constantly picked on. She put in her two-week notice and quit, without discussing it with her parents. For the first time in her life, Mary saw Steve lose his temper at one of the children. She cringed, as shades of her father engulfed her. She began to tremble, her hand shaking as she reached for her water glass.

Steve told Margaret in clipped, firm tones, that this was her own problem and none of anyone else's, that he knew Rueben and Annie well and had no reason to believe Margaret was treated unfairly. This led to Margaret yelling back about having old-fashioned parents who didn't stick up for their kids. She threatened to leave the Amish and said there wasn't a thing they could do about it.

Margaret was in hot, frustrated tears as she stormed up the stairs to her room, Mary watching Rebecca's pale, shocked face. Logan's eyes were downcast as he picked at his food while Chris loaded peas on his spoon, saying, "one, two, three," completely oblivious to his surroundings.

Ach, my dear children, so precious. So soon the years accumulate and bring us sorrow, responsibility in the form of shaping, helping to mold a stubborn will.

That evening, on the stone patio, the solar lights casting a yellow glow across their chairs, Steve told Mary this was only the beginning, and he was concerned about Mary's well-being as well as Margaret's.

"I'll be okay, Steve, really. I'm just depending on you to steer me through. It seems as if she hates me."

"She doesn't."

"But why? Is this the reaping my father always talked about?"

"Mary, don't. Don't even go there."

"But why? Why is she like this? What do I do wrong?" An edge of panic crept into her voice.

Steve shook his head, watched the swirl of disoriented moths and other night insects in their dizzying spiral around the lights.

"Could it be she has my mental illness?"

"*Ach*, Mary. I know it's not easy to talk about this, is it?"

"Not really. But what if she is bipolar?"

"She's young. She's very self-willed. Stubborn. Remember how we recognized that at a young age?"

"At fifteen, I wasn't aware of the fear and anxiety, the high moods, or the lows, so perhaps we can't tell yet. And to approach her about a mental disorder at this age . . . I don't think is very wise."

Steve nodded. "We better get ready though. Sixteen is coming up, the age they're pushed right off the diving board."

Mary laughed. "It's not funny. But an apt description."

"Sink or swim."

"Absolutely. I sank many times."

"I remember the painful years so well, trying to find my way. Didn't fit in with anyone. Girls were silly, everyone putting on airs. Hunting and fishing and hiking got me through it, pretty much."

"There is always prayer. For Margaret. You have to shift it over to God, to allow Him to catch her when she falls, as she inevitably will."

"Smart woman. Good mother."

He put his hand on hers, and she curled her fingers around his, as the bugs chased themselves around and around the lights. The moon rose and cast dark shadows beneath the trees heavy with thick green leaves.

As MARGARET'S SIXTEENTH birthday approached, Mary did her best to win over the contemptuous daughter, to create a better relationship, knowing it was essential at this stage in her life. She offered to help Margaret redo her bedroom, which was met with unusual enthusiasm.

The first thing was to paint her room in the color she chose, which proved to require a round of tedious trips to Lowe's, then to the Sherwin-Williams store, where she deliberated for an hour, then finally settled on a shade of olive green for one wall, and the perfect white for the remaining three.

Next they picked out a small sofa, curtains, pillows, quilts, and pictures for the wall. The cost was astounding, but Steve said not to worry, it was fine.

But after the furniture was all in place, the windows cleaned and curtains hung, Margaret decided she didn't like the green. It wasn't right. So Mary helped her paint it over with a lighter shade. Then it was her quilt. She wanted a comforter, like Mary Beth had. You could send for it online.

She acquired a cell phone, without her parents' approval. In fact they didn't even know about it until she needed money to pay the bill, saying she owed Danny two hundred and twelve dollars.

Steve looked up from his recliner, slowly folded the paper, and asked where her own money had gone.

Margaret shrugged. "Spent it, I guess."

"You know we don't approve of you having a phone."

"Dat, that's ridiculous. Everyone has them."

An answer to that would only result in a power struggle, so he merely looked at her with a level gaze, before saying, "This is it, then. After I help you out with this, you're on your own. And I expect to be paid back. Another thing, be respectful with your phone."

"Thanks, Dat." She hesitated. "Dat?"

"Yes?"

"Thanks. And I mean it. You're the greatest."

"Margaret, if you want to do something for me, be nice to your mother. It's hard for her when you don't treat her with respect."

"I do."

"Not always. But try."

Margaret nodded curtly and left to be alone in her bedroom.

HER SIXTEENTH BIRTHDAY party was an eye-opener. Steve and Mary expected their daughter to be in her element as the center of attention among her friends, but she wasn't nearly as confident as they had imagined. In fact, Mary could barely believe this was Margaret, this hesitant girl biting her nails at the edge of a circle of girls dressed in brilliant colors, like birds in a jungle. But she did stand and smile while everyone sang "Happy Birthday," And Mary's heart swelled to see her daughter, this beautiful young woman, ready to embark on her *rumschpringa*.

Mary took note of all the group dynamics and felt new compassion for Margaret. There was so much to navigate at her age. Groups of boys, huddles of girls, each young person so aware of all the others. They were each growing into themselves, finding out who they truly were, a task so hard to do when so much energy was spent trying to copy anyone perceived as prettier, cuter, or cooler.

The volleyball games lasted far into the night, long after Mary had gotten the younger children settled in their beds. Steve went to bed too and urged her to do the same, assuring her the youth were old enough to look out for themselves now. Mary stayed up for a while, but at midnight, she noted most of the buggies had turned right at the end of the drive and disappeared. Margaret would be coming in soon enough, so Mary climbed into bed and tried to relax. She turned one way, then another, still listening for the door. When she glanced at the clock and realized an hour had passed, she got out of bed. *Where are you, Margaret?*

Tiptoeing to the living room, she peered into the black night, pressing herself against the window, the palms of her hands on either side of her head for a better view. What she saw sent a chill through her blood.

A vehicle was parked beside the driveway, the lights off. Dimly, she could make out two silhouettes in the half-moon's light, standing side-by-side against the hood of the car. She turned away and slid down on the couch, her knees too weak to support her weight.

On the evening of her sixteenth birthday, and she was with a man who owned a car. This truth was like a gong, sounding over and over in her ear. Who was this boy? She thought she'd known everyone at the party. Had he shown up after everyone went outside to play volleyball?

What was a mother to do? How could she confront Margaret without driving the bitterness toward her even deeper? Should she wake up Steve and ask him to go out? Then again, she was now officially in *rumschpringa*, free to make her own choices. But what if this man wasn't safe?

Her breathing accelerated, her heart began its staccato rhythm. She fought the rising panic, leaned back, and took deep calming breaths. God would watch over Margaret. This was only a phase, only her first step into *rumschpringa*. Perhaps this was an acquaintance of hers, only talking, getting to know her. As she sat, her mind slowed, eased, righted itself, and her thoughts remained clear.

She jumped when the door swung open, and Margaret rushed through the kitchen. Mary shrank against the back of the couch, hoping to go unnoticed, but Margaret caught sight of her.

"Mom! Whatever."

"I couldn't sleep."

"I was talking to Ivan. He's so funny. Mom, he's twenty-one. He could probably have any girl he wants, he's so handsome. He picked me to talk to. You know what he said, Mom? He said he'll wait, 'cause I'm not old enough, but I know he's going to ask me out. Like, on a date. Can you imagine riding around in that car? The girls will be so jealous! For sure when Betty finds out, she'll lose her mind. She can hardly wait to have a boyfriend, and the other boys aren't half as cute as Ivan."

She stopped for breath, peeled off her apron, started pulling pins out of her covering.

Part of Mary knew she should just listen, just be grateful that Margaret was sharing this with her. But she couldn't stop another part from taking over. Was it fear? Her conservative upbringing? Just responsible parenting? She didn't know, but the words came tumbling out. "But . . . but really. I don't know if your father and I will allow it. We never imagined a young man who owns a vehicle."

"There you go again, spoiling my life. You're the most negative person I know. You two may as well get used to it, because nothing you say will make a difference."

"Margaret, it's for your own good. We care about you, and what is best for your soul."

"You don't care about my soul. It's your pride. All you care about is what people will say, thinking you have a wild daughter, and you're not good parents."

"Stop. Go to your room. We'll finish this conversation in the morning."

With a derisive snort and a toss of her head, Margaret flounced up the stairs, leaving Mary alone with her racing heart and thoughts.

She returned to her bed, and found she was trembling, but listened to Steve's even breathing, the slight rattle in his nose as he slept deeply. She pulled the blankets up to her chin, but no matter how hard she tried, she could not go to sleep, her daughter's words like painful darts stuck forever in her quivering, fearful mind.

Was her harvest so painful? She had sown so much rebellion, hated her own father many times, dismissed her mother for being unconcerned, soft, without protecting her when she needed it. Had she been unfair? How much could she blame on her mental condition? Or was none of this through a fault of her own?

Surely, after she had sought and received forgiveness, there was closure. *Jesus wipes our slate clean every time we ask, and this I believe with my whole heart,* she thought.

Oh, but Margaret was maddening, talking like that. Mary would never have dared at her age.

Should she confide in Steve? What if he lost his temper again, gnawing away at the broken rope that barely held them together?

She prayed a broken mixed-up prayer for Margaret, for wisdom, for guidance, and fell asleep about forty-five minutes before the alarm went off.

Steve was happy, talkative, drinking coffee as she packed his lunch. She decided not to mention anything at this point. She said next to nothing, just answering him when necessary.

"Didn't sleep well?" he asked.

"Not very much."

"Guess it's exciting, huh? A *rumschpringa* in the house."

"I guess."

He kissed her goodbye and was out the door, swinging his lunchbox and Thermos jug, happy, unperturbed. But he knew nothing of last night's events, and so guilt gnawed at her all day, making her irritable and short with the glowing Margaret. Finally, after lunch, she decided to have a talk with her.

"Margaret, listen, we need to talk. This guy, this Ivan?"

"What about him?"

"Not every guy can be trusted, okay? He's so much older and you're so young. I just don't feel as if you should take him seriously. I have no right to judge him, not knowing him at all, but don't get too serious. And it troubles me a lot about you thinking it's okay to make your girlfriends jealous. It's not good, this competitive spirit. It's worldly, and not what we want for our children."

"That's quite a speech, Mom."

"Please go slowly. You're still really young."

"Mom. I'm not going out with him. Not yet, anyway. You're over-thinking everything, as usual. Calm down. Anyway, I'm sixteen. I can pretty much do what I want."

Mary let it go at that. She hid her fears from Steve, wanting to create a peaceful environment, smooth, calm waters, without a single ripple of discipline or words of anger that might drive Margaret away.

Her precious daughter. It was painful to remember that at first she had not wanted her. Would things have been different if they'd been together for the first six weeks of Margaret's life? She had to admit she did not have the same bond with Margaret that she shared with Rebecca and the others. She knew the illness was not her fault, but she wished desperately that she could go back in time and do things differently. If only she had listened to Steve and gotten help sooner.

Dear God in Heaven, preserve her, be with her, protect her. I do love her. She's just so difficult. Allow me the chance to make those six weeks up to her. Somehow.

CHAPTER 9

MARGARET STARTED HER NEW JOB AT THE MARKET THAT THURSDAY. She rode to work in the backseat of a fifteen-passenger van, most of the girls asleep or staring out the window, the driver slurping coffee and talking nonstop to Margaret's new boss, Elmer Lapp of the famous barbecue place.

Margaret didn't want this job, but she wanted the cash. Market jobs were all the same, long exhausting hours with a check that should have been twice as much.

The alternative was cleaning English people's houses, which was even less fun, swabbing toilets and scrubbing floors. She could work in a restaurant, but people made her too angry with all their petty demands, then left a skimpy tip. Amish girls had it rough until they got married. That kind of life wasn't ideal, either, but what else was there?

She dreaded this day, dreaded navigating the maze of a new market stand. She knew it would be confusing, everyone so capable and businesslike, except her, standing there feeling like the biggest joke.

Her mom said she'd owned a bakery, bought the building and everything. Sometimes she could hardly believe her mom was capable of that.

Her mom had also been mental. She was on medication now, but it sure didn't do much for her. She tried liking her mother, but the truth was, she couldn't find much to like about her. She was such a turnoff, with her mouth pressed together till it resembled an earthworm when she disapproved or disagreed, which was basically all the time. She was so strict, so worried and serious about stuff. Ordinary stuff that didn't matter at all.

She hadn't seen Ivan since the night of her birthday party, but she hoped desperately she'd run into him again soon. She knew he was her meant-to-be, knew it with every fiber of her being.

She'd be the one everyone watched from here on out, riding around with him, windows down, music blaring. She shivered a little, thinking about it. No doubt, her mom would try and stop it, but she was sixteen now and could make her own decisions.

As she'd predicted, she had a terrible day, messed up the cash register, dropped a whole chicken out of the rotisserie, and made countless mistakes on orders. An older woman named Nancy dogged her steps, looked over her shoulder, and bossed her around till closing time. And all she had to look forward to was another day of this, and then more of the same after that.

But she made twenty-five dollars in tips, which wasn't too bad. She bought a pair of sunglasses at the leather shop, which cheered her immensely.

At home, she showed her mother the sunglasses. She told herself she didn't care what her mom thought, but she was hurt when she waved a hand, rolled her eyes, and said there was nothing Amish about them. Unsure how to handle the feeling of rejection, she retaliated with the first thing that came to mind. "You're hopelessly depressing, Mom. Have you been taking your meds?" Her father overheard and was told firmly never to speak to her mother like that.

Rebecca watched in silence, her fourteen years having been spent quietly in Margaret's shadow. She was content, comfortable, unassuming, watching the drama unfold around her. When her mother slammed pots and pans into cabinet doors, she knew she was upset.

ON SATURDAY, THE market was humming with people, a steady line of them coming to the register. Margaret was sent to the back to mix barbecue sauce, where she had to listen to Elmer's fourteen-year-old son tell her what to do. Joel Raymond Lapp was a pimply-faced boy with greasy hair and a camouflage bill cap.

"Hey, you have to measure that paprika. You can't just pour," he said.

"I wasn't just pouring. the measuring cup wasn't quite level, so I added a bit more."

"You can't do that. Dat is precise."

In answer, she glared at him, hoping the blank stare would chase him away. Instead, he told her she was pretty, but had a bad attitude. Then he got chatty, telling her he was the best on his basketball team because he was tall for his age and quick on his feet. He asked if she played, but didn't wait for an answer before saying he guessed if she did, it wasn't very seriously. Whoever had heard of a famous Amish basketball player?

"That's the thing about being Amish. You're just so Amish. You can never *be* someone. I guess that's supposed to be a good thing, a Bible kind of thing."

"Yeah. Well, I don't read my Bible. It's scary."

"Nah. No, it's not," he snorted, followed immediately by a, "Hey, not so much vinegar."

"Eight cups. Eight cups is two quarts. This is a two-quart container, so what are you yelling about?"

He laughed.

"You have it right, looks like."

"Looks like I do."

Joel told her to stir that batch of barbecue sauce better, and she told him her shoulders were tired, she wasn't going to.

"Don't you listen to your mom either?" he asked, narrowing his eyes at her.

"No. Not always. My mom's depressing. Every single thing I do is wrong."

"Oh, come off it. I don't believe it. I love my mom."

"Good for you."

He narrowed his eyes, reached up to pick his face.

"Don't pick your face. It only makes it worse."

"I don't care about stuff like pimples."

"Oh, you do, too. Or you will when you're older."

Elmer Lapp stuck his head in the door.

"You done with that yet?" he asked briskly, coming over to the kettle to give it a stir. "Looks about right."

He told Margaret to give Nancy a break at the register, and told Joel to empty the trash, and hurry, there was a line a mile long. He looked frustrated, tense, and a bit too warm, but that was every market stand owner. It was all about making money, and half of them were already wealthy, owning two or more homes.

Margaret stood at the register, disliking Elmer Lapp, the market, and every person in the long line snaking around the corner.

"Good morning. May I help you?"

The old lady peered at her through rheumy eyes, adjusted the blue surgical mask, and mumbled. Did anyone even wear masks anymore? The man behind her sighed, shifted his feet, lifted his wrist to look at his watch.

"Excuse me?" Margaret asked.

Another mumble.

"I'm sorry?"

Margaret simply could not hear, the mask hiding the movement of the elderly lady's mouth, so she asked her to remove it, please, resulting in a sharp rap of her cane and a louder garble from beneath the mask.

"I'm sorry?" Margaret said again, trying to hear.

The line behind her held a sea of faces registering impatience, disgust, a few pairs of eyes merely curious, but to Margaret they suddenly seemed threatening. Her heart began hammering in her chest. Nausea rose in her throat. Incredulous, she looked down at her hands, which were shaking, a tremor going up her arm.

The mumbling from beneath the mask was turned up a decibel, but still she could not hear. Helpless in the wake of her anxiety, Margaret turned away and tapped her co-worker on the shoulder.

"Help me, Lavina."

One look at Margaret's ashen face, and she hurried to the register, while Margaret gripped the edge of the counter, steadying herself.

"You alright?" Elmer Lapp asked, noticing the pale sheen of her skin, her agitation.

Margaret nodded, gave him a weak grin. "Too much caffeine."

He nodded, moved on.

But the incident left a mark on her, a bewilderment. She was not quite sure what to make of it. But she tossed her head, shored up her reserves, and laughed it off to Lavina, saying she had to lay off the energy drinks.

She told her mother she wanted to quit her job. She simply had no interest in market work, it was a dead-end job going nowhere, and she'd had enough.

Mary turned slowly, holding a wooden spoon, her face impassive. The late Saturday afternoon sunlight cast a golden light on the white cabinets, turning the white walls into a honeyed color. Her daughter was sprawled on a kitchen chair, her strawberry blond hair afire, the small freckles like thrown stardust, her eyes hooded, dark with unhappiness, her mouth petulant.

"What happened?" she asked quietly.

"I hate market. It's stupid."

Mary sighed. "Can you tell me what happened though?"

"Nothing happened." Lifting her hands to the side of her face, she wiggled two fingers. "It's just a boring, dead-end job going nowhere."

"Do you have anything else in mind?" Mary asked, turning to insert the wooden spoon into the bubbling caramel pudding.

"No. I hate any job. Why can't Amish girls go to high school, then on to college, have an interesting career?"

"Oh, come on now, Margaret. You know better."

"You don't even know why, do you?"

"Of course I do."

"Then what's the reason?"

Mary gave the pudding a final stir, set it off the burner, and turned to face her.

"It's the Amish way of teaching our girls to be keepers at home, to marry and bear children as the Bible instructs. We don't feel it's right for women to have a career, to divide her time between duties at home and in the workplace. It's traditional, the way it was a hundred years ago."

"Not a very good reason," Margaret snorted.

"Oh, come on, Margaret. Be reasonable and try to understand."

Margaret tossed her head. "Well, I'm not going to be Amish. I'm also quitting my job."

A dagger of fear sliced through Mary. Her daughter not being Amish? It was unthinkable. Every ounce of her resisted this terrifying thought. Their status as good parents would be smashed into a thousand pieces. Her pride. There would be nothing left.

The true mark of successful parenting was keeping all your children in the fold, safely shepherded by the *ordnung* the bishop announced, guidelines to a life lived in Christ.

She swallowed her fear, and said she'd talk to Margaret's father.

"It doesn't matter what he says. I'm quitting. You can't tell me what to do. I'm sixteen."

She flounced off to her room, her sneakers creating dull thuds as she went up the stairs, leaving the kitchen to Mary, who stirred the pudding absentmindedly, her thoughts in a careening torment. Was this the harvest of her own rebellion? Was God a God of punishment, visiting the sins of the fathers—or mothers—into the second and third generation? The old anxiety threatened.

Steve found his wife in tears, Rebecca burying her face in yet another book, the boys at the table strewn with Legos.

His eyes questioned her, and he mouthed, "Margaret?"

She nodded. He shook his head, his mouth in a thin line.

A few hours later, there was a patter of feet on the stairs and Margaret was on her way out, dressed in her Saturday night favorite, a rose-hued dress and matching bib apron, one she'd bought from Betty Sue.

Mary noticed there were no strings on her covering and rose from her chair immediately.

"Margaret, where are your covering strings?"

"I ripped 'em off," she called back, heading straight for the front door, where the idling of an engine could be heard.

Mary walked toward her. "You're not leaving the house like that."

"Sorry, Mom. Nobody wears strings on their coverings Saturday night."

"But I forbid you to go."

A pop song jangled from her phone. She lifted it, swiped, and giggled, "Be right out."

"Margaret," Mary said firmly, lifting a hand as if to restrain her, then letting it fall helplessly to her side as the door opened and Margaret flew through it, a blur of rose color.

Steve emerged from the bathroom, his hair wet after a shower. Mary turned, irritation wrinkling her forehead.

"Where were you when I needed you? Margaret just left with no strings on her covering. I told her she's not allowed, but she simply ignored me and walked out the door."

Steve sat down on the recliner and pulled the lever to bring up the footrest.

"Aren't you going to say anything?" Mary cried.

"Come Mary. Sit down. Let's wait until the boys are in bed."

"But I need to talk."

"We will."

Mary sat with Chris and Logan while they fixed bowls of graham crackers, peanut butter, and milk, a concoction they loved to eat before bedtime. Logan told her they were building a fort with their Legos and tomorrow the Indians would attack. The only problem was not having enough horses.

"Maybe we can find a few at Walmart when I go for groceries on Wednesday," she said, breaking a graham cracker in two before spreading it with peanut butter. She broke it in two again, dunked a portion in milk, sighed, and asked why it was so good.

Chris grinned. "It just is."

"Yeah," Logan echoed, his smile as contagious as Steve's.

For a fleeting moment, Mary wished the boys would always stay this age, their winsome ways coloring her days with vivid hues of laughter. They were both well-adjusted, happy individuals who were a great help around the property, keeping the barns swept, using the blower on the driveway, with seemingly endless energy.

After everyone was in bed, Mary sat in the chair opposite her husband, and waited. He put down his magazine, smiled at her and said, "Shoot, Mary. I'm ready to listen."

She did, starting with the market job and ending with the covering strings, her voice reaching a high wail as she finished.

"She's bound and determined to take her own way, and I'm absolutely helpless in the face of it."

Steve took a hand and swiped it across his face, a gesture he often displayed when he was agitated. He waited too long to speak, so Mary took up where she'd left off.

"I mean, what is most troubling is I did exactly the same thing, except I didn't leave the Amish."

"She hasn't gone yet, and likely never will," Steve said calmly.

"But you don't know that."

"No, I don't, but don't you think lots of young people go through this same thing at sixteen?"

"Surely not to this degree."

Steve raised an eyebrow, his gaze meeting hers.

He said, "I think we're all guilty of disobeying in our youth. Whether it's having a fit about covering strings, going in someone's car, or something else. She's just spreading her wings, trying them out. It's all a part of growing up, wanting to be cool, to feel accepted."

Mary leaned forward, gripping the arm of her chair.

"You're making light of this. You're sticking up for her. You have her back instead of mine. How can we expect her to turn out right if we don't work together?

She began to weep, quietly, her distress showing in the slump of her shoulder, the color of her face.

"Don't, Mary. I wasn't finished. I will support you, and I will stand with you. I just think you might be blowing this a bit out of proportion."

"No, I'm not, Steve," Mary cried out, dabbing at her eyes.

"Look, we always knew she was going to be a boundary pusher, right? Even in school, we knew."

Mary nodded.

"So, I'm not surprised at the group she has chosen. No, it's not what we want, but it's what she wants, and I doubt we can change that right now. Think about it, Mary. How did your father make you feel when he refused to honor your choices? If we threaten hell and damnation, would it do any good at all?"

"I think so."

"Really, Mary?"

She could not meet his eyes, but instead kept hers on her twisted hands.

"I don't know. Maybe not. But don't you think she needs the fear of the Lord to keep her from doing things we don't approve of?"

"What kept us from leaving the Amish? Was it threats?"

Mary paused. "No, I suppose not. I mean, I always had my father's voice in my head as a warning. But in the end, I guess it was my own conscience that kept me from leaving the Amish."

"Of course. In all His mercy, God cares for the youth, taps a bit here, straightens a bit there, allows them to find out for themselves the things that matter most."

"But what can we *do*?"

Truly bewildered, Mary lifted honest, pleading eyes to her husband.

"She already knows our boundaries, and she's broken every one. So we wait, and give her to God. She is in His care. We remind occasionally, we provide spiritual advice, but as far as forcing her to comply, I'm not sure it's the thing to do. If it's even possible. With a child like Margaret, we're basically along for the ride."

Mary shook her head. "Steve, I simply can't agree with you. You mean you're going to let her quit her market job, go out with this Ivan? And that cell phone. Her dress. Her covering. It's all blatant disrespect."

Far into the night, the battery lamp burned on as they exchanged views, troubling thoughts aired for the other one to see. But what came clearly to view was the fact that Steve leaned toward the more liberal approach to child rearing, and Mary the conservative. They took Mary's upbringing into consideration, the way her father always threatened damnation if she did not obey, plus Mary's mental illness.

"Do you think Margaret is bipolar like me, Steve?"

"I don't like to think about it. You're doing so well now, and it hurts to remember the hard times."

"But what if she is? We both know ignoring it would be the worst thing we could do."

Steve sighed.

Mary added, "I'll ask her sometime, see if she's experienced anxiety. That is how it all started for me."

She paused, then rose to her feet. "And Steve, I want to thank you for talking to me. You have no idea how much it means to have someone to lean on. You are my pillar, my stronghold. I overthink things, and I need you."

Steve took her into his arm and held her gently, murmuring his love and pledging to be the man she thought he was, creating a union of truth and love like a fortress of spiritual and emotional safety.

A few miles down the road, at the home of her friend Rachel, Margaret sat in the vehicle with Ivan, talking. She felt lucky, felt on top of the world, reveling in his handsome profile, the excitement of being chosen at such a very young age, the first one of her friends to have a real boyfriend.

She didn't want to leave his company, and certainly did not want to play volleyball, but he thought it was expected of them. He walked with her to the circle of light, where powerful batteries fueled pole lights, illuminating the entire yard. Standing with Ivan, she felt victorious, ahead of the pack, a winner.

The whole evening was a dream. She never left his side, playing volleyball beside him, filling a plate with snack food when he did.

He was showing her off, she knew he was, and she felt pretty and popular, the envy of every other girl.

When Betty Sue came and led her away, hissing quietly in her ear, Margaret drew back, horrified at what she'd heard. She told Betty Sue she was just jealous. They were joined by Rachel, who listened with a serious expression, backing what Betty Sue had told her. But Margaret would have none of it. They were just jealous. They knew nothing. She tossed her head, straightened her stringless covering, and tried to reclaim the exultant feeling she'd reveled in a few moments before.

She went back to the volleyball game and looked for Ivan. He was nowhere to be found. Taking matters into her own hands, she left the group and went to look for his car, thinking he might be waiting for her, wanting her to sit with him and continue their conversation.

His car was gone, and so was he. She texted him, asking where he'd gone and if everything was okay. For a long time, she stood by the side of the white fence, alone in the dark, checking her phone obsessively and waiting for his return. Maybe he had to help someone, or maybe he went to pick up a few buddies.

She did not want to rejoin the group alone, and especially wanted to avoid her two friends, so she moved through the dark till she found a large hedge and made her way beside it, hidden from view.

He'd be back soon, or at least he'd text her, explaining why he had to leave so suddenly.

She chewed her lower lip, changed her position, and waited. She texted again, then tried calling. Finally, she realized the lights were being taken down and groups of young people preparing to leave. Suddenly, she was truly afraid of being left alone. She got to her feet, did her best to appear unconcerned, and walked over to her group of girls.

"Marge, what's up? We thought you left," Rachel cried.

"No, I'm still here."

She yawned casually, or tried to, and asked if she could hitch a ride home, adding about Ivan having car trouble, maybe, which she hoped was true.

CHAPTER 10

WEDDING SEASON WAS APPROACHING. NOVEMBER WAS ALWAYS full with buying wedding gifts, sewing new clothes, washing buggies and harnesses and horses, and attending the wedding festivities. Invitations in different colors and designs were pegged on corkboards in kitchens.

Mary went to the local dry goods store with her daughters on a Saturday morning, driving Trixie, her beloved brown mare who was safe and good natured. They weaved in and out of traffic. Mary checked the rearview mirror, flipped the switch for the left turn signal, and crossed over as soon as the road was clear.

"Look at this, guys," Margaret muttered, eyeing the full hitching rack, cars lined up in front of the building. "Lancaster is so crowded. I'm going to move to Florida."

"Do you have any idea what Florida is like?"

"Course not. You'd never go."

Mary let that one go as she drew back on the reins, slid the buggy door open, and climbed out, followed by the girls. They helped tie Trixie to a fence post, then turned to walk across the parking lot and into the store. Mary lifted her purse to look for the list.

"Why, Mary," she heard.

An aging lady, bent at the waist, her black shawl and bonnet hiding most of her form, peered up at her, the bright blue eyes behind round eyeglasses appraising her with gladness.

"Sarah. *Vee bischt* (How are you)?" Mary answered.

"*Goot. Ich bin goot.* (Good. I'm good.)"

She looked the girls up and down. "These are your girls?"

"Yes."

With a curt nod, Sarah moved on, her cane tapping the floor, and Mary swallowed hard. She knew what Sarah was thinking. Knew she had been a disappointment to the old matriarch. Mary cringed, wishing she'd never allowed Margaret to wear the fur-lined hooded coat. It was disrespectful, flashy, exactly the kind of thing the older generation would shake their head at. Mary's pride was injured, but she recovered as much as possible, consulted her list, and moved to the black fabric aisle, Margaret in tow, preparing for battle.

"Not that, Mom. Don't even think of it," she hissed, when Mary drew a bolt of fabric from the shelf.

"What's wrong with it?"

"It's Spring Melange. Mommy stuff."

Mary sighed. "What do you want?"

"I want something stretchy."

"Do you know how hard it is to make a belt apron with stretchy fabric?"

"I don't care. I'll make it."

"No, you can't," Mary whispered, hoping to avoid being heard.

"Why not? Plenty of girls do."

And that was only the beginning.

Margaret chose a fabric in brilliant orange. "Melon," she said. Margaret told her no, absolutely not. When she shrugged her shoulders, Mary realized she might simply be doing that to test her authority, but then she moved onto a shocking shade of pink.

"Margaret, please."

"What? It's beautiful."

Mary shook her head. Margaret rolled her eyes and swung her shoulders as she traversed another aisle.

"This."

She held out a golden yellow, shiny, flimsy fabric that was suitable only for a nightgown.

"Stop it, now. Of course not."

"Then I'm not getting one. I won't go to any weddings."

"Well, that's up to you."

Rebecca came over holding a 500-piece puzzle, her blue eyes alight. "Mom, Chris and Logan would love this. See? It's a dogsled."

Mary shifted her attention to it, held it up to the light, then smiled and nodded. "Good choice, Rebecca. Yes, let's get it for them."

Margaret was furious.

"Of course, here's Rebecca, the dear soul. Immediately we hear a yes, yes oh yes."

"It's a puzzle, Margaret."

But she had already moved away, her breath whooshing in disgust, which Mary chose to ignore, knowing anything she would ever suggest now would be dashed to the ground. It was so maddening.

And how was one expected to love them both the same, when Rebecca was such an angel? So slight, so blond haired and blue eyed, with Steve's dimples, the cleft in his chin, always thinking of others, never herself?

Wisdom, dear Lord, just give me wisdom.

In the end, Margaret did not purchase fabric for a new dress, saying she had no interest in going to any weddings.

They stopped for groceries at Creekside, and afterward Rebecca perched on Margaret's lap, since the back was filled with bags and boxes of food. Trixie trotted happily as they shared a bag of Cheetos, drinking iced tea and chatting, the power struggle in the dry goods store forgotten.

Rebecca chewed a mouthful of Cheetos, swallowed, then said, "I'm sort of jealous, Marge. Invited to all those weddings. And you get to go to the table with all those young men. It seems so exciting."

"Not really. I doubt Ivan will be there."

Mary slid a glance in her direction, shocked to see the set of her jaw, the real hurt in her face. She asked what had happened Saturday evening, but Margaret did not want to talk about it. She locked away the humiliation of hovering over her phone, alone, texting and calling, with no reply. She'd sulked for a few days after that, and then remembered how he'd told her he wanted to wait till she was older, and she felt a little better. She alternated between the sting of feeling rejected and the hope that he still wanted her.

He was so terribly handsome. By far the best-looking guy she'd ever seen. She couldn't stand the thought of being married to someone inferior. For a moment, she imagined herself fat, tired, surrounded by too many children, and tied down to a husband who wasn't even cute. She shuddered. She would wait on Ivan, bide her time until she was older. In a way, it was gentlemanly that he wanted to wait so the age gap between them would seem less important. She tried to convince herself that's all it was—that he was just being respectful.

THE FIRST WEDDING of the season was a cousin on her father's side, Ruthie King. The whole family, even Chris and Logan, were invited, which meant there were new clothes all around—white shirts and black suits for the men, a dusty blue for Mom, and a dark mauve for the girls, a color Margaret pronounced "deplorable," though she reluctantly agreed to wear it. The truth was, she did want to go to the wedding. There was always a chance Ivan would be there.

They all looked so fine, Mom said, and if they were English, they'd take a group picture before they left. But really, Mary was ashamed of Margaret's hair. She had asked her softly to abstain from rolling it up in the new style, which she found ridiculous. It was humiliating, having that Margaret of hers so completely out of the *ordnung* with that tiny covering.

For the hundredth time she felt her father's pain, his humiliation, his shame. Steve assured her it was mostly her pride, cringing over what others thought, afraid of being dubbed a weak mother, an insufficient parent. Having a headstrong daughter never seemed to bother him much, or if it did, he rarely showed any sign of anger or impatience.

And could she truthfully say she was proud when the line of color-ful girls filed into the wedding area and sat on benches, her Margaret the prettiest of them all? Of course she was. Any mother would be. But it was hard not to long for the ideal of a daughter, versus the real one she had to raise.

After the girls were seated, her sister-in-law turned to her. "Well, Mary, do you want to go first?"

Puzzled, Mary knit her brow, stared back at the blue eyes regarding her. "What do you mean?"

"Crawl under a bench for a while. Did you see my Ida's hair?"

Mary didn't mean to snort, the laugh escaping her before she could hold it, so she slapped Katie's arm, and felt a solid bond of motherhood between them.

They understood one another's feelings, which was priceless, and in the afternoon when the single young men chose a girl to "take to the table" from the assembled group stationed at a certain spot for that purpose, Mary was with the mothers straining their necks, on tiptoe to watch for their own daughter, then settling down, relieved to find their own daughter had been chosen so soon. And my, the young man was really rather good looking.

So they returned to the cooking area, smiling only a bit remem-bering their times of "being taken to the table" to sit with a young man they might or might not be acquainted with, to eat the delectable dishes, snacks, candy, platters of cheese and crackers, fruit punch, all while singing the German wedding songs, which rose in a great swell-ing crescendo as more and more of the *freundshaft* (extended family) from the working area chimed in.

And behind the scenes, the harried sisters and sisters-in-law man-aged, fussed, squabbled a bit, setting out lasagnas, asking assigned friends and relatives to do their tasks, cutting up heads of romaine let-tuce for salad, grating cheese, mixing lima beans and corn. Inevitably, some item was misplaced, or they ran out of butter.

In this case, they couldn't find trays for serving the lasagna, which was just like Sadie, forgetting an item as important as that.

"Well, what's wrong with serving lasagna in glass dishes?" asked Sadie. "If you let them set a while, the handles won't be hot and you're supposed to let it set for at least ten minutes. Sets it up, you know."

Sister-in-law Lydia said she never heard of it. "Wouldn't that cool it off?" Then she threw her hands in the air and walked off, her backside as substantial as a wheelbarrow, and Mary told Katie she must be going through "the change," that one.

Somehow they had far too many dinner rolls. What were they going to do with them? Put them in Zip-loc bags and freeze them. Katie said they could always use them for *roascht*, and Lydia asked who wanted to eat more *roascht* during November. Not her. Stout Aunt Barbie said she could live on *roascht*, with a side of pecan pie and ice cream, which reminded Mary, where were the pecan pies? She couldn't remember seeing them at all, resulting in a flurry of skirts and aprons looking for the necessary pies. Not a pie in sight, so an aunt was dispatched to wade through the crowd, bend over the bride's mother, Sadie, and ask for the pies.

"In the cooler," Sadie whispered back, her threadbare nerves and exhaustion threatening to unravel her completely, thinking to herself about how sisters had no common sense at a time like this.

But the following day, when everything was over, sleepy-eyed relatives back on the job for the third day, they laughed and joked, forgot the tension of the previous day, and wished one another well.

And on to the next wedding.

"Who'd you have at the table?" Mary asked Margaret the following morning.

"Some Ben." Her voice was low, plangent, her eyes downcast.

"Nice guy?"

Margaret shrugged. "Sort of simple."

"Oh, come on."

"He was. Said he flunked his driver's test for the third time in a row, so he has to wait six months. I wouldn't go around telling folks that if I was him."

"*Ach* my."

"And he spit when he talked."

Mary smiled, in spite of herself.

"It's not funny, Mom. I despise weddings. All those people. When I get married, I will not invite more than two hundred, if that."

"That's a long time yet, sweetheart." Mary smiled.

"You bet it is. You have no idea. I'm never getting married."

There wasn't much to say to this, so Mary reckoned she'd be better off staying quiet.

"Did you see Ivan? He sat so close to Ida, he may as well have swallowed her. He is so good-looking and I will never date anyone else. But he never even glanced at me. It's like I had leprosy or something."

"Looks aren't the most important thing."

"He's too cute for words, but it's like he doesn't even know I exist. I don't get it. Before, we talked and talked. I *know* that he liked me."

"Isn't he much older than you? Am I right, thinking he's the one who picked you up on one of your first weekends?"

"Yes, that was him."

"I'm sorry, Margaret. There's still time. Perhaps he's serious about waiting till you're older. Just go out and enjoy your *rumschpring* years, and leave it up to God. He will lead you in the right direction if you let Him."

"I hardly know God. I never pray."

A burning jolt shot through Mary. Her piercing gaze went to her daughter.

"Margaret, seriously. That is exactly how I used to be." She took a breath and then decided she had to ask. "Do you ever experience anxiety, like your heart seems to go out of control, like a hammer in your chest? Maybe you feel like throwing up?"

"So now you're saying I'm mental, like you?"

"No. Just asking."

"No. Well, once. Once when I was at the register at market."

"Tell me."

Margaret did tell her, in her usual brusque manner. Mary told her if it ever happened again, it was important to let her know.

"I still hate that job."

"Well, sometimes we have to do what we don't want to. It's an important part of learning to be a responsible adult. Life is hard sometimes, and how can you be prepared if you never have to?"

"That's morose."

"Morose or not, it's the truth."

"I'm going to be English then."

"You want me to pack your bags?"

Margaret's eyes flew open, alarm registering on her face, till Mary smiled and they both burst out laughing.

"You're so strange, Mom."

THERE WAS ANOTHER wedding the following day. Steve was up at three, in his office for a few hours of paperwork before he had to eat breakfast and be on his way. It was the church wedding, where Mary would be assigned a job of making gravy, or creamed celery, or coffee.

She yawned as she drank her coffee, picked at a thread on her sleeve, and said it was only the second wedding of the season, with four more to go.

Steve sat down to a dippy egg on a piece of toast, salted and peppered it, nodded in agreement.

"Maybe we can come home early today."

"What about Margaret?"

"Oh, yeah. Well, guess we should stay for her sake."

"She probably wouldn't mind, actually."

Steve smiled at her. "You two seem to be getting along."

"A bit better."

"Mom!" The loud wail thundered down the stairs.

Mary rose to her feet, hurried to the stairway.

"What is it, Margaret?"

"I don't have anything to wear."

"I'm not going there. Come on, we're almost ready to leave."

"You have to help me with my cape."

Resigned, Mary climbed the stairs to find her daughter in a huge disarray of clothes, shoes, pillows, books, drinking glasses.

She said nothing, but quickly pinned the navy blue cape to the dress, then pinned the black apron. She asked her to use hairspray please, and then left the room, shaking her head as she reentered the kitchen.

Steve raised his eyebrows but she shook her head, then smiled at Rebecca, saying the boys' lunchboxes were in the laundry room, and to have fun babysitting with her cousin Amanda.

A flurry of steps, and Margaret hit the kitchen in a half-dozen strides.

"Mom, my covering string tore off. I never heard of anything as senseless as covering strings. This navy blue makes me look like Grandma Moses. I don't even care. It's only a church wedding."

Mary concentrated on gluing the covering string, then handed it to her, noticing how pretty she looked in the navy blue dress, though she said nothing.

"I'm not staying all day," she announced defiantly.

"We might not either."

Another wedding with a different group of people. Some were acquaintances, some Mary had never seen before. She was busy making chicken gravy with Aaron sie Sarah, mixing the flour with chicken fat, and missed the entrance of the long line of young men and women, her daughter among them.

While serving gravy, Margaret rushed up to the stove. Her job as a church girl was waiting on tables.

"Mom. He's here," she hissed in her ear.

Mary drew back. "Who?"

"You know, Ivan."

Mary raised her eyebrows and went back to serving gravy, filling trays of gravy bowls as servers waited. So much for going home early, she supposed, but was curious to see the object of Margaret's desire, or despair, depending how you looked at it. Oh my, it was an adventure, having a sixteen-year-old daughter.

After dinner, Mary's job was done, so she settled down with a group of church women to talk and laugh, eat potato chips and blueberry donut holes from bowls on the table, and sip a cup of coffee with cream.

"Here they come," Lydia whispered.

They rose as one and strained to see across the crowded shop, watching, waiting for their own son or daughter.

Oh my, but the young man beside Margaret was arresting. You almost had to look twice. Oh, poor Margaret. Her face was deathly pale, her nostrils dilated, and she looked as if she might faint.

Mary sat down, regained her composure, and ate a potato chip that turned dry in her mouth.

She took a swallow of water, said, "*Hesslich.*"

Lydia leaned over and said, "I'd choke too, if that was my daughter. Who is he?"

"I think his name is Ivan."

"My goodness, he's handsome."

"Looks are not what's important."

"Mmhmm, sure."

AT THE AFTERNOON table, Margaret's head spun and her hands shook, but she took deep breaths to steady herself.

She was seriously afraid of heart failure when he looked at her and said, soft and low, "Hi."

She tried to speak, but nothing formed.

"How do you know John and Rose?" he asked

"Church."

"Well, I'm glad you're here."

"Mm-hm."

The truth was, she was terrified. How had she lost all the confidence of her former month, those first few weeks of *rumschpringa*? She was certain he had chosen her as a joke, perhaps on a bet from his friends. He'd disappeared that first evening, never answered her texts.

She should leave him, now, let him sit there looking foolish. How would he like that?

"You probably wonder what's up with me, huh?"

Margaret shrugged.

"I'm a first-class coward."

She blinked, swallowed, toyed with her fork. When brimming glasses of meadow tea were served, she did not dare lift the glass to her lips for fear of spilling the whole thing into her quaking lap.

Chapter 11

It was Friday, the long, tiring workday she so disliked, but she didn't sleep at all during the ride there. Her eyes were wide in the semi-dark of the fast-moving van, the usual annoying chatter from the other market girls only a distant hum.

She felt the hovering fear of allowing herself the smidgen of a dream, the vulnerability of hope. Ivan was everything she had ever wanted, but she could still feel the sting of being dropped like a piece of unwanted trash, the hurt and humiliation of texting him over and over with no reply.

He was a coward, he'd said, softly, and she had been too nervous in his presence to ask him what he meant by this, and he'd moved on to lighter subjects.

"How have you been?" he'd asked. "Haven't seen you around."

Her hands shook, her palms sweated, her heart beat so hard and fast she was actually afraid of fainting. She answered in quiet monotones.

She replayed every moment in her mind, cringing at how she'd acted around him. She would never have another chance at redeeming herself. Only once had she looked straight at him, and quickly away. That fine dark hair, cut so neatly, his dark eyes and perfectly arched eyebrows, the dark skin. His mouth sculpted to perfection, the white shirt and black vest setting off the sultry good looks. Her self-confidence had been completely obliterated, wiped away by remembered pain.

Frozen, she'd endured the evening, managing to eat only a few bites of the casserole, dropping the tongs in the salad.

There was one moment she returned to again and again in her mind. Their eyes had met as they flipped the pages of the hymnbook. His dark eyes were infused with a warm, gentle light. And hers had lingered a few seconds too long. They'd both smiled.

She sighed, leaning the side of her head against the van window. She must leave this, whatever it was. She must forge ahead, gather her self-confidence, that arrogant toss-her-head control over her life, and forget about him. That was the smart thing to do.

He'd asked her where she worked during the week, then laughed after she told him she did what all Amish girls did—worked at market, cleaned houses, gave most of her money to her parents.

"You sound a bit miffed," he said, still smiling.

"Oh well, you know. It's life. Doing what the forefathers did."

He laughed again, and that was something, wasn't it? She'd been witty, entertaining. She cringed again, though, thinking of her plain dress, that old navy blue church dress, as unappealing as an old rag, but whatever.

"You could train horses. I know some Amish folks who make good money doing that."

"Yeah? I guess, I don't know."

"Girls are doing a lot with horses these days."

"I don't think I'd have the ability."

"You certainly have the confidence."

She had said nothing to this, thinking if he only knew.

THE MARKET DAY moved on like an inching caterpillar, her eyes repeatedly turning to the large, round clock on the wall. She was tired, so terribly sleepy, having slept only a few hours.

"Who'd you have at the table?" her coworker Mellie Lantz asked, her small brown eyes like shiny raisins set in a bowl of milky oatmeal, her skin pockmarked with old acne scars. Her name was Malinda, which had soon been shortened to Mellie, matching her adorable personality.

She was friendly, cheerful, always interested in others' welfare, dating a fine young man who was quite taken with her, seeing past the physical flaws to the heart of gold beneath.

Margaret was used to being asked this during wedding season. Either a young man asked you to sit with him, or the bride and groom seated you together, which meant they thought you would be a good match. There was always a lot of curiosity about who was pairing up with whom.

"Ivan Stoltzfus," she said quietly.

Mellie did a double take. "Oh really? Wow."

Margaret nodded, gave her a sheepish grin.

"Well, good for you, Marge. A perfect fit. I bet you were a stunning couple."

Genuine praise from a genuine person, but Margaret shrugged it off. "I think he's a player, with those looks."

Mellie nodded. "They often are, but he comes from a really nice family. His dad is at the Plain Homestead, that place for troubled people."

"You mean, he's there?" Margaret asked, taken aback.

"No, I mean, he's like, a counselor or something."

"Hm."

"Yeah, his mom is a sweetheart. She works with my aunt."

Margaret said nothing. Everyone was a sweetheart to Mellie. Margaret turned away and went to the cooler for sliced lettuce, fresh in her resolve to step away before she got hurt again. It was absolutely nothing to her whether his mother was nice or if she wasn't.

She arrived home late, unable to sleep in the van, wide awake and stressed out from the wearying, churning kaleidoscope of thoughts in her head that had grown to monstrous proportions as the day wore on.

Worst-case scenarios played out in her head, creating a churning stomach, no appetite, and a dull thumping headache above one eye.

Her mother's recliner thumped as she lowered the footrest, then came to the kitchen to greet her.

"How was your day?" she asked kindly.

"Long, hot, and stupid. Market."

"*Ach*, Margaret. You're probably tired after the wedding."

"Yeah. Well, I hate market. You know that."

"Yes. It's a shame. We keep hoping you'll learn to like it."

"Well, I won't."

Mary recognized that this was not the time to ask Margaret about her time at the table with Ivan Stoltzfus. Instead, she mentioned there was leftover lasagna and some raspberry tapioca if she was hungry.

"I'm going to bed," Margaret replied curtly, leaving her mother to stand alone in the kitchen, doing a slow turn to watch her daughter go through the living room and up the staircase.

She sighed, looked out the window at the light in Steve's office. Working late again. She went back to her recliner, picked up the book she was reading, before sending up the breath of a prayer.

He came through the door of the laundry room, whistling softly as he bent to wash his hands at the sink. She heard him opening cabinet doors, getting the jar of peanut butter, the graham crackers.

Oh, she could eat half a dozen slabs of them dipped in milk, but she felt across her rounded stomach with the palm of her hand and thought she had better not.

"Mary, put your book down and come have a snack," Steve called.

"*Ach* Steve, I shouldn't."

"Come on."

So she did, sitting across from him at the oak table, straightening the place mat beneath the wooden tray holding salt and pepper shakers, a square of napkins, a small pewter pitcher of toothpicks.

This was their place, this kitchen table, a shrine to their connection. Here was where they talked, shared, laughed, cried, the hub of the family, creating a secure foundation for their sleeping children.

He handed her the jar of peanut butter, raised his eyebrows as she pushed it away.

"Fat, Steve. I feel fat. You know how I love lasagna and I ate too much supper."

"You know I don't mind if you gain weight or not. You're still as beautiful as the day I met you. Eat."

She broke a graham cracker in two, smiled at him.

"You spoil me."

"I love spoiling you. You're my wife."

"And I don't deserve it."

"Margaret home?"

Mary nodded. "In a bad mood."

"Why?"

"She doesn't like market."

"She doesn't like housecleaning, either. She doesn't like any job. She has to learn that life doesn't hand you everything. It takes giving up your own will, learning to do what you don't always like. It's called growing into your role as a mature person."

"I heartily agree, you know that. But it's so hard for her."

"You know, Mary. I'd say let her quit, but the next job is going to be the same. I wish she had a hobby, an interest in something other than *rumschpringa.*"

"But what? She shows no interest in anything." Mary sighed, the weariness of constant concern for Margaret showing on her pretty face. "And she takes all her frustration out on me. Sometimes I don't think she likes me at all."

"We've been through this before. For some teens, it's normal. Life kicks you around at that age sometimes, and you take it out on the ones you love most."

"Huh."

Disgruntled, tired of worry, tired of not eating graham crackers and peanut butter, she took herself off to bed, leaving Steve to drink the last of his milk and head to the shower.

Upstairs, Margaret hashed and rehashed her evening again, replaying his words, "See you around." She convinced herself that was only a nice way of saying he didn't care if he never saw her again.

He didn't like strawberry blonds with freckles and blue eyes. Or maybe he didn't like her because she had a mentally ill mother and was afraid she'd turn out to be the same. Yes, it was all her mother's fault. Why couldn't she be normal?

She finally fell into a troubled sleep, waking at two with her heart racing, her mind doing tricks of its own.

She felt as if she was losing control of her life, her own sense of hanging on to whatever a normal person hung on to. She shot out of bed, her breath coming in ragged heaves, and stood in the middle of her room with nowhere to go, no idea what was wrong or who to call. Gradually, she calmed herself by pacing her room, before falling into bed and covering her head with the quilt.

She was afraid, abandoned, condemned to suffer some unnamable punishment, caught like a rat in a trap. She must find courage, and no one must ever know what she had just experienced. The last thing she needed was rumors going around that she was mental like her mother.

She wasn't. She couldn't be. It was stress, leftover stress from the stupid market job and being at the table with Ivan. That's all it was.

She rose at her leisure on Saturday morning. Elmer had told her to take the day off since he was training two new girls, which suited her just fine. She stretched, luxuriating in the sun beginning its golden light between the slats of her blinds, with absolutely no obligations at all. Perhaps she would sew a new dress or go shopping with Rebecca.

She rose slowly, grabbed her robe, and went downstairs, finding her mother at the stove, frying scrapple, slicing bread.

Rebecca looked up from placing knives and forks beside plates.

"You're home?"

"I got the day off."

Mary turned, her eyes wide. "You didn't tell me."

Margaret ignored her, turned to Rebecca. "What're you doing today?"

"I dunno. Nothing special."

Logan looked up from tying his shoes. "Yeah you are."

"What?"

"You're going to the horse sale in New Holland with me and Dat."

"Who said?"

"Me." Logan grinned.

Steve came in from the barn, where he was feeding the two driving horses, the twelve brown chickens in their run, and the two miniature ponies the boys drove around the place.

He spied Margaret. "You're home?"

"Don't worry, I didn't quit. Elmer just gave me the day off." She tried hard to hide the pleasure she felt in seeing her family glad to have her there on a Saturday morning.

The golden November sun highlighted her pale face as she sat at the breakfast table, and Mary noticed the dark circles beneath her eyes, the droop of her eyelids, the downturned mouth as she picked at her toast, moved a piece of egg from one side of her plate to the other. A stab of concern waved across her features.

Steve asked Margaret if she wanted to go to the horse sale.

Margaret looked up. "Who, me?"

"Yes, you."

"What would I want there? I don't even like horses."

Mary opened her mouth, closed it again. Her eyebrows drew into a straight line as she lifted her coffee cup.

"You might actually enjoy it. Lots of guys." Steve grinned.

Rebecca chimed in, "Yeah, Marge. Western guys, like rodeo people. They're the real deal. I love watching them. They're the best riders you will ever see."

"They're not really from the West," Margaret scoffed.

"Some of them are." But Rebecca's voice was quiet, subdued, her sweet countenance having been swiped with the cold cloth of her sister's superiority. Mary quickly tried to change the subject.

"Margaret, you haven't eaten. Everything okay?"

"What? You afraid I'm anorexic or something? Maybe I'm just not hungry."

Steve frowned. "That's enough, Marge."

She shrugged her shoulders, turned her face away.

Mary contemplated the power of one person to ruin the innocence of a happy Saturday morning breakfast.

But Margaret did decide to go to the horse sale, telling Rebecca she was curious now, which made her shine, jumping up and clapping her hands. She adored Margaret, loved to be responsible for her happiness, and while they were getting dressed, broaching the subject no one else had dared.

"Who did you take to the table?"

Margaret leaned over the bathroom sink, rolling her hair up as far as she possibly could, smoothing, combing, spritzing hairspray. She clipped a barrette in place, looked at Rebecca in the mirror, and said quietly, "Ivan."

"*The* Ivan?"

Margaret turned her head to the left, began to twist a thick wad of hair. "Yep."

"Weren't you nervous?"

Margaret clipped another barrette into place. "He's stupid, I don't want him."

Rebecca gave her a long, level look. "Don't tell lies."

"Regardless of what you might think, I don't lie. I just don't want to get involved with him. Someone like him can have any girl he wants, and he didn't treat me well. So, I'm moving on and never looking back."

She placed her small white covering on her head, pinned it, and they went downstairs together. When she drew her coat over one shoulder, Mary turned and frowned.

"Must you wear that to the horse sale?"

Margaret snorted through her nose, a derisive sound showing the impatience she felt.

"Who cares, Mom? I can never do one thing right. You're always on my case. Every single time I go anywhere, you find fault."

"I don't like that fur-lined hood. Why can't you wear something decent?"

"Because I am not a member of the church, and I can do whatever I want. All the girls wear coats like this."

"Not all of them," Mary said quietly.

Margaret flounced off in a huff, Rebecca in her wake, casting a pitying look at her mother, who went back to the sink, the hot, sudsy dishwater offering a kind of solace.

Mary felt the looming demons of her past, the times when her own parents felt helpless and afraid of their headstrong daughter, the times she found her father repulsive, her mother weak and unassuming, sloppy and spineless, agreeing with him even when she was not fully convinced of his harsh ways. How long did the sins of the fathers reach down to the next generation? And the next? Oh, her poor parents would have a fit, seeing their modern, beautiful home, the lifestyle, the children's clothes, the stretching of boundaries, until they no longer resembled the dress and lifestyles of old. Hadn't her father's rumbles warned her of this gradual, terrifying drift into the world? She thought of how her steadfast siblings retained the old ways, handing down the importance of *ordnung*, the stringent rules set in stone.

Well, her conscience had always been different. She was only being who God had made her to be. It had taken time, but she had found the deep inner peace which surpassed all understanding, and this not of herself, but through Christ Jesus, a relationship more precious than anything on earth.

She listened to the song in her heart as tears plunked into the dishwater.

"Alas, and did my Savior bleed
And did my Sovereign die.
Would He devote that sacred Head
For such a worm as I?"

She would have patience with Margaret, as Jesus had patience with her. But even as she resolved this, the fear of losing her rose within.

What if? What if Margaret chose to go out into the world and make a life for herself, away from everything she had ever known?

Mary's spirit shrank within her.

But she found the silence of the house calming, found peace in the solitude as she plied the can of Pledge, the dust rag, and the Swiffer. She thanked God for His saving grace and asked Him to keep Margaret in the palm of His hand.

STEVE FOUND SEATS high up in the bleachers. The place was so packed he was fortunate to find seats at all. Margaret wrinkled her nose, said the smell in there was disgusting, slouched in her seat, and got her phone out till Steve asked her to put it away out of respect for the surrounding Amish folk.

She sniffed and mumbled something under her breath, but obeyed, then told her brothers to sit down and behave. It was embarrassing being out with these little rowdies. She shouldn't have come, she decided. It smelled bad, and she had yet to see any real Western cowboys.

The auctioneer got on the stand, lifted the microphone, and tested it, his florid red face beneath the white cowboy hat like a ripe plum, his western shirt straining at the pearl snaps.

He certainly wasn't a real dyed-in-the-wool horseman. She became bored, yawned, looked around for distraction.

"Sit down!" she hissed to Christopher, who punched her in the arm, Logan glaring, taking his brother's side.

The first horse was a skittish paint, his hipbones jutting, his ribs like bed slats, a wild look in his rolling eyes.

"Poor thing," Margaret said, nudging Rebecca.

Rebecca nodded, shook her head.

"We need to buy him," she hissed.

They both leaned over, tapped Steve's knee. "Dat."

He looked over, raised his eyebrows.

"Buy him," Rebecca said, blushing a little at her own audacity.

Steve shook his head. "He's headed for the kill pen."

"That's why we want him. The poor thing," Margaret mouthed.

Steve looked at the wild-eyed creature, then back at the girls.

The auctioneer held the gavel high, his nasal voice pronouncing the final cost. Up flashed Steve's card. The men taking bids yelled, which escalated the bidding to eight seventy, seventy-five, sold for eight-seventy-five.

Margaret was caught up in the excitement, high-fiving her sister, telling Steve they needed another one, for practicing.

They watched them go, one after another—prancing palominos, black horses, brown ones, and just about everything in between.

An Appaloosa went for over seven thousand dollars, setting the tone for the Morgans and Quarterhorses, a few Thoroughbreds, and then the driving horses began.

Bored, the girls pushed their way through the crowd to the food stand, where they stood in a long line. There were Amish men in tattered black hats, Mennonites in narrow-rimmed fedoras, and yes, leathery-skinned old cowboys wearing shapeless greasy hats, their worn boots hitting the floor hard, their tough, steely gazes labeling them as true ranchers.

Children dodged the crowd, running between startled bystanders, and old men sat on benches with canes propped in the palms of their hands as the thundering, microphone-enhanced yelling of the auctioneer rose and fell.

Sitting at a greasy booth with Cokes and fries, they ate in silence, the noise around them too clamorous for conversation.

A shadow crossed their table, stopped. They looked up.

"Imagine seeing you here," Ivan Stoltzfus said above the din.

"Hi," Margaret said quietly.

Rebecca looked up, puzzled.

CHAPTER 12

"How are you, Margaret? This your sister?" he asked.

"Good. Yes. Rebecca, Ivan."

Rebecca smiled, nodded, and blushed when he said hello, then went back to her fries as if they alone would save her.

"This is my brother."

Margaret smiled at the younger boy, said hello, nodded when he said his name was Jake.

After that, things became awkward in a hurry, with Rebecca intent on her fries, Margaret afraid she would faint dead away, not having eaten or slept and not wanting to see Ivan Stoltzfus at all.

"Buying horses?"

The words rained down like hail, unwanted.

Go away, Margaret thought.

At this, Rebecca perked up as if some kind of spell had transformed her into a much more outgoing version of her own sweet self. "Actually, we are. We got Dad to buy the first one. He's a pathetic-looking thing, but we'll change that."

She smiled her angelic smile, her blond hair almost white in the winter sun, her blue eyes alight with excitement. Ivan looked down at her, then over at Margaret, who kept her eyes on her congealed fries, soaked in ketchup, uneaten.

"Plus, he's buying another one, so we can learn together," she went on. "We don't even own a saddle. Well, the boys do, but they only ride the minis."

"Wow, that's great. I hope you enjoy learning to ride."

"Oh, we're going to. But first we need to get that poor thing in shape. I bet in a year or so, you wouldn't know him."

"We'll have to come around, see how you're doing."

"Yeah! That would be great," Rebecca said, bouncing a bit.

Ivan looked at the long line, shook his head. Rebecca offered the rest of her fries to Jake, then slid across the booth and told him to sit. There was nothing for Margaret to do but slide over so Ivan could sit with her. It was stiff, awkward, and now her shy sweet sister was talking to Jake as if she'd known him her entire life, which was beyond embarrassing. She did not want Ivan to know she planned on having anything to do with a horse. She was way too cool for that. She didn't like horses, only cars.

Jake looked like a younger version of Ivan, but Rebecca didn't seem to notice at all.

Ivan turned to Margaret. "Any weddings this week?"

"No, thank goodness."

"I have two."

"Really?"

He nodded, asked if that was it for her. She shook her head, held up a forefinger. "One. One more."

"Lucky. Whose?"

"Cousin wedding."

Before he could ask, Jake jumped to his feet. "Come on, Ivan."

And after a quick "see you later," they were off, hurrying into the crowd and through the swinging doors.

Margaret exhaled long and loud, bent to drink some of her Coke, and refused to meet Rebecca's searching eyes. There was nothing more to say.

"Margaret, why aren't you friendly to him?"

She merely shrugged, feeling more miserable than ever.

Rebecca's soft hand crept across the table, then closed around hers.
"It's okay, Marge. I understand. It'll get better."

"What's that supposed to mean?"

"What I said. Come on, let's go see if Dad's bought another horse."

THEY CAME AWAY from that horse sale with three new horses, each one in worse shape than the previous one, all for a grand total of seventeen hundred and thirty-three dollars, plus the additional cost of saddles, bridles, halters, minerals, and shampoo.

It would turn out to be a family effort, the restoration project of three horses slated for the kill pen.

At first, Rebecca spent most of her days alone in the barn, a wide well-lit area away from the sound of traffic, neighborhood sounds, or any other distraction. Steve had built the original barn out back by a cluster of pine trees, then built an addition as the boys grew. It was a unique barn, with odd angles of the roof, dark brown board-and-batten siding, a large pasture surrounded by woven wire fence, and more trees along the north side, separating their property from the neighbor's.

Rebecca fed, shampooed, and brushed the horses. She dodged flying hooves and those mean teeth like tobacco-stained rows of corn. She learned the warning of flattened ears and shifty rumps, watched the horse dentist file down those awful teeth, observed her father's patient ways. Her brothers joined her sometimes, but Margaret avoided any contact.

"She's too cool," Logan said drily.

"Too highfalutin," Chris echoed.

"It's okay," Rebecca said. "We got this."

WEDDING SEASON CAME to a close. Margaret ran with the usual crowd, the thought of seeing Ivan around dogging her weekends, stirring up an unease, a certain discontent she could never discard entirely.

In February, the rain was icy cold and there had been no snow worth mentioning. The dark winter days dragged. Lowering clouds churned restlessly, creating portent, as if they would unleash a winter storm, but instead it was just one steel-gray day after another. Housewives yawned and took long afternoon naps, went to quiltings, and gossiped more than usual just to relieve the winter doldrums.

Sourdough bread rose on scrubbed countertops, and everyone seemed to have advice on making the best loaf. Einkorn was the favored grain suddenly, with everyone touting its amazing health benefits. Margaret told her mother she should try making sourdough, and Mary stood in the middle of the kitchen with hands on her hips and said if she heard that word one more time she was going to yell as loud as she could. No, she did not want to mess with the stuff.

Margaret said that Caitlyn's mom made artisanal sourdough, and it was so good she wouldn't believe it.

Thoroughly fed up with the virtuous women stretching and folding their sourdough every half hour, she snapped at Margaret. "What's wrong with my bread? I used to run my own bakery, you know. If Caitlyn's mom wants to spend her life feeding sourdough starter and stretching dough, well, good for her. I won't be wasting my time. I'll never understand why we have to go catching yeast from the air when you can buy it in a packet and move on with your life. And then the endless feedings . . . I don't need to worry about keeping one more thing alive in this house."

"Geez, Mom," Margaret said, surprised by her mother's vehemence.

"Let me tell you something, darling. There is high fashion and style in the world, but we lowly Amish have our share too. All these women comparing their sourdough loaves, bragging about having the best 'crumb' or 'lift,' or fancy design on top. Not to mention the money they spend on some 'heirloom grain' or another. The way I see it, it's all just a shameful display of pride masquerading as being a good housewife."

"Okay then," said Margaret. "It was just a suggestion." She rolled her eyes and left to find a bit of normalcy with her sister Rebecca, who basically lived in the barn.

She climbed the fence separating the box stalls from the forebay and sat quietly, observing as Rebecca braided pink ribbon into the paint's thickening mane.

"Tell me their names again," she said.

Rebecca looked up. "This one's Charlie, the brown Quarterhorse is Darling, the black Morgan is Dragon."

"Why those names? They're all ugly."

"Thank you."

Rebecca went back to her intricate work, ignoring her sister who had no hand in the rehabilitation of these animals, then made fun of their names.

"Why Dragon, though?" she persisted.

"He was wild like a dragon. Bit, kicked, hocked his front feet at you. He was vicious."

"Is he still?"

"Sometimes."

"You know why I came out here?"

"No clue."

"Mom's going haywire, yelling about sourdough bread. She's a mess."

"She doesn't have to make sourdough if she doesn't want to. Her bread is delicious."

"She's mental."

"So are you."

Margaret's eyes flew wide open. In a scared voice, she asked, "What do you know about it?"

Rebecca looked up sharply. "What do you mean?"

"Nothing."

But she did mean something. More frequently now, she woke during the night, sure she was having heart problems, kidney failure, a brain tumor slowly spreading across her brain. She often experienced dizziness, nausea, towering rages, then a deep trough of depression in which she would hide herself away, saying she had a migraine.

Margaret slid off the fence, stood beside Charlie, and slid a hand beneath the braids, stroking the silky hide. Suddenly, something in her gave way. She told Rebecca she thought she might have what her mother had, and she began to weep softly, making mewling kitten sounds that frightened Rebecca.

Quickly, she left the braiding half-finished, took up the ribbon, and left the stall, holding the door open for Margaret, who stumbled a bit through her blurry vision. She leaned against the watering trough, took up the corner of her apron, and inhaled deeply.

"I'm just so afraid sometimes, Rebecca."

"Why don't you tell Mom?"

"I'm . . . I don't want to be like her, and I'm afraid I am."

"You have to talk to her."

"Don't tell anyone."

They both looked up as the door opened, letting in the cold, wet air, stirring wisps of hay and scattered sawdust.

"Hey, Dat."

"What's up, girls? Mom says supper's ready. What's wrong, Margaret? You look upset."

"Got some dust in my eye."

"Okay, come in for supper."

Mary smiled as she served a large square pan of homemade pizza, complete with home-canned sauce, fried sausage and green peppers, and a mixture of good cheese. She served heavy slabs on each plate, then passed the salad and bottle of homemade dressing.

"Sourdough crust?" Steve asked with a twinkle in his eye. He laughed when Mary cast him a look.

"The days are finally getting longer. Surely the sun will shine now. It's been over a week of rain and drizzle." Steve tried to cheer the stodgy family, quell the irritation of bleak days.

No one answered. Rebecca ate small bites of her pizza, contemplating her sister's confession.

Steve tried gamely, "Dragon doing any better?"

"Some days."

Conversation lagged. Mary yawned, wiped her eyes, said, "Boy."

"Boy what?" Logan asked, checking responses to see if it merited a laugh. Apparently it didn't.

"It's just so dark and dreary. I went for groceries today and I know I have never seen so many glum people. Pushing grocery carts with bent heads, looking straight ahead and avoiding eye contact. It's amazing how grumpy people are in this kind of weather. Oh, that's right, Margaret. I found a new over-the-counter pill for migraines. Do you want to try it?"

"I doubt it."

She kept her head lowered, and Rebecca tore off a crust of bread, balling it up between thumb and forefinger.

MARGARET TOOK TO going with Rebecca to the barn in the evenings, and before she was aware of it, she was brushing, feeding, mucking stalls. As they worked, they talked, and by the first spring breeze, Rebecca knew all of Margaret's history of panic attacks, uncontrollable thoughts, anger, depression, all of it.

They worked a lot with Dragon, whose unpredictable temper still kept them safe distances away. Even on a lead rope, there was never a time to relax, never knowing when he would lash out, his stained teeth hovering, or a twitching hindquarter.

And still no one told Mary about her daughter's condition, as Margaret fought on by herself, disliking the thought of medicine, of depending on a manufactured drug to keep her normal.

Her beauty multiplied as she grew older, her features settling into themselves, a certain maturity serving her well. In two weekends she was asked out by three different young men, each one afraid to approach her and not surprised when the answer was no, each one believing she'd spoken the truth when she said she wasn't ready to date. There was always tomorrow, and the chance of acceptance.

To say she was popular among the youth wasn't exactly truthful. Some days she was outgoing and friendly, others she was withdrawn, suspicious, with hooded eyes and no smile.

There was talk of her being like her mother, but that was all it was, guesswork, surmising. Margaret knew. Though she had told herself she wanted nothing to do with Ivan, she also found every other young man repulsive in comparison. She always watched for him, knew the sound of his car, could decipher his voice from surprising distances.

She decided it was better to be alone for the rest of her life than to marry someone she did not love. She honestly had no idea what her mom meant when she talked about giving yourself up to God's will.

Sometimes Ivan talked to her, stood beside her to play volleyball, included her in conversations, but each time she seized up, froze like an ice cube, and could only utter monosyllables. She never imagined her anxiety, the condition she so tried to hide, had anything to do with her inability to interact in a normal way.

ABOUT TWELVE MILES away, across level farm country dotted with clustered buildings, Ivan Stoltzfus walked out of a large brick house beside a macadam road winding along till it dropped down a sharp incline and up over a bridge spanning little Pequea Creek.

The old stone gristmill resided over the flowing water, the huge wooden paddle wheel silent forever, only an object to be photographed by tourists, appreciated by the elderly remembering a sweeter, simpler time.

A pair of mallards followed their instinctual habits, moving against the current, searching for a suitable eddy with a grassy bank, a quiet place to raise their brood. To the left of the bridge, a sleek heron stood as if made from cement, its rounded eyes missing nothing, as it waited on unsuspecting fish. Buds were pushing on willow trees and new dandelion shoots emerged thickly by the water's edge.

Ivan breathed deeply and took in the scent of new growth, the earthy smell of moving water and wet earth. His mind was not on simple things, however, after experiencing another battle of wills at the supper table, another episode of his food turning tasteless, his mother leaving the table in a temper as his father bent his head to his plate in frustration. Raised to keep up appearances, these arguments were never fully acknowledged, but they were frequent enough that Ivan preferred not to be home more than necessary.

He walked down the well-maintained drive, past the old oak trees along the row of hosta, hydrangea, heuchera, and ferns to the edge of his neighbor's property where he parked his vehicle. Young men with cars were required to park them elsewhere, not on their parents' properties, making it clear that the parents did not approve of the vehicles.

He unlocked it as he approached, reveling in the fine lines of the black Mustang. He felt the usual thrill as he started the engine. He enjoyed owning a car. Enjoyed driving it, felt proud to rev the engine and watch pedestrians turn their heads in appreciation. Like most young men of the Amish, he knew vehicle ownership was not a permanent way of life, but could be enjoyed for the short years of *rumschpringa* before he joined the church and gave up the things of the flesh to serve God.

The low throbbing of the engine sent the mallards into a cover of tall shrubs, but the heron remained, his constant vigil unperturbed. Ivan glanced at the creek, adjusted the rearview mirror before backing out on the road, his foot pressing down on the gas pedal as he moved slowly away. He had no real destination on a Wednesday evening in early April, only the need to put distance between him and that table surrounded by parents and siblings.

He tried to keep his mind on more pleasant things like baseball season, his friends—lighthearted subjects that were far from his troubled family. There were only three kids left at home now that four were married, beginning lives of their own, even if there was no great distance between them. The four older siblings—two brothers and two sisters—were swept up in having children, working, creating a home according to the things they had been taught. Taking on the traditions from one generation to another. Work hard, go to church, support the community, raise a family, fit in without rippling the waters of peace and harmony.

As he drove, he wondered idly how many other families' tables were turned into a veritable hornet's nest by the end of the meal. Sometimes he felt the blame lay on his mother, other times he felt the burden of his father's coldhearted reserve. He never did understand why he was voted on the board of the Plain Homestead, but perhaps he turned into another person when he was away from home.

What was home?

A showplace, for them. A restored showplace of brick and replaced windows, oak floors refinished to perfection, costly furniture in a beautiful flagstone patio surrounded by luxurious landscaping.

And it was never enough. He knew his mother was insatiable, always wanting what she didn't, or couldn't, have, choosing to open the subject at the evening meal, throwing the young adults into the melee.

His father was rarely at home, and if he was present, he was working, or in his office. He kept busy as a board member for several establishments among the Amish. A man of honesty and valor, a man of wisdom, he presided over many things, having made a name for himself as a hard worker, a good manager, standing a head above others.

As he drove, Ivan's thoughts went to Margaret, the girl with the spun gold hair and the bewildering personality. She occupied his thoughts too much of the time, left him guessing, feeling like an outsider. It was better to disentangle himself before he got caught in a snare, like a helpless rabbit dangling from a rope, like his father had. He was afraid of a serious relationship going sour, afraid of thinking he'd found the perfect girl only to discover she was, well, like his mother.

All his life, he'd known the bitterness of discord, of verbal warfare, doors slamming behind hurled accusations. Then there'd be days of polite silence until things were smoothed over, every wrinkle of their existence as a bickering family erased, smiling faces showing the peace and harmony in which they lived. Fine. Everything was fine. It had to be fine. Real emotion was tucked away and only acceptable things presented.

So Ivan felt fine as he drove along, felt fine as he turned in at Sheetz to fill up his tank, felt fine as he greeted an Amish man in a carpenter's pickup truck. It was fine if the man gave him a stare of disapproval. He didn't mean it if he didn't allow it to penetrate his armor of fineness.

He paid for his gas, bought a Gatorade, and left, then decided to drive to his sister Sarah's house, just off the New Holland pike. She was closest to his age, married only a few years, living in a rented bungalow on the outskirts of New Holland.

As he passed horses and buggies, he remembered his own brand-new carriage, sitting in the shop, the shafts propped up to allow more room for his parents' carriage. He hadn't used it for years, couldn't imagine using it now, but it was there if he ever needed it.

He found Sarah in her small kitchen, mixing brownies, her husband Dave at the table holding six-month-old Arlan. They seemed glad to see him, so he agreed to a cup of coffee. They made small talk about the weather, Dave's job as a roofer with Stoltzfus Roofing, and caught up on local interests, the way siblings will do.

Ivan noticed the simplicity of the house, the freshly painted white walls, the aging cabinets, the worn linoleum. He raised his eyebrows, asking how long she'd be okay with this tiny house.

Sarah raised her fine, dark eyebrows. "I'm not Mom."

"Obviously," Ivan commented.

"Hey, we're trying to save for our own property, but the way things are, we may have to move out of Lancaster County," Dave said seriously.

"Didn't Dat offer to help?" Ivan asked.

Sarah shook her head, avoided her brother's questioning eyes.

"No. He doesn't help."

"Never? None of you?"

"Nope."

Incredulous, he stared at his sister.

"He has his organizations he supports, and you know Mom requires a lot. She's pretty high maintenance."

Ivan nodded.

"So, we respect that. 'Honor thy father and mother.'"

"I guess."

"And everything will be fine," Sarah added, with a laugh.

CHAPTER 13

"STILL NO GIRLFRIEND?" SARAH ASKED IVAN AS SHE SLID THE PAN of brownies from the oven.

Ivan shook his head.

"Time you get on that."

Who was to say he had the wisdom and understanding to marry someone? There was no guarantee in matters of the heart. He was afraid—that was what it boiled down to. Afraid of marrying a sweet-natured girl who simply turned sour, made unreasonable demands, and looked at you as if you were a cross to bear. A girl could be attractive one minute and then a weight around your neck the next.

And Margaret certainly didn't qualify as sweet. She never said much, was terribly rough around the edges at times, especially around her friends, the gaggle of girls in brilliant colors, chewing gum, snapping it, laughing too loudly, flirting too much. Margaret always seemed shy around him, but around other guys she lit up. Didn't that mean she had no interest in him?

She was in a league all her own, of this he was convinced, which was why she spent far too much time in his mind. The color of her hair, her aquamarine eyes, the way her cheekbones created a contour of movement when she talked, the flashing of perfect white teeth.

"Who did you have at the table?" Ivan's mother had asked him.

When he told her, she'd frowned, shook her head.

"Mental. Her mother is mental. Comes from some community way out in New York. You don't want her."

"I didn't say I did. I just had her to the table."

"Good. That poor father of hers went through a lot with his wife. I think she's still mental at times, you just never hear about it."

SPRING WAS IN the dips and hollows, by the bank of the creek, in the planting and plowing across the patchwork of fields in Lancaster. Everywhere, farms and small homes were a beehive of activity, humming with energy, gardens being planted, horse stables cleaned, barns pressure washed.

Mary was in a frenzy of housecleaning, washing windows and bedding and curtains, wiping floors on hands and knees, cleaning and organizing throughout the house. She loved it, to stand in the doorway of a freshly cleaned room shining in the golden glow of late afternoon sunshine with a sturdy sense of accomplishment.

Rebecca was a good, willing helper until the horses in the barn began to occupy her mind and she lost focus. Margaret refused to help except for tidying own room, and even that was a struggle.

"Mom," Margaret yelled as Mary glanced into her bedroom. "I see absolutely no sense in this. Housecleaning is a ridiculous, unending chore and I'm not doing it!"

"Yes, you are." She said it firmly, but in a quiet, level voice.

Alarmed, she watched Margaret pick up her alarm clock and throw it against the opposite wall, shattering the glass front and creating a dent in the drywall, before storming off down the stairs in a white-hot fury.

Mary was frightened but stayed calm for Rebecca's sake. They picked up buckets and mops and went downstairs. "Let's call it a day," she said, freeing Rebecca to head to the barn. They left Margaret's room untouched. She could clean up the broken glass when her anger subsided.

It was a beautiful, balmy spring evening, the air as soft as the golden sunshine, the daffodils already withering as the bold red tulips upstaged them. New lambs skittered beside their stoic mothers. The wind had settled, which made a perfect afternoon for volleyball at Jonas King's, and Margaret wore her newest spring dress in lime green, setting off her peculiar hair color and accentuating her unusual eyes.

She was unaware of her parents' close observation of her mood swings, from the episode in her room, to the maniacal high following, laughing hysterically at something Logan described that no one else found quite humorous.

But Sunday morning, she seemed okay. Mary caught her breath as she saw her come down the stairs, dressed and ready for church. It was prideful to notice her great beauty, but just this once, she allowed herself a bit of luxury.

After church, Margaret scootered off by herself, the group of youth being less than a mile from home. She seemed to be in a normal, even state of mind.

Margaret walked her scooter up the gravel drive, her eyes going to the line of vehicles parked in the field, searching as always for the black Mustang, which was never there. Her friends greeted her, and she was swept up in the circle of colorful girls, saying soft hellos to a few young men, glad to see the volleyball nets being set up.

She loved to play, and knew she was becoming one of the best. She jumped into the first game and played with abandon, experiencing a genuine rush from the fierce competition. She was totally swept up in the game when she became aware of the tall, dark presence beside her.

"Hey," he said, very low.

She looked over, wide-eyed, her cheeks flushed with the activity. She smiled, said nothing, then looked away before focusing on the ball.

When they rotated, she was aware of him following her, but she tried to stay calm, focused on the game.

"How have things been for you?" he asked quietly.

"Good. And you?"

"Fantastic, with the weather and all."

"Yeah. Me, too."

And he was gripped with impatience, a rush to continue the conversation, to really get to know her. But that would mean asking to take her home that night, which she'd likely say no to. She'd been so childlike and trusting that first weekend, and he'd dropped her like a hot potato.

He was embarrassed, the way he kept watching her, the grace with which she moved, her motion like a song, a piece of poetry.

His mother's words rankled, cut into his joy of being here with her. *Mentally ill.* The words seemed like an unfair label. He had googled a bunch of mental illnesses, and none seemed to fit Margaret.

When she went for the ball, she was so quick, and so unaware. She plowed straight into him, knocking him away with a few quick backward steps, then sent the ball up and over the net before giving him a sideways look of apology, a quick "Sorry."

"You have to let me take you home for that," he said quickly, so only she could hear.

Startled, she said nothing.

Then, "I scootered."

"It'll fit in the trunk."

Her eyes followed the ball as she hopped from one foot to the other before moving away and giving him the thumbs-up signal. Even her hands were astonishing, he thought. He raised his eyebrows and asked if it meant yes. She nodded, and his world exploded in fireworks.

FINALLY, THE LONG line of young people filling their plates was over, and the singing started at eight o'clock, voices rising and falling in the soft spring evening, the mist settling down and bringing a decided chill. After the goodbye song had been sung and the crackers, cheese, and cookies passed around, Margaret's heart began to bang against her chest, all the confidence of volleyball seeping away.

But there he was at her elbow, a hand touching it lightly, his voice in her ear.

"If you tell me where your scooter is, we'll load it."

She nodded, moved through the crowd, found the scooter, and tried to maneuver it into the trunk, which barely closed, and then they left quickly, before anyone would see. He drove slowly, and both were unaware of a certain tall young man in a dark shirt, the light going out of his eyes as he watched the black Mustang turn to the right on the main road.

Back at Margaret's house, she asked if he would like to come in, as was the custom, but he said they could sit in the car for a while, if that was okay. Surprised, she asked for a reason, and he shrugged his shoulders. "I don't know. I told you I was a coward. Afraid of dating, I guess," he said sheepishly.

There was an awkward silence, an awful space of time in which they were suspended by their own inhibitions. The longer the silence prevailed, the more Margaret's panic increased. She had to say something, anything.

"I guess I could get my scooter out of the trunk."

"I'll get it. Stay."

When he returned, she forced herself to ask him about his job, then his parents and siblings, and the conversation was off to a halting start. She was a bit taken aback at how unusual his answers were—always upbeat, always fine, everything about his entire life was wonderful.

"You certainly have a beautiful place. I hear your dad is a successful stonemason."

"He is. Always too busy, though, according to Mom."

"Yeah. Parents. But I have good parents."

"That's cool. My mom drives me up a wall, but Dat's a good soul."

He looked at her, wide-eyed. Who would ever admit to a mother's shortcomings? Her, evidently.

She noticed his shock. "What?"

"Sorry, it's just . . . that's a bold thing to say about your mom."

"Well, not everyone can have a perfect family like you seem to. My mom's fine, she just such a *mom*. I mean, she worries so much about what people think, and she's always on my case. She and I don't get along all that great. Never have."

Ivan was shocked. He couldn't imagine talking about his mom that way.

"What about your mom? You get along?" she asked suddenly.

"Oh sure. She's fine."

"Must be a winner, letting you driving this car around."

"She is."

The conversation stalled after that, but he picked up the frayed ends and told her how nice it was to have married siblings he could visit often.

"So, you're a big, happy family?"

"Yes, we are."

"Well, you got us beat. We can be real losers sometimes. At least I can. Probably all of us except my sister Rebecca. She's pretty close to perfect."

He laughed softly. "You're so honest. We were raised to keep all the bad stuff hidden. It keeps things peaceful."

"Like putting a lid on a can of worms," she blurted.

"No, no, no. It's just . . . you know, it's better not to talk about feelings and stuff like that."

"What? What on earth are you talking about?"

He drew back in alarm. "Sorry, I just meant that staying positive helps to keep disagreements at bay, you know? If you admit to failures, you're weakening the family structure."

Margaret breathed deeply, steadied herself.

Slowly she said, "I see."

He took a breath and shifted the subject. "So, I have wanted to ask you out, but I wasn't sure how you felt about me. And I also thought I should wait till you're older. You're seventeen, right?"

She nodded, feeling like she was being measured and weighed.

"I'm a lot older."

"I know."

"Your parents will think I'm robbing the cradle."

"Do you care what they think?"

"Of course."

"Dat won't care. He's pretty easygoing and he's kind of, like, old, as in graying hair and all that. Mom is a lot more to worry about. She's weird."

"Margaret, really? The way you talk about your mother, I find hard to believe."

"Why?"

"Well, I told you. In our family, things are much different."

"Everything's great?"

"Well, yes."

"I doubt that."

He felt caught, trapped in an uncomfortable place where his half-lies bumped against his conscience. He had never thought of them as lies before—he was just being respectful of his parents. To talk about the bad parts—the fighting at the dinner table, the constant tension in the home—*that* would be wrong. Wouldn't it? Suddenly he felt confused and uneasy.

Perhaps that was why he merely touched her waist lightly as he walked her to the front door, then stepped away after confirming next Saturday night at eight. And she went through the door in a daze, but not quite as ecstatic as she imagined she might be if he ever asked her out.

What was the deal with his "perfect" family? Really? It almost made her mad, the way he described keeping the peace. Really? She'd be stuck away in some facility if she couldn't speak the truth. Well, he'd get used to her way of seeing things in time. Why wouldn't he, when she was obviously right?

IN THE MORNING, she bounced down the stairs with the amazing event spilling from her mouth before she reached the kitchen, her mother looking up with a glad expression and the proper congratulations.

"Tell me about it, Margaret. This is so exciting."

"Never thought it would happen. He just walked onto the volleyball game and never went away, then asked if he could take me home. A perfect evening, a dream come true."

"I'm so glad," Mary said, voicing her true feelings.

Margaret slid into a chair, picked at a leftover piece of toast. "The only thing . . ." Here she told her mother of his view on family harmony.

Mary listened, then said, "Oh, wow. Sounds a bit iffy."

"Yeah, seemed weird."

"But you know, there are lots of families like that, where you simply don't speak of emotion and honest feelings, just like he said. And sometimes I wonder if that isn't the reason marriage problems develop. No one talks."

"Well, he's so handsome, and I am thrilled. If we get married, I'm sure I can convince him that being open and honest is the way to go."

"Whoa there. Never assume you can change someone after you're married," Mary cautioned, wagging a finger.

"Well, I don't see why he wouldn't agree with me once I explain it."

Mary spoke to her daughter, imparting the wisdom gleaned from experience, until Margaret flounced off to her room, shouting about how nothing she ever did was good enough, and why couldn't she ever just be happy for her? But by the time Saturday evening rolled around, the disagreement was forgotten, and the whole family was on hand, watching without being seen as she floated down the walk in her light pink dress, a cloud of her signature scent following her.

Mary turned away after the low throbbing of the car faded.

"My poor father. What would he say? *Ach*, Steve, I'll never be free from the ties that bind. The guilt I still carry about my brothers and sisters living real Amish lives, while I'm only half Amish. It's just so hard at times."

Steve listened, really listened, then asked if she really thought anything in their lives disqualified them from being fully Amish.

"I know now that we can't be saved by our works," she said thoughtfully. "But the Amish are supposed to stay separate from the world, and sometimes I don't feel that we're doing that enough."

"But don't you think your father went a little too far?"

"Yes, that's true," she said, and then let the conversation go. Steve would never fully understand her upbringing.

Steve was proud of his daughter, but concerned about her display of temper, the highs and lows, the refusal to get a proper diagnosis. He hoped this Ivan was no foolish young man, but one who would pick up on the mood swings.

Ivan smiled at Margaret from the driver seat, reached over and took her hand, then told her she looked so pretty, so unlike anyone he'd ever met. Margaret knew they were off to a much better start and wondered if the first lack of agreement had merely been an attack of nerves.

"How was your week?" he asked.

She said it was okay, nothing exciting, and that she had a hard time getting along with one of her English coworkers. "How was yours?" she asked.

"Great. Absolutely great."

"That good, huh?"

"Yep, it was great."

She nodded, smiled at him, and let it go, telling herself she was overreacting, and she might as well get used to his upbeat ways.

She loved his profile, liked the way he dressed, enjoyed listening to him talk, so what was there to become peeved about? Nothing.

She settled herself into a softly lit booth at Texas Roadhouse, and smiled and talked and laughed. She felt as if she had to pinch herself to make sure this was real. What young girl would not be thrilled to sit here at this fine restaurant and enjoy such a handsome man's company?

By the end of the evening, she felt relaxed in his presence, entertaining, and capable of impressing him with her views on a number of subjects. She knew they made a striking couple, turning heads as they walked out of the restaurant, her confidence at an all-time high, her happiness reaching to the stars.

The night was in their favor, one of those beautiful spring evenings so lovely it actually made her heart ache, the scent of lilac mingling with early tea roses.

"Would you like to go for a drive since it's such a nice evening?" he asked softly.

"We could do that."

"You have church tomorrow, right?"

"I do, and my mom's pretty strict about me going."

"Okay. Fine with me. I suppose she's pretty strict about dating practices as well, huh?" he asked quietly.

"We talked about it."

"And?"

Margaret shrugged.

"You don't want to talk about it?"

"No."

But when they drove up the Welsh Mountains and stopped at the overlook, the night as sweet as a dream, and he put his arms around her as they stood beneath the magnificent stars, the heady scent of budding mountain laurel as sweet as old wine, everything her mother told her was forgotten.

HER FACE WAS pale and drawn as she came downstairs carrying her white cape and apron, standing silently, waiting on her mother to pin it onto her navy-blue dress. From the laundry room came the sound of running water as her father returned from getting the harness on the horse.

"Oh, there you are, Margaret. Is Rebecca ready to have her cape pinned?"

"I don't know. Didn't see her."

"How was your first date with Ivan?"

"Good. We had a good evening."

Mary detected the worrisome note in her voice, saw the set of her jaw, the hooded eyes, and felt scratched by claws of fear.

The world was such a frightening place for her innocent daughters and, more than ever, her conservative background came up to taunt her. Her own daughter, out in a vehicle with a young man seven years older . . . it was not a good idea. Not now, not ever.

She would have to take matters into her own hands if Steve was planning on sitting there like a nesting duck thinking everything was going to turn out peachy.

CHAPTER 14

IVAN'S MOTHER, BARBIE, WAS HAVING A MELTDOWN OF HER OWN. She had gotten him to go online and order two swivel rattan rocking chairs for her new pergola on the flagstone patio, but when they arrived via FedEx, they were small and cheaply constructed.

Ivan was getting dressed to go out with Margaret when he heard his mother's footsteps on the stairs, muttering to herself, which was not good, not good at all.

"Ivan," she shouted, banging on the door.

"What?"

"Those chairs. I could just cry. They're all wrong."

"What am I supposed to do about it?"

"Tell me how to send them back."

"Not tonight."

"I know. But Monday. You know Dat won't bother with them. I can't have those chairs on my porch, and it's your fault, I hope you know."

This was all spoken through the closed door as Ivan combed and styled his dark hair and pulled on an expensive leather belt. He felt the burning sensation in his collarbone, that bundle of nerve endings she lit with her strident demands. He rubbed it with the palm of his hand, grimaced.

"Okay. I'll see what I can do Monday night."

He heard her turn away, heard the receding footsteps. He didn't allow the resentment to get a toehold, but stuffed it in the airtight box marked: CAUTION. FLAMMABLE. KEEP CLOSED AT ALL TIMES.

As he left the house he skirted the back patio, her thin frame bent over a potted plant, pruning, fertilizing, achieving perfection, her mouth drawn in a thin line of concentration.

He used the front porch, avoiding her as he walked to his car.

"Ivan!"

He gritted his teeth, turned to answer, the set of his shoulders giving away his resignation.

"What?"

"Come here. I want you to look at these chairs."

"What's wrong with them?"

And so he endured her tirade about the inappropriate chairs, and the fact his father didn't care, wouldn't look at them or listen to her. What was she supposed to do without his support? The old feeling of helplessness enveloped him, the same thing he'd experienced growing up when he was expected to fix a situation beyond his means. It was always his job to step up to the plate and take responsibility when his father refused to satisfy her demands. Chicken wire for pea vines, a lost water hose, a broken screen, a hornet's nest under the eaves, the list went on and on.

Ivan tried to shrug it off, but the feeling lodged in his chest like a festering sore he could never escape, so when he picked up Margaret he appeared preoccupied, a certain part of him not present.

"How was your week?" Margaret asked, settling herself in the passenger seat as she smiled at him.

"Great. I had a good week at work. Helped my mom in the garden."

"I bet she appreciates you a lot."

"She does. We're pretty close. Couldn't ask for a better mother."

Margaret smiled to herself. What was the old saying? "As a young man treats his mother, so he will treat his wife."

She asked when she could meet his family.

"Soon."

But one weekend turned into another, the beautiful spring days turning into the heat of summer, and she was still in the dark about where he lived, and had yet to meet his parents. Then one Sunday evening, when they sat on the back patio, he told her church was at his parents' house the following Sunday and did she want to come Saturday night and attend services in his district the following morning?

She smiled to herself on the darkened patio, but asked if he was sure she wasn't a bother to his mother. He assured her that his mother would love to meet her, but then he left earlier than usual, leaving her standing by the screen door and wondering.

Mary sensed an air of anxiety about her daughter and asked what was making her so jittery.

"If you have to know, church is at Ivan's place on Sunday, and he wants me there Saturday night. I haven't met his parents yet. He only has good things to say about them, but sometimes I wonder. I mean, who *only* has good things to say about their parents?"

"Not you, I'm sure."

Margaret looked at her mother, wide-eyed. "How did you know?"

"Oh, you're my daughter, and every word out of your mouth is unfiltered. You speak the truth, no matter where it lands."

"Absolutely."

"I know I get on your nerves."

"Absolutely, but I love you, Mom." She draped an arm over Mary's shoulders, and said, "You're the best."

Mary closed her eyes and soaked up the unusual display of affection like a dry sponge.

"I love you, too."

ON SATURDAY EVENING, the air was sultry, heavy with thunderclouds, the trees so still a bird flitting from the tips of branches was the only movement. In the distance, heat lightning quivered.

Margaret walked up the road beside Ivan, clutching her overnight bag, anxiously searching her mind for anything she might have forgotten. White cape and apron rolled precisely, dress folded, new covering.

Black shoes, pantyhose. She had agonized over dress color, not wanting too bold, or too plain, too mousy. Rebecca had finally chosen the green, and Margaret agreed.

They neared the formidable brick structure, the groomed lawn, the edging so precise it seemed to have been done by a laser, the garden a portrait of perfection. There were no lights in the windows, but string lights shone from the flagstone patio.

She touched Ivan's hand, needing assurance, but he drew away quickly. His father sat on a wicker chair, his bare feet on an ottoman.

He looked up, watched their approach, then got to his feet. Tall, like Ivan, with dark hair and a graying beard, he extended his hand. Margaret took it and said hello when he did.

Ivan said quietly, "My dad. Dad, Margaret."

"Nice to meet you, Margaret."

"And you. Ivan speaks of you often."

He smiled, and somehow Margaret felt the air of defeat.

"Good things, I hope."

"Of course."

The screen on the French doors was pushed back, and a thin middle-aged woman stepped into the dim lighting.

"Amos. How . . . oh, here you are, Ivan. And this is Margaret?"

Ivan stepped forward, a hand on Margaret's back.

"Yes," he said quickly. "Margaret, my mother. Mom, Margaret."

"Hello. Where did your parents find such a name?"

But she took her hand, shook it, then turned to her husband.

"Amos, you have to do something about this screen door yet. I told you a hundred times it needs some WD-40. It pushes too hard. Do you have any? And did you turn the clock back? Where's Jake?"

Margaret had opened her mouth to answer about her name, but closed it again, waiting to see what his father would do. He did nothing, just eased himself back into his chair, without answering.

Ivan took her elbow lightly in his hand and steered her through the sliding screen door, saying nothing. He led the way upstairs, then turned to her at the top.

"I . . . we aren't allowed to be in my room."

"Oh."

Perplexed, she searched his face in the dim light, but his dark eyes slid away.

"So, you'll have to sleep in the guest room. If we want to spend time together, we'll have to be downstairs. Or you can hang out with my sisters."

"But I don't know them."

"I'll introduce you."

The wind rose, sending a curtain at the end of the hallway billowing in, a potted plant rustling beneath. Lightning flickered, followed by a faraway rumble of thunder.

"Storm coming," Ivan remarked, as if he was making small talk with a stranger at the grocery store. "I think they're calling for hail and high winds."

He seemed ill at ease, antsy, watching the opened doors of the hallways, as if waiting for an appearance.

"Here. This door is the guest room."

He led her to a dim room, the bed high and wide, made up as if being photographed for a magazine. She took in the plush comforter with matching shams, fronted by an array of gray and beige pillows, an expensive throw positioned at just the right angle. A beautiful wooden rocking chair, elaborate mirrors, paintings on the wall, an Indian rug on the flawless floorboards.

Lightning flashed again.

"There's a closet for your church clothes. The bathroom is across the hallway."

Bewildered, she looked up at him. "But where are you going?"

"Downstairs. You can join me."

Glad to be invited, she slipped a hand in his. Gently, he shook hers loose and walked ahead of her. Rejection slammed her chest, but she said nothing, wondering how he had turned into a different person in an hour's time.

They met his three sisters, all teenagers, each one tall, willowy, and dark-haired. They were dressed in immaculate dresses, bib aprons, and white coverings. Ivan introduced them as Anna Mae, Suzanne, and Emma Sue.

She felt herself being scrutinized as they extended hands politely. Margaret found their handshakes weak, limp.

"We finally get to meet you," Emma Sue remarked, but Anna Mae and Suzanne merely said softly, "Hey."

The sky was filled with a blinding flash of lightning, immediately followed with a deep, hard clap of thunder. A high shriek sounded from another room, followed by a shout for Amos. Footsteps reverberated. Another flash of lightning.

"The windows!"

Ivan and his sisters turned, shoving down on windows, closing doors. The wind increased as rain battered the sides of the house.

Lightning snaked across the sky, illuminating the downstairs rooms. Thunder crashed, and Ivan's mother let out another high shriek, a sound of pure terror mixed with despair. Then there was the unmistakable sound of ice, hail pinging against the windowpanes.

"Oh boy," Ivan muttered.

"Let's go out on the porch," Margaret suggested. "Watch the storm go by."

"Are you kidding me?" Ivan asked.

"Why not? I love watching a storm."

Before he could answer, they heard a high keening noise, and Ivan told her to go upstairs, that he'd be up soon. She asked why, but he shook his head, so she went, stumbling a bit on the dark steps, with the door below shut firmly into place. She didn't know what else to do, so she sat on the rocker, hoping she wouldn't displace the cashmere throw on the back of it.

She became aware of muffled sounds from below, feet scurrying along, voices raised, then lowered. She rocked and watched the storm through the windows, the willow trees along the creek moving like hula dancers as the storm lashed.

She lifted her overnight bag and unzipped it, hung her dress and white cape and apron in the closet reeking of mothballs and lavender.

Where was Ivan? Why did he banish her to the guest room? Her eyes felt heavy after a hard day at market, and soon she dozed off. She woke to a completely dark room, shivers of heat lightning dancing in the distance, the sky clearing its throat with weak rumbles, the rain diminished to a few weary drizzles. She became aware of light thrown across the ceiling, flashes interrupted by movement, scissored shadows, followed by loud voices.

Quietly, she got to her feet, peered down on the scene below.

Everywhere, battery lamps floated like enormous fireflies as Ivan and his sisters held brooms, rakes, and garbage bags, dashing from one area to another, the movements punctuated by the loud shrieks she now perceived to come from the mother, who was obviously frantic.

Incredulous, she watched the activity below, the garden hose unwound, jets of water aimed at patio furniture, the flagstone floor. Plants were being shaken, fluffed up, wiped and polished, while rakes were dragged through the precisely cut grass.

Blinking her eyes, she finally covered her mouth to hide the smile threatening to turn into a laugh. Another shriek. Slowly, Margaret slipped her fingers beneath the window, raised it a few inches, intent on hearing what was actually going on.

"Amos, I told you we didn't want to *hondle* (switch) with Ephraims. Whoever heard of going on vacation and not being able to take church? I wouldn't have done it, but oh no, of course you have no backbone, had to say yes, and here we are."

The tirade was stopped by a rumbling injection of unintelligible words from the accused father, resulting in a hysterical comeback.

Below the window, Ivan stopped raking.

"Hush, Mam. We have company."

"Company? You call her company? She's as mental as her mother. You can see it in her eyes. Emma Sue, I told you to keep that rake off the porch. This is the worst mess I have ever seen, and I kid you not. The evening before church. Amos, you better check the driveway, where it washes out there beside the barn. You never did a thing to fix that like I told you to."

"I fixed it," the father yelled.

"Whatever. Probably not right."

Ivan ran off, the battery lamp bobbing in the direction of the barn.

Margaret turned away and sat down weakly, the chair still. "Please tell me it isn't true," she said to no one in particular. The hurt was like a burn, a searing pain.

Mental. She'd said her eyes were "mental." Surely she didn't mean it, she was just upset on account of the severe storm before services at their house. For a long time, she sat alone, her mind doubling down, playing tricks with her imagination.

But Ivan said his mother was the best. She must have caught her at a bad time. She was fine, likely. And as if to reassure her, she heard his footsteps on the stairs, a light knock on her door.

"Yes?"

"You okay? I'm sorry about all this."

"I could have helped."

She got to her feet, went to him, needing reassurance. She lifted her arms to put them around his shoulders, but was met by his hands removing them firmly. They fell by her sides, leaving her as awkward as a child on the first day of school.

"Not here. Not now."

She swallowed her disappointment but searched his eyes. His slid away. He cleared his throat.

"Look, I'm going to bed. We get up at four when church is at our house. I'll wake you."

Margaret swallowed, nodded.

"Goodnight," he said, in a small voice.

"Goodnight."

It was a long night punctuated by distant heat lightning, water dripping, old eaves popping and snapping. She played the scene on the patio over and over, incredulous, thinking of her own mother. Her mom would have laughed and said no one would notice a few leaves around the yard. She seemed dear, close to her heart now.

Well, everyone had their low moments when stress got the best of them. Things would be better in the morning.

IT WAS DARK at four o'clock, but she sprang out of bed, went to the bathroom before the sisters, and tried her best with her hair, using liberal amounts of hairspray. She dabbed on a bit of makeup, the beige colored foundation hiding flaws.

"Good morning," a girl's voice came from the shadows of the hallway.

"Oh, good morning to you," Margaret returned. "Hey, can someone help me with my cape this morning? I'm okay with my apron, but my mom puts my cape on."

"Really? I'm surprised."

With a sniff, Suzanne pushed past her into the bathroom.

Miss Better-than-thou, Margaret thought bitterly.

She resisted going downstairs, but finally found the courage, dressed in the green Sunday dress without the white cape and apron, her covering pinned neatly on her head, her hair rolled expertly.

Everywhere she looked, there was frantic activity, windows being polished, floors swept, rugs shaken. Hurried greetings were mumbled in her direction, the mother like a whirling dust storm in summer, shouting instructions, slamming doors, carrying folding chairs.

"Cereal. We have cereal for breakfast. Help yourself," she said quickly while passing in the kitchen.

"Can I do something to help?" she asked politely.

"You probably don't know how we clean our sinks, so no, you don't need to. Just eat your cereal so that's done. Cornflakes in the cabinet on top of the fridge."

Margaret stood, her hands at her sides, and looked at the door she had pointed out. How was anyone supposed to reach the cabinet without standing on a chair? And she had the distinct feeling that standing on a chair would be severely frowned upon in this home. There was no sign of coffee anywhere. She felt ridiculous standing in the middle of the kitchen with no coffee cup, no food, and no job to do, so she decided to go back upstairs.

She resolved to pin her own cape into place, no matter what. The three sisters couldn't be bothered, and she certainly wasn't about to ask Ivan's mom to help.

But when she met Ivan coming from his room, dressed in the traditional white shirt, black vest, and trousers, he was undeniably the best-looking man she had ever seen. Her knees turned weak with the pure happiness of being his girlfriend, obliterating every frightening thing she had witnessed.

Why then, that night, in the darkness of his car, when he turned to grab her roughly into his arms, holding her tightly in the August heat, did she feel herself shrinking away? She couldn't push away the thought of not being good enough for him when he was with his family. Yet alone in the dark, it was okay to let his desire rule him?

No, no.

And yet she didn't push him away.

HER MOTHER, SENSING something amiss when Margaret returned, gently questioned. But it was well into the week before Margaret admitted there was anything out of the ordinary. She described his home, his family, even going so far as telling her how he refused to allow her to put her arms around him. She stopped herself before revealing the evening in his car.

"Hm. Well, perhaps, like you said, you caught them all at a bad time. I suppose a storm like that just before services could be stressful."

"Huh," was Margaret's reply.

"How do you feel about Ivan?" Mary asked, pressing on.

"I definitely love him. He's the best-looking guy ever. He treats me really well."

"Does he?"

"Well, yeah. Would I lie to you?"

"I'm not saying that. I just . . . well, those good looks have very little to do with a good marriage. That's all I want for you, Margaret."

"How could it be anything but good if I love him the way I do?"

Mary nodded, knowing now was not the time to push her daughter. The next day, she gave her a book on Christian marriage, which Margaret looked at suspiciously, but later read late into the night.

IVAN AND MARGARET were dating seriously, the hot winds of summer turning into the brilliance of autumn. Fields were dotted by orange pumpkins and an October moon created haunting shadows at night. Ivan's black car left Margaret's house later and later as time went on.

It was Steve who brought up the subject to Mary, smiling sheepishly as he spoke.

"I don't know, Mary, but I lie awake when Ivan's here. You can tell me I'm overprotective, but it seems to me, there's very little communication between those two. I mean, shouldn't we hear low voices? I strain to hear, and this is to my shame, but all I hear is, well . . ." He stopped.

"The couch creaking?" Mary supplied.

Steve burst out laughing, and Mary put a protective hand over her own mouth, pointing to the ceiling toward Margaret's room.

"It isn't funny," she said.

"But it is. It explains her moods. I'm not convinced she's happy. And what is a parent to do?"

"You mean with a daughter like her?"

"We can't tell her anything."

"We have a power far beyond our own strength, you know."

"Absolutely. God be praised forever."

They went to bed after kneeling together, their prayers reaching the throne of Grace, while Margaret lay awake with her own set of doubts, hashing and rehashing the troubling events of a chilly Sunday evening in October.

CHAPTER 15

Ivan paced the floor of his room. He lifted the window blind to stare through the heavily shadowed night, his thoughts tormented by Margaret, a frequent event. It was the way she talked, the way she went through life speaking the truth about everything and everybody. There was no glossing over anything, and hardly anything was fine, which seemed to upset all he had ever known.

One simply didn't talk about the things she found perfectly okay to talk about. How mad she was at her mom, what a putz her dad was getting to be. A few weeks ago, she'd told him his family was so proper they were as cuddly as a cement block, then laughed at the cleverness of her own joke. He'd winced at the truth.

And she asked impossible questions. How did he feel when his mom irked him? Didn't he mind if she was being a real pain? How could he respect her, the way she acted?

He would shrug and avoid a direct answer.

She had latched on to this respect thing. She'd even asked if Ivan respected her, Margaret. Sometimes he felt as if he didn't know what respect was. She was beautiful, he desired her, what more did she want? Their sessions in the Mustang showed her how much he loved her, didn't they?

Lately, he'd felt her drawing away, an unconscious act of no longer being there one hundred percent. He panicked at the thought of losing her, couldn't bear to think of her with someone else.

His mother did not approve of Margaret, however, and never hesitated to make it known, which really messed with his mind.

Was it fair to Margaret? To him? His mother was a powerful force, one who could trouble him endlessly. Did she sense something in Margaret?

"Ivan, she's not as healthy mentally as she should be. I heard they didn't detect it in Mary till after she was married, so think about it. A mental wife. Think what you'd go through, especially when children are involved."

But Ivan loved Margaret. The way she walked, talked, smiled.

She had even told him she'd probably be a bit chubby like her mother once she started having babies, an announcement that left him totally baffled. Where did she find the courage to say such things?

By November, Ivan and Margaret were an item, the best-looking couple at his friend Omar's wedding, turning heads and fully aware of it. Other couples sat at the wedding tables, deep in conversation, or exchanging smiles of recognition, clearly enjoying each other's company, while Margaret and Ivan sat, bored and stone-faced, their view of each other's faults multiplying as weeks passed.

Margaret had told him flat out he did not respect her, and he flew over the truth as efficiently as an airliner thousands of feet above the earth.

But despite their misgivings, their lives became more and more enmeshed. His friends became her friends, his family was inserted into every get-together, and they spent nearly all their free time together. She still believed her love would see them through.

When Christmas arrived, she bought him many expensive gifts, while she received a poinsettia in colorful foil. Ashamed of it, she set it in the garage till it froze, and told her mother her boss had given it to her and she'd forgotten it.

Wisely, Mary hadn't asked about the absent present from her boyfriend. She talked it over with Steve, and let it go.

MARGARET, HOWEVER, CONFIDED in Rebecca, who listened quietly and came up with a wise solution—taking a break for a while.

"I can't," Margaret groaned, her head in her hands, her soiled bib apron from market reeking of grease and mayonnaise.

"I can't let someone else have him."

"That's not a whole lot of foundation to go on," Rebecca quipped.

But that same Sunday evening, Ivan broke up with Margaret, citing their differences. He hadn't meant to mention his mother's concerns about Margaret being mental like her mom, but when Margaret responded with a burst of anger, then tears, he got flustered and defensive. "This is what I'm talking about," he said hastily. "You're nothing like me. You're so emotional, and outspoken, and you fly off the handle. I'm just not sure I can be with someone who struggles . . . you know, mentally."

"Mentally?" she said, truly shocked. "So, you think I'm crazy? Is that what this is about?"

"That's not what I meant."

She told him with a wobbling mouth, red eyes, and a Kleenex held to her nose that he was married to his mother and until he started thinking for himself, he'd never be ready for a real relationship. She said she hoped he'd find someone who would live up to her standards, some straitlaced, quiet, "sane" iceberg to love. Then she slammed the door of the Mustang and stalked off through the wild winds of January.

The bitter cold of winter blew straight through the walls of their house and into her heart as she nursed her heartache, self-pity pooling inside the frosty demeanor she presented to the world.

She went to market, cleaned houses, performed chores at home, and tried to forget Ivan. Rebecca wrote Ivan off as a handsome loser, which bolstered Margaret's spirits. Margaret had never appreciated her little sister so much.

In March, when mounds of gray snow lay beside slushy country roads and horses shied at hissing tires throwing wet snow, Margaret pulled back on the reins of her horse and turned toward Rebecca.

"I'm going to quit running around," she announced. "I can't face one more boring volleyball game or stupid supper or singing. Not one."

"Oh, come on, poor sport. I'll be there for you."

Rebecca dug in her heels and the tough little Morgan horse dug his hooves into the field and took off. Margaret chased after her on a horse simply named Pony, a white horse with gray spots.

They were both panting by the time they reached the barn, the wet March air turning their faces crimson, their scarves pushed off their heads.

"I meant what I said back there," Margaret emphasized, unmounting in one swift move.

"I forget what you said."

They both laughed, then turned to unsaddle their mounts.

"We can just spend every weekend in the barn."

"Or we can go away somewhere. Get an Airbnb, just the two of us."

"I know!"

Without words, each one understood what the other was thinking. They'd find an Airbnb with a shed for the horses, truck them there, and go trail riding. They made phone calls and found a place only a hundred miles away along the Juniata River, with miles of trails through state game lands.

"Let's ask Kathy to go," Rebecca suggested.

"Kathy who?"

"You know. My best friend."

"Then what would I do?"

Margaret could not think about trail riding by herself, the loss of Ivan still sharp in her heart. She encountered him from time to time, always experiencing the same deep sense of bewilderment, followed by days of self-loathing, which Rebecca dispelled eventually.

"You couldn't change who you are," Rebecca kept insisting. "There were too many strikes against you. His mother, the way they're raised, the way we are. Forget it, Marge. Do you want to walk around as stiff as a poker the rest of your life?"

They found a driver with a pickup and a horse trailer, who said he'd be there on Friday morning the twenty-eighth of April.

Margaret did agree to go to one more supper gathering before they left, only because it was held at her friend Rachel's house.

"And I'm not staying late," she told Rebecca.

She did stay for the singing, sitting beside Rachel to sing the first song, unaware of the tall youth in the back row who kept glancing her way.

Her boss, Elmer Lapp, was not thrilled at the prospect of finding a substitute, but grudgingly gave his consent, which Margaret felt was unfair, venting to her mother as she packed the Igloo with food.

"Well," Mary said, shaking her head knowingly, "that tells me you are a very valuable worker, or he'd be more lenient with you."

"You think?"

"I do."

"Thanks, Mom. That's a huge compliment."

"I meant it as that."

By Friday, their favorite horses were groomed, the tack polished and oiled, and provisions and clothes packed, and they were waiting eagerly on the back porch. Mary admitted for the first time in her life that she was appreciative of the fact she'd be able to get ahold of them. She didn't use the words "cell phone," which sounded much too worldly, but both girls winked at each other and smiled.

The black pickup truck whined up the drive hauling a white horse trailer detailed in black and gray.

Rebecca whistled, her eyes shone. "Traveling in style," she quipped.

The driver leaped out of his truck, all business in dark glasses, a bill cap pulled low, without bothering to introduce himself. He talked briskly about the horses, got the address for the GPS, and waited impatiently while they said goodbye.

The day was overcast, so Margaret kept glancing at the dark glasses, hoping he had good vision through them.

Finally, she said, "What did you say your name was?"

"I didn't say."

"Oh, pardon me."

"I know who you are."

Margaret blinked, turned to give him a sharp look.

"I have no idea . . . A market customer? I don't know."

In one swift move he removed his glasses, then his hat. When he looked at her, she had a glimpse of blue eyes, a shock of longish brown hair.

She felt confused, sure she had never seen him in her life.

"You're Margaret Riehl."

"Yes. I am."

"I'm Amish. Well, my mother is. I'm not yet."

"Who are you? Should I know you?"

"Probably not. Although I've seen you around. Came to your group a couple times."

"How about a name?"

"Mike. Mike King. Quarryville."

Margaret shook her head.

"Anyway, now you know. And I'm pleased to meet you. When you called, I knew immediately who you were. And Rebecca back there, good to meet you, too."

He looked in his rearview mirror and smiled.

"Yup. You too. And my name is Rebecca Back There."

He laughed, an infectious sound rumbling up from his stomach, then turned to look at his left mirror before pulling onto Route 340.

"You two don't look much like sisters."

"We are. Same parents, same bloodline," Margaret quipped.

After a while, they stopped for a Starbucks, pulling up to the drive-through window. Rebecca ordered a hot chocolate and Margaret got a vanilla chai latte with sweet cream foam and brown sugar syrup.

"Fancy," Mike teased Margaret in a friendly way, before ordering a black coffee.

"We're on vacation," Margaret defended herself. "And at least I'm not boring. Black coffee? What's even the point without cream and sugar?"

"Caffeine. Caffeine is the point."

They all laughed.

The drive went quickly as they talked easily, mostly about horses, his life's occupation and his father's before him.

"I'm actually being *grosfeelich* (prideful), driving this expensive rig around. I'm pretty Amish at heart, just haven't decided to join. Don't see any hurry."

"You must not be very old school."

"Not really."

"Well, you know. Some people would list you as walking the perimeter of perdition."

He looked at her sharply. "You mean you're beautiful *and* smart?"

Flustered, Margaret had no reply.

"I don't mean to offend you or anything, of course. I'm just saying it how it is."

Her thoughts reeled through her head like an old movie. Ivan had never told her she was beautiful, or even remotely mentioned her appearance. He seemed attracted to her when they were alone together, but he never said so. She recognized it now as a form of control, keeping her guessing if she was good enough for him, for his family.

"Thank you," she said softly.

He swallowed, looked straight ahead as they moved onto Route 30 on their way to Harrisburg, merging into traffic.

From the back seat, "What kind of horses do you have?"

"A bit of everything."

"As nice as your rig?"

"Nicer, I think. I love horses. That's why it won't be hard for me to be Amish."

"We're not really that Amish anymore," Margaret said. "My mom comes from a place in New York where they're like, Amish a hundred years ago. They dress plain, for real, and have to obey the rules like you wouldn't believe. I have eleven aunts and uncles from there, Pinedale Valley. Terribly strict and sober. But loving. They don't condemn my mom the way they used to."

Margaret realized the ease with which she'd been conversing as the miles evaporated behind them. She couldn't believe how soon they came upon a charming green chalet by the swollen river. All around them, trees stood like tall, brown soldiers, their branches showing the green mist of buds that would provide a thick canopy of leaves later in the season. The small house was built into an incline, and the barn-like shed looked like it was from the Swiss Alps. There were window boxes everywhere, and tulips pushing through borders along picket fences. The river moved along in its springtime fullness, hurrying to join forces with the Susquehanna before emptying into the Chesapeake Bay.

"This is great!" Rebecca shouted.

Margaret shared her enthusiasm, although not quite as loudly. She was smiling as they led the horses off the trailer, and then unloaded the hay and grain. The combination worked on the lock, and they stepped inside to find a life-sized dollhouse, complete with tiny rooms, plump beds, a quaint table and chairs.

"I could stay here with you," Mike suggested, grinning.

"You don't have a horse," Rebecca said quickly.

Margaret said nothing, unsure how to handle this very different young man. Ivan would never have admitted to wanting to stay. Instead, he would have made her feel as if he thought she didn't want him to stay, and therefore he would leave. She was never sure how he truly felt, the way every situation was tied up in knots.

She must stop comparing, thinking of Ivan.

"True." Mike smiled. "And besides, I've got things to do. If you need anything, here's my number. Be careful. Two girls alone. Things happen. See ya."

They saw him to the door, watched him leave, then unpacked food into the fridge and tiny cabinets. They hung their dresses in closets and placed their toiletries in the bathroom, chattering the entire time.

"We do need to come here with the rest of the family," said Rebecca. "The boys would love it. Dad, too."

"What about Mom?"

"As long as she has something to eat, she'll be happy."

They both laughed fondly.

As they were on the way to the barn to saddle the horses, the clouds lowered even more and the first sprinkles hit their heads.

"Shoot," Rebecca offered. "Rain."

"Looks like it."

"Which means we'll have to rough it. It will be just miserable watching television and eating microwave popcorn." Rebecca gave a sideways smile.

"Absolutely no pleasure in it," laughed Margaret, running for the house.

Having no access to television at home, this was a rare treat. They were overwhelmed by the barrage of channels, but finally settled on a Discovery Channel show about Alaska.

They made a pot of popcorn and smothered it in melted butter, plunked on the deep couch, drew cozy crocheted afghans over their laps, adjusted pillows, and were transported to the mountains and lakes of Alaska as the rain fell dreamily on the little green house by the river.

IN THE EARLY morning, they were awakened by a series of yipping sounds, followed by long drawn-out howls. Rebecca leapt from her bed, but Margaret stretched and yawned, told her it was just coyotes, rolled over, and went back to sleep until the light of the sun breaking through clouds woke her.

They made pancakes and scrambled eggs for breakfast, then fed and watered the horses. The new grass sparkled with raindrops and the wind was picking up in the treetops.

They rode out mid-forenoon, the wind tugging at their light scarves and sweaters, the horses dancing, their ears pricked forward, taking in the unusual surroundings, shying away from boulders and undulating mountain laurel.

"Rocky," Rebecca observed.

The trail wound away from the river, across the top of a ridge, and down a steep incline to a marsh complete with bulrushes and velvety skunk cabbage. The high, shrill trilling of tree frogs was deafening.

A black snake sunned himself on top of a flat boulder, and snapping turtles raised their prehistoric visages, slowly blinking odd eyes. The air was heavy with moisture, the rich scent of moss and lichens. The horses' hooves made a wet, sucking sound as the trail went even lower.

They stopped their horses, allowed them to nibble at new growth, sat relaxed on their saddles, and watched the swaying of trees far above them, the raw spring wind only a soft breeze in the marsh.

"Look, Rebecca. Check out that spider web."

Margaret gazed at the intricate design still glistening with dew suspended between two branches. It was magical. Margaret was not well-versed in things of the Spirit, but the beauty of the woven cobweb spoke to her heart. She experienced a deep inner longing, as if her heart expanded to include the beauty around her.

A red-winged blackbird set up its plaintive call, and she spotted the red and yellow on the coal black bird. A hawk spread its wings as it soared overhead.

They started moving again and the narrow trail widened, turned uphill. As far as they could see, through the half-bare branches of trees, it wound up a steep and seemingly unending hill.

"Up we go!" shouted Rebecca, goading her horse.

Margaret whooped and gave chase, the horses lunging in great, powerful strides, the girls leaning forward to keep their balance.

Iron horseshoes clanged on loose stones, but the horses wanted to run, so the girls loosened the reins till the horses' breath came quick and fast, nostrils flaring. When they reached the top, they were surprised to find a grassy clearing, the trail turning left, away from the river.

"Cool. Let's rest them."

They both climbed down, stretched their legs, and listened to the birdsong as the wind played with the branches of trees, shivered undergrowth, and played along clumps of grass. Overhead, clouds like cotton balls were pushed along by the gale.

"So, how far do we go?" asked Rebecca.

"According to the map, we can tun left, double back, or go right and end up at the river again. Which one?" Margaret asked.

"The horses are doing okay. Why don't we go right?"

"Fine with me."

They mounted and rode off, relishing the creak of leather and the scent of horse sweat. With trees everywhere, it was hard to see what was ahead, but they knew their elevation was high above the river. They'd be turning downhill soon, they supposed, but no matter, they had all the time in the world, two good horses, a cute Airbnb, and the whole weekend to themselves.

They paused at the brown signpost with white words engraved in it: DANGER. TRAIL CLOSE TO OVERHANG. KEEP LEFT.

Hmm, thought Margaret. *No guardrails?*

CHAPTER 16

Margaret stayed to the left, the sign engraved in her mind, although she longed to tug on the right rein for a view of the river.

She heard the ring of hooves on rock behind her, turned to tell Rebecca to take it slowly, when the undergrowth parted and the round eyes of a startled black bear emerged. Like lightning, Margaret's horse snorted and shied sideways, leaving her with the sickening despair of having no control over a panicked mount. She was vaguely aware of the sensation of loose rock and crumbling soil.

She clung to the saddle horn for only a second before her feet were ripped from the stirrups, her body thrown into space. A terrified scream from the horse, the knowledge she was falling, falling, then a gut-wrenching impact and a blinding explosion of pain. She opened her eys in time to see her horse's descent, an awful scene of rocks, dirt, broken branches as the force of gravity pulled him to the rock below.

She heard Rebecca scream, but since there was no air in her lungs, she couldn't respond. Movement was an impossibility as pain ripped through her body.

She wondered briefly if she was going to die, lying here like a broken doll, barely able to suck in life-giving air. She tried lifting an arm, a signal to tell Rebecca she was alright, but the tiniest amount of effort ignited a roar of hot agony.

She had to stay still. Rebecca was there, had seen her fall. She'd figure something out.

Taking small sips of air, she stayed conscious, determined to stay aware of her surroundings. The brown water lapped at rocks, her feet likely inches from the edge. She rolled her eyes to the right, wondering how long the water would continue to rise after yesterday's rain.

She began to shiver and became aware of a stickiness on her forehead before the sight in her left eye was obliterated by an approaching wetness, and she knew her head was bleeding.

She tried to move her foot, her hand, but there was absolutely nothing. An anguish unlike anything she'd ever experienced sliced through her. A hoarse cry emerged from her mouth, a primal call for survival, a beggarly cry of desperation.

Not paralysis, her mind wailed. *Please.*

The please was directed to God, the only One who could do anything about this situation. But she felt as if she was begging from a stranger who didn't know her, had never seen her.

Oh God, help me.

The air was so damp and chilly, the wind so harsh. She was cold, shivering, the rocks below her unforgiving. Her head rested on a tuft of river grass. She heard heavy breathing, loud grunts, then bellows of pain as the horse struggled to regain his footing.

So, he was alive?

Her tongue was swelling, her mouth dry. A drink of cool water would be soothing, she thought, as wave after wave of burning pain surged through her side. It hurt to breathe. The sun was warm enough on her face, but why couldn't she feel it on her body?

God, if you hear me, have mercy. Don't condemn me to a wheelchair for the rest of my life. You wouldn't be that mean, would you? But you never know what God was going to do—that was the thing.

Where was Rebecca? How would she find her way down? The cellphone was back at the cabin. There was no service anyway, so they hadn't seen any reason to bring it.

She wasn't sure she could stay conscious much longer. The spinning void seemed to be sucking her in. *Rebecca, please.*

Suddenly, she was aware of discomfort, cold and wet, on her right foot, then the calf of her leg. She was not paralyzed. She could feel the cold, wet river lapping at her. She squeezed her eyes shut to stop the tears, but they came through anyway.

For real, God in Heaven, thank you.

Where was Rebecca? *Come on.*

The river continued to rise, inch by inch, climbing to her knees.

She became aware of a whole other danger, that of being drowned, slowly, excruciatingly, by creeping brown water.

I have to move. She gritted her teeth and squeezed her eyes shut with the effort, but an electrifying pain shot from her neck to her feet, disabling her completely. She tried moving her fingers, her hand, resulting in the least bit of movement coupled with searing pain.

She cried, she begged hoarsely, her throat clogged with sound. She felt as if she was roaring, but there was no sound. The cold water reached her thighs, and she shivered uncontrollably. Hysterics built up like shrieking demons taunting her.

I can't lie here. I have to get out.

Again, she tried turning her body, twisting it, creeping away from encroaching water. *Rebecca, where are you?* She must have gone for help, but how long would that take?

She heard hooves on stone for a moment, but her hope faded as the sound disappeared. Had the horse wandered away, or merely gotten to his feet? Would he stay, or was she going to be entirely alone? She had no way of knowing.

I have to get out. The water reached her hips now, excruciating, wet and cold. She could smell the mud, the silt, that fishy scent of a river in spring. It was a creeping enemy now, perfectly capable of snuffing her life out like a blown candle.

I don't want to die. I don't think I'm ready. What will happen to me? I barely know who God is.

Despair took her breath away, and she knew in that moment that drowning was imminent. If only she could take a deep breath, perhaps she could muster more strength.

She'd always been determined, strong-willed, fighting her way through life. Surely she could draw on that strength now. With every ounce of willpower, she tried to suck in more oxygen, but knew defeat immediately. She allowed tears to flow down icy cheeks.

She was aware of thirst now. A deep longing for water, any water, even the muddy river water lapping at her waist now, moving past with no beginning or end in sight.

She thought of her parents, and imagining their shock and sorrow brought a whole new element of pain. She felt remorse at her own self-ishness, the sadness she had caused them.

Sorry, Mom. Sorry, Dad. I'm so sorry.

It was when the water crept up to her chest that she began to let go. She'd heard somewhere drowning was not unpleasant, perhaps like falling asleep. When the time came, she'd simply give in to it. She noticed shadows on gray-brown, pockmarked rock, and knew the afternoon was wearing down. Would they find her body? Likely they would.

She heard voices, but thought she was only hallucinating, imagining things. She heard a question. An answer.

Could it be Rebecca?

She called out frantically, desperately, but the only sound was a hoarse croak. She tried to move one hand across the rock.

She heard a change in the water. A slopping, like hands in dishwater, then a distinct call. More splashing.

"Hey! Hey, you! There."

"It is someone."

There was a dark figure above her, then another.

"Hey, you awake? My God. It's a girl. The river's closing in. Honey, can you talk?"

A face above her, jowly, gray-bearded, frightened eyes behind steel-rimmed glasses, a camouflage shirt.

"Yes . . ." But her voice was a croaking whisper.

Clearly shook up, the man discussed the predicament with his companion. He'd been taught never to move an injured person, but if they didn't, the river would claim her. Margaret lay in a state of gratefulness for being found, a calm she would never be able to describe.

Again, the faces above her.

"Listen, honey, we're going to have to get you out. I have no idea where you're hurt, so we'll do our best. If we don't, you won't survive. Does anyone know where you are?"

She nodded slightly.

"You think there's help on the way?"

She croaked again. They bent to hear. The water rose slightly on her back.

"Okay, Gary. We're gonna have to do it. Gently now. You go under one arm, and I'll take the other. Easy. Look, this is gonna hurt, but do the best you can. Here we go, honey."

The kindness in his voice created weak tears. She gritted her teeth, then heard a horrible sound as the pain tore through her body, and a merciful blackness held her in its powerful grip.

SHE AWOKE TO humming voices, radios crackling, medics, stretcher. Blankets. Needles in her arms. She gathered that she'd been carried out somehow. The pain was more distant now, and she saw Rebecca, white-faced, crying.

Doors closing, lights above her. An engine starting, followed by the wail of an ambulance.

When she awoke the second time, there was morning light through a window with slatted blinds, a series of beeps and clicks above her head. She tried turning her head to see if anyone was in the room and found her mother and father, both asleep in chairs, a sight she would always carry in her memory.

"Mom?" Only a whisper, but she tried again. Instantly, Mary's eyes flew open. She leapt to her feet, hurried to her bedside.

"Margaret. Oh, Margaret."

Mary broke down, racked with heartfelt sobs. Steve was beside Mary then, an arm about Mary's shoulders, his own eyes filled and spilling over with tears, overwhelmed by the powerful emotions wracking him.

"You almost died," her mother managed after a length of time when her mouth wobbled too much for one coherent word to escape.

"Am I okay now?" Margaret choked out.

"You broke all the ribs on one side of your body," her dad answered. "Punctured your lungs and crushed a vertebra in the middle of your back. You were in surgery for most of the evening."

Her mother took a deep breath to steady herself. She smiled and bent over the rail of the bed to kiss her cheek. She put a hand to Margaret's forehead, smoothing her hair, as if she were a small child again.

"How did I get out?" Margaret whispered.

"Well, two fishermen found you. They would have glided right past if it hadn't been for the white scarf on your head. One of them spied it, thought it was snow, then looked again. A few hours longer and I'm not sure you would have survived. Rebecca was very level-headed. Knowing time was important, she took off to get help. But on the way there, she was ripping downhill as fast as she could go, when her horse fell, throwing her. The horse took off, so she ran the remainder of the way.

"She directed the medics, amazed to find the fishermen. All this took time, of course, so I can't even think of what might have happened had God not sent the men in the boat. And now listen to this. They'd gone fishing, weren't counting on the river being that high, decided to go back home without even unloading the boat, but Gary, the older one said, ah, they're here now, let's check out where the river forms an eddy there below the cliff on state game lands. And there you were, half-drowned and helpless."

Fresh tears spilled onto Mary's cheeks. A hand went to Margaret's shoulders, rubbing, assuring herself she was warm, alive.

For a long moment, Margaret stared unseeing, then slowly began to talk in a hoarse whisper, gaining strength as her voice was put into use.

"I was cold. That river water was horrible. I tried so hard to get myself away from it. Out of it."

She swallowed, pursed her lips to keep from crying. "Was Rebecca hurt?"

"Just bruised. She's at home with the boys. They'll be in tomorrow after school."

"Where am I?"

"You're in Johnstown. A hospital."

"How long?"

"We have no idea."

"The horse?"

"He had to be put down. Broken leg, which is doom for a horse. But the touching part is, he stood there, waiting a few yards from you, as loyal as you've ever seen a creature."

"And Rebecca's?"

"He's fine."

"Good." Margaret sighed. A great weariness overtook her, and she slept.

WHEN THE DAY finally came for her release, she was wheeled into the late spring sunshine, birdsong, and peonies.

Margaret breathed the scent of freshly mown grass as deeply as possible, her lung that had been punctured still restricting her intake significantly. She understood gratitude at a whole new level.

Rebecca was beside her, helping her into the car. The discomfort of the ride was far more than she'd anticipated, but the sight of home was pure relief.

Logan and Chris, for once in their life, were quiet, standing in awe of the sister who lived through an ordeal like that.

Margaret's friends came to visit, brought flowers, gifts, cards, and listened wide-eyed as Margaret told her story.

Then, on an evening in June, when she was back on her feet, but still not back to work or spending weekends with her friends, there was a knock on the door, just as the light was fading from the sky. Margaret shuffled slowly to open it, her parents having gone to a school meeting, the boys on a camping trip with their cousins.

"Oh, it's you."

It was none other than Ivan Stoltzfus himself, looking more handsome than ever, his dark hair outlined in the sinking light as the sun disappeared.

'Yes, it is. May I come in?"

"Of course."

She stepped aside, but clung to the opened door, her eyes on his face, questioning. He didn't look at her, just walked inside, looked around, commented on the many vases of flowers.

"Your parents home?"

"Actually, they're at a school meeting."

"Good. Then we can relax. So how are you? Heard about it." He sat on the couch, smoothed his jeans over his thighs, adjusted the collar of his shirt, flicked an imaginary hair off his forehead, and looked out the window. He cleared his throat, clenched and unclenched his hands. "Must have been pretty bad."

"It was."

"Do you want to talk about it?"

"With you? Ivan, you know I talk about every single thing in my life. I have to, and I actually think that's healthy. But not with you, not anymore. You broke up with me because you thought I was crazy, remember?"

"I never said that."

"Pretty much. You never said much of anything, if we're being honest, but we both know the truth."

"Margaret, I came here to say, I thought maybe we could patch things up and start over again. I regret some things and would like to work on them."

"What do you regret?"

He shrugged his shoulders. "Some stuff I did."

"What stuff?"

"Just . . ."

"Go ahead."

"You know it's always hard for me to find the right words."

"Well, I can only guess then, but I'll tell you what I regret. I regret mistaking all the makeout sessions in your car for actual love. I really let myself believe you loved me, but it's so clear to me now that love takes a deeper connection, an emotional and spiritual one, a meeting of hearts. And I'm not settling for anything less than that."

She barely heard the words then.

"Well, hopefully, you'll find that with me."

"I doubt very much if that's possible."

"Will you give me another chance?"

"You, know, I never felt very close to God, but He turned that boat in my direction, so I figure He cares an awful lot about me and wants me to live my best life. And not just for myself, but for Him."

"Oh, so now you're all goody-two-shoes, all born again and ready to rumble."

She saw his sneer, heard his mocking tone, and decided it was better not to reply.

"See? You don't know what to say to that, either."

Margaret sighed, her shoulders slumped. "Yes. I know what to say, but there's no use saying it. We truly do not love or respect each other. Never did, never will. I have come a long way in a short span of time, but that, too, is only by the grace of God."

"Give me a break," he said, as if to himself.

"I think it's best if you go now," she said evenly.

"You know what? There are plenty of girls out there who are normal, who don't overthink and overanalyze every single thing, and who aren't so full of themselves."

"Then you'll have to go find one, I suppose."

"I will," he ground out, leaving the house without looking back.

Why was she weeping, then, wiping silent tears as he drove slowly down the curving driveway? It was sad, in a way, but sadder still would be their pathetic union, she knew. No, it was better this way, much better.

BY LATE SUMMER, she had experienced a dramatic healing. Her back fused miraculously, ribs and lung healed, and the scar on her head was already disappearing. She had gone back to work, but Elmer Lapp allowed her more than her share of breaks, reminding her often not to push herself too hard.

She often wondered why God allowed that fateful weekend, but her mother told her you could never understand God's ways, that it wasn't Biblical to think human beings could or should. "We live by faith," she said.

And Mary often watched Margaret go about her life, a still, peaceful version of the former hothead. It was a wonder, but sometimes that was the way when one was born again, born of the spirit, that great mystery Jesus explained to Nicodemus.

She knew, then, when she saw her daughter swinging on the porch swing with Logan, laughing, smiling, asking questions, reaching over to pat his hair, bending down to stroke the cat as she purred against her leg, that it was the work of the Holy Spirit in Margaret's heart.

Mary sang praises with her hands in the dishwater, she sang praises as she hung towels on the line, and knew she was unworthy of the goodness God had bestowed on her time after time. She spread this newfound happiness by planning a quilting for the church women, then donating the quilt to the school.

CHAPTER 17

STILL HERE, MARGARET THOUGHT. *STILL AT THE SAME OLD MARKET. I am so sick of this job. My back hurts. My feet are buzzing with fatigue. Twelve and a half hours is too long in the middle of summer. I have to talk to my parents about being allowed another job.*

Everything irked her today. Everything. Especially the coworker who did only the jobs she liked to do, took long breaks, and was never reprimanded for it.

Muttering to herself, with hardly a cheerful thought in her head, she looked up to find the next customer in the endless line.

"Next!"

Too loud, rife with irritation.

"Yeah. Hey, how are you?"

She looked straight into two very blue eyes, a tanned face, and a shock of too-long brown hair.

"Oh."

She gathered herself together, felt the dreaded blush. "Mike. You're the driver."

"Yeah. Heard about you. I'm so glad you're okay. What a crazy accident. I remember getting the call that someone else was taking the horses back."

"Horse."

"Only one?"

"Had to put one down."

"Move along, buddy. You wanna talk to the girl, take her out."

Mike looked over his shoulder. "Sorry."

"Your order?" Margaret asked.

"Bacon, egg, and cheese on rye toast. Mayo, lettuce, tomatoes. You have a phone number?"

"Seven-fifty. For the sandwich."

"Oh, right."

He paid, told her he'd be back.

Irritation fled. She hummed, rang up customers, smiled. How did he know where she worked? Coincidence? When Jolaine said she was going on yet another break, Margaret said okay, but take the garbage, knowing she'd head past the dumpster on her way to her car for a cigarette break.

When Jolaine returned with a message that she'd run into a guy outside who wanted to meet Margaret at four that afternoon, Margaret felt her face on fire. When the time came, she asked Elmer for a fifteen-minute break and then turned to see Mike standing at the counter holding a cup from Starbucks.

"One vanilla chai latte, with sweet cream foam and brown sugar syrup," he announced, handing it to her.

"What? How did you know?" she asked.

"I remember your order."

They found an empty table and sat down. He merely looked into her eyes for a long moment before asking if she was willing to talk about the accident.

And she did tell him in detail, becoming emotional about the man named Gary, the rising river water, the way she felt about dying.

"You knew you weren't ready?"

"I knew. And yet I wasn't afraid. Almost as if . . . I don't know. I'm not exactly an authority on matters of spirituality."

"Tell me. I really want to know."

And she believed he did, so she continued telling him about her thoughts. How she'd begged God for help, even while realizing she hardly knew Him. How now she knew without a doubt that God had answered her and had a plan for her life.

"Man, that gives me cold chills. It sure does. Amazing."

For a moment, they simply looked into each other's eyes, experiencing a moment of mutual awe for God's mysterious ways. And then Margaret remembered the time. Surely they'd already talked for more than fifteen minutes. "Hey, I probably need to get back to work."

"Okay, so, could we exchange phone numbers?"

"I suppose we could. Although I won't call you first. That's not common etiquette among our people. Tradition, you know."

They both laughed, then exchanged numbers. He got up to leave, said thanks, smiled, and was gone.

A WATCHED POT never boils, her mother said. The same rule must apply to the phone.

Margaret was peeling neck pumpkins, standing at the sink, grimacing as she drew the paring knife through the thick outer shell. Next she and her mom would cut them into chunks, add water, and put the pots on the stove to boil. Finally, the chunks of pumpkin flesh would be mashed, spooned into jars and cold packed, and carried down cellar, where they'd be placed among the rows of colorful jars on the wooden shelves.

She wiped the sweat off her forehead with the crook of her arm without releasing the paring knife, and blew a snort of air from her mouth to get rid of the annoying strands of hair.

"Why do you put yourself through this?" Margaret asked, leaning on the counter with one elbow.

"I can't even tell you the difference between these home-canned pumpkins and store-bought canned ones," Mary answered tersely. "And you, lady, put that phone away. You know only half your attention is on what we're doing. He's not going to call."

"He might, and if he does, I don't want to miss it."

"Well at least set it aside so you don't get pumpkin strings all over it."

Margaret heaved herself away from the counter and put the phone on the stairway.

"Oh my, what would my father say? We should not allow you that device of the devil."

"Stop it, Mom. Don't be scary. Cell phones are here and they probably won't go away anytime soon, Mother dear."

"Oh, but it pains my conservative heart," Mary answered.

"You're not as strict as you think you should be," Margaret quipped.

"How does that even make sense?"

"You know exactly what I mean. Children see straight through their parents. You know, you're the one who told me that."

Margaret gripped a paring knife, grabbed a large pumpkin, and cut it into sections, her eyebrows drawn down as she concentrated.

"This is impossible," she whined, as Rebecca came in to join them.

With Rebecca's help, they had twenty-two quarts of pumpkin bubbling in their hot water bath by the time Steve arrived home from work. Mary was crowing about the accomplishment, saying everything from the garden was finally canned, frozen, or dried. All except the grape juice, and she had a notion to let that go this year, seeing there were still twenty or twenty-five jars in the basement.

"I didn't think the grapes were anything to write home about this year," Steve said, without taking his eyes off the intricate work of spreading peanut butter on every available surface of his stalk of celery.

"I agree. We can just drink orange juice," Mary said.

"We're going to have to clean up the garden tonight, so everyone get in the mood," said Steve. "Lyons said there's a hurricane on the eastern shore, and we could get up to five inches of rain."

"That's exciting," Logan buzzed. He lived to hear of floods, thunderstorms, blizzards, but most of all, the infrequently announced tornado watches.

They lugged enormous pumpkin vines, tomato stalks, and brown, brittle rows of lima beans. They chopped dry cornstalks, tilled the soil, and sowed tillage radishes, a ground cover serving to loosen and nurture the soil all winter long.

Everyone was worn out by the time twilight settled in. Margaret wiped her face with the hem of her skirt and announced she was not planning on having a garden, ever.

Christopher took this very seriously, saying Amish people all had gardens and what would her family eat in winter? Logan said she probably wouldn't have a family, seeing how husbands were derived from boyfriends, which she didn't have. Margaret replied that she would have a boyfriend if Mom and Dat weren't so strict about her phone, and that half the time she couldn't hear it when it rang. Logan, who was a bit big for his britches, said that if a guy ever called or texted, surely she could see if they did or not.

Margaret said, "Maybe, maybe not," in a teasing manner, which infuriated him. He threw a small pumpkin at her, which she caught like a football and the chase was on, Christopher goading him on.

"Go, go, go! Go, Logan!"

Steve laughed so hard he had to lean his elbow on a tree, and Mary set down the wheelbarrow she was pushing to catch her breath. Mary whispered a prayer of gratitude, thanking God that Margaret had healed so quickly from her accident. She could be paralyzed, or worse, and here she was, running after her little brother.

The horses in the pasture were only a dark silhouette and the mourning doves heralded the oncoming night as they all made their way to the house. *Now let the rains come,* Mary thought. The garden was put to bed for the winter and she was glad, ready to rest her weary bones in the winter months, quilting, baking, or simply enjoying a good book. She'd get around to sewing Steve's pants once the snow flew.

Bedtime snacks were in order. The boys decided on Oreos with milk, Rebecca peeled a tangerine, Steve spread a graham cracker with peanut butter, and Margaret was about to eat a spoonful of peanut butter straight from the jar when she held up a finger and cocked her head.

"Shh! Listen! Yep, my phone," and she raced to the stairway. *Oh my word,* she breathed, and raced up the stairs to answer.

"Hi."

"Yes, hello."

"It's me, Mike."

"How are you?"

Margaret thought she might still die young of heart failure, and all that after her rescue in Bedford County.

Oh, she couldn't do this. It was too soon after Ivan. So, she said the right things, answered the proper questions, but was absolutely frozen on the inside. Here she was again, all excited, fairly bursting at the seams with eagerness to have another boyfriend, and what if it went south like her relationship with Ivan did?

"Is something wrong?" he asked, catching her off guard.

"Uh, no. Well, yes. I'm just sitting here in my room beating myself up, thinking 'here I go again.' My last relationship left me feeling pretty sour, so I guess I'm a little wary of starting something new."

"I haven't asked you out yet."

"Yeah, but you're going to."

The line was quiet, for a long moment, before muffled laughter was heard. "You *are* different. Someone told me you were."

"Good. I am. I have no interest in trying to be like anyone else."

"So, what if I tell you I don't want to ask you out?"

"Then I'll wait until you do, I suppose."

"You want me to?"

"Of course."

He grimaced, smiled to himself. This girl was as refreshing as a cool rain shower on a hot summer day, no doubt. She most definitely wasn't like other girls, and he liked that. She had an air of confidence, yet it seemed to be laced with mystery. He had never imagined the phone conversation going like this.

He hated the way most girls gave mixed messages and kept the boys guessing. You could never tell if the girl actually wanted you and just wouldn't let on, or if she really had no interest. Or maybe she wanted another guy, but would spend time with you just to make him jealous. It was all so frustrating and silly.

And here was Margaret, simply shooting straight with him.

"Well then, Margaret, will you go out to dinner with me?"

"Yes. Yes, I will."

"You're not just messing with me?"

"Why would I? I said yes and I meant it. I've been waiting for you to call ever since you were at market. That's the truth."

When he hung up, he let his phone drop on the rug, put his elbows on his knees, and lowered his face, a smile spreading as far as possible. All he could think of was, *Wow.*

He listened to the night sounds around him, the swish of dry oak leaves outside the window, his mother's cough in the living room below. He was the youngest of a family of four, and his father had passed when he was twelve years old. He had lived with his widowed mother for four years, alone, and she had been fighting weak lungs since COVID-19 almost killed her.

There had been plenty of talk about the way that youngest boy drove around with that horse trailer and wide pickup truck, showing no respect for his poor mother, all alone and suffering with congestion. The small painted bungalow with one big dormer in the roof and a deep front porch was all they could afford. She quilted, went to market a day or so, but everyone guessed that Mike handed over a portion of his paycheck, which was the truth, though he never talked about it. He didn't care much what people said about him.

Neighborhoods were rife with talk, folks minding one another's business far too much. His mother knew he would never hurt her feelings, and no one had to know the times they spent in conversation, the loneliness he eased, the love he had for his mother. She had a feeling the real reason he stayed single was on her account.

But Mike went through his days with no ill feelings toward anyone. He was unabashedly who he was, and that was that. In that way (although he was not aware of this) he was a lot like Margaret.

He went downstairs, his mother putting down her book as he approached, doubling down a corner of the page.

"Mom?"

"Hm?"

He looked at her small, thin frame encased in the oversized house coat, the gray and white hair tucked into her white *dichly*, and suddenly he felt selfish, ashamed to take this important step.

"I asked a girl to dinner, and she said yes."

"Why Michael, that's wonderful. Congratulations. May I ask who this lucky girl is?"

"No one you know. Steve Riehl's Margaret."

"Oh, Susie Belier told me about her. An unusual name. She dated Amos Stoltzfus's Ivan a while back. Amos is my second cousin. They say his wife Barbie has never made his life easy, but I guess there are people like that. Always will be. So, tell me, how old is Margaret? I can't wait to meet her."

Mike smiled at her. "That's great, Mam. Thank you. It's just . . . you know, if this develops into something, it means I might get my own place, and you'd be alone here."

She shook a misshapen arthritic finger at him.

"You know that isn't a problem at all. The girls have it all figured out, have for a long time."

"I imagine they have."

"Yes. So, you enjoy your date with Margaret and don't worry about me. They talked to me about moving into someplace where I can get more care, and that will be just fine. Mike, I know this house isn't much, but it's yours."

"Thank you, Mam." He wrapped one arm around her and, for a moment, rested his head on her shoulder.

MARY GOT OUT the trusty Fisher book, an Amish publication with page after page of families listed alphabetically. It was a guide to look up distant relatives and a who's who for the curious. It was especially helpful at times like this, when a veritable stranger asked your daughter for a date, and you kind of knew about where his mother lived but had no real idea of her family tree.

Genealogy was an important part of Amish life, and Mary felt strong ties to tradition. She hoped the young man in question would prove to be worthy of her daughter.

"King. Abner King, deceased. Five children."

Hmm. Interesting. She wondered what had happened to him. She turned pages to look up the daughters, and to see to whom they were married. Here was a connection. One of them was married to a Mark Stoltzfus. His father's name was Jonas of Honeybrook. She wondered if it was the Jonas Stoltzfus who was a bishop in that district.

When she heard Margaret's footsteps on the stairs, she closed the book, quickly, and was sliding it into the bookcase as she appeared.

"Caught you, Mom. The Fisher book," she announced.

"Guilty as charged," Mary answered sheepishly.

"You're so old-fashioned."

"Maybe, but I prefer to think of it as caring."

"Mom, I need a new dress. Can we go to the fabric store?"

As THEY DROVE along country roads, Mary felt the cool breeze coming through the window and noticed the colorful array of leaves carpeting green lawns, an occasional bare branch emerging through the thick foliage. White barns dotted the countryside, with plodding mules drawing equipment as the heavy stalks of corn were cut, bundled, and stacked.

All the neighbors gathering from one farm to another to fill silos, putting the cumbersome bundles through the cutter, blowing the pieces of dried cornstalk, the ears of corn with husks intact chopped along with it. Silage for hungry cows, fueling their bodies with wholesome nutrition, enabling them to produce gallons of rich, creamy milk with a good butterfat content.

Fresh silage smelled like fermentation, a strong, acidic odor that took her straight back to the old barns in New York, where the life of the Amish was so very different. And here she was, traveling along to help her own daughter choose a fancy new dress to go out with a young man showing no signs of belonging to their plain sect. The uncomfortable wave of guilt accompanying these memories was her own thorn in the flesh, the curse she bore.

What would her father say? She visibly bowed her head as the dishonor boiled up and over, wrecking her own peaceful, meandering thoughts. Like a quiet, deep river, the speedboat of guilt roared against the current, creating giant ripples, waves of remorse.

I'm sorry, Dat, please forgive me my lossheit (uncaring).

"Watch where you're going. Mom! Geez," Margaret yelled. Drawing on the left rein, Mary corrected her course and grinned sheepishly before shaking her head, then turning into the parking lot of the dry goods store. A few cars were parked in front, with a black horse hitched to a gray buggy at the rail, and a small brown pony beside it. Expertly, she steered her own horse beside the black one, then climbed down and retrieved the neck rope, before noticing Margaret's slow descent on the opposite side.

"Ow. Ouch," she grimaced, her voice hoarse in her throat.

"My, Margaret. Is it that bad?"

"Sometimes, like today, everything hurts."

They exchanged a look that could only be interpreted as understanding and Mary breathed a prayer of thanks for her precious daughter, that her life had been spared.

She looped an arm around her shoulder and drew her close.

"I love you, Margaret."

"Mom! Not in public."

She shrugged her shoulders to rid herself of the display of affection, and Mary laughed out loud. A thread of joy like a dust whirl made the yellow chrysanthemums blend with the orange pumpkins on the steps, creating a golden scene on this wonderful afternoon.

A young mother with a baby on her hip, two toddlers in tow, carrying a heavy plastic bag nudged the door open, held it till the children came through, then let them down the steps before her.

They stood aside to let her pass, said hello before going into the store. It was quiet, the lines of shelves packed with bolts of fabric, sectioned into parts labeled by the name of the cloth itself. Amish women had their preference, some choosing plain, dark colors, others choosing stretchy fabric crisscrossed with a pebbled design in brilliant colors.

Mary allowed Margaret to wander off on her own, determined to avoid the usual power struggle and stick to her own list of thread, fine-toothed combs, and trouser buttons.

She rounded a corner to find her next-door neighbor, Annie, poring over the small bags of snaps.

"Hey there, Mary," she said over her shoulder.

Mary grinned at her. "What's up?"

"Boy, aren't you looking young and fresh as a teenager today?"

Mary shrugged. "You know what they say. The company we keep rubs off on us."

"You're here with Margaret?" Annie asked, smiling.

"Who else? What are you doing, plucking a bag of snaps off there? Do you still use snaps?"

"Of course I do. I'm not sewing my dresses down the front in this new style. I can't imagine the acrobatics getting out of the thing. Twisting and turning with your arms straight up trying to tug your dress off."

Mary laughed good naturedly. "You'd love it."

"I brush my teeth, then I comb my hair, then I get dressed. I can't imagine sticking my head in that tiny neckline, then combing my hair with my dress on. My whole back would be covered in hair, the way yours probably is. Turn around, let me see."

"*Ach*, Annie. There are no hairs on my back. They blow off during the day."

They laughed together, each one comfortable with the other's preference, although Mary shook her head, saying she couldn't imagine applying those old snap buttons.

"Well, if you ever see me walking up your drive, stuck in my dress, you'll know I tried," Annie said, throwing a few packets of snap buttons into her basket dangling on one arm.

Mary gave her the thumbs up, and they parted, smiling, but she couldn't help thinking of her dresses growing up in New York, closed down the front with straight pins, the very conservative way still used years later.

And here she was, joking with her neighbor about something so far out of the most important aspect of her father's life, *ordnung*.

CHAPTER 18

MARGARET WAS NERVOUS. THERE WAS NO OTHER WAY TO DESCRIBE her feelings. Afraid of being disappointed, afraid of her own ability to carry an intelligent conversation, afraid of liking him more than he liked her. Her confidence seemed to have evaporated.

Her new dress was green, a hideous, nauseous green she simply couldn't wear, she told Rebecca, after agonizing over the sewing machine for almost an entire day. Mary got into the fray when the dress was draped over a chair, discarded, and Margaret stormed off into her room.

"You're not getting away with this, Marge," she said, holding up the dress to inspect the workmanship after she'd cooled down and made an appearance at the sewing machine room door.

"What?"

"We paid for this fabric, it's a beautiful shade of green, and you'll wear it," Mary said firmly.

"Sorry to disappoint you, Mom, but I don't think so. It's the color of vomit."

"Margaret, stop."

"I won't wear it. It's a market dress."

Always the mediator, Rebecca sat on the couch, looking from one to the other, her lips pursed in deep thought, watching her mother's frustration and Margaret's obstinate face, the usual battle of wills.

"We made a special trip all that way," she ground out.

"You didn't have to go. The horse needed exercise, so what are you wailing about?"

Rebecca got up, slipped the dress over her head, took a few steps with her arms held out, then twirled across the floor gracefully.

"It's pretty. Very different. The fabric falls in a great way. Like, it drapes perfectly."

Margaret frowned, her eyebrows drawn. "It's green, in a horrible way."

"It feels nice, though."

"I'm not wearing it, Rebecca."

And so the discussion came to a halt, the way it did so much of the time, with Margaret holding court and Mary disappearing to draw on reserves of patience, thinking how useless these arguments really were.

The new dress was hung with Margaret's everyday dresses, and she spent a long time picking and choosing from the layers of colorful dresses in her closet, Rebecca sitting on her bed, her knees drawn to her chin, her eyes bright with curiosity.

She had never seen her confident sister so completely unhinged.

"You know, Rebecca, I don't think it'll work out with Mike, so why am I worried about what color to wear?" she said finally, flopping back on the bed.

"Sweater. Did you forget you'll wear a sweater? Always black. That will tone down the vibrant green."

"I'm not wearing one. It'll ruin the whole effect."

"What's that even supposed to mean?"

Margaret pushed Rebecca to the side, putting her into a fit of laughing.

"Get off of me."

The cobalt blue was worn for a few minutes, then exchanged for a purple one, which gave way to a navy blue which was discarded in favor of a rust color, which Rebecca told her quietly made her look like an overripe neck pumpkin.

"Rebecca, you have to stop saying things like that. I mean it, he said eight o'clock, it's almost seven, and I haven't done my hair yet."

Below them in the kitchen, Mary was putting the chocolate chips in a double boiler, adding peanut butter, making the triple layer bars she would leave beside the coffeemaker if he came inside when he dropped her off. She was humming low under her breath, the way she did when she baked, but the song in her heart was actually more a prayer than a hymn. When Steve wandered into the kitchen, following his nose to the melted chocolate, she grabbed his arm when he went to the kitchen drawer for a spoon.

"Huh-uh, Steve. Date night."

"Come on, Mary," he begged.

"Wait till they're finished, okay? The boys will want some, too."

When Margaret appeared, she was wearing a navy blue dress without a sweater, which Mary promptly tried to remedy, but was waved off, with a "Not tonight, Mom."

Mary stirred the chocolate, peered past the woodwork as headlights wound their way up the drive, the decreasing light of evening obscuring most of her view. Upstairs, Rebecca knelt on Margaret's love seat in her room, parted the curtains, and stared. On the recliner in the living room, Steve craned his neck sideways, trying to see whether the young man would get out of his vehicle to open the door for his daughter.

He did. A good sign. He settled back in his chair and breathed deeply, anticipating the taste of the chocolate bars.

Margaret found Mike to be polite, his voice low, a little rough. She sat stiffly, trying to match his politeness.

"There's a volleyball game, you know. You want to go afterward?" he asked, in his low, gentle voice.

"After what?"

"Dinner. I'm sorry, I thought I told you we were having dinner together."

"Dinner?"

"You know, supper. I was trying to impress you by being classy."

Margaret laughed genuinely and began to relax.

Seated in a small booth with the yellow glow of a dim bulb above the table, Mary was delighted by the cozy ambiance of the Asian restaurant. He introduced her to new dishes, and she was surprised to find herself enjoying a variety of foods she would never have thought to try.

They talked easily then, and she found herself drawn to him in a whole new way, something much deeper than physical attraction. His quiet voice gave her a feeling of belonging, as if she'd been on a journey and had finally reached her destination.

At the end of their two-hour dinner, she laid down her fork, looked him straight in the eyes, and said she felt as if she'd come home, and wasn't that mysterious?

He was wiping his mouth with a napkin and was taken completely by surprise. He could only fold it slowly and lay it beside his plate, before steadying himself with a deep breath.

"What do you mean?" he began, then picked up his napkin and lifted it to his mouth, buying time.

"I just feel as if I came home. Like, you know what I mean. You're gone, then you come home where you can relax, be yourself, you know. Home. But you wouldn't believe the case of nerves I had earlier this evening. I bet I tried on ten dresses and none of them were good enough. I was a nervous wreck. I was so worried you wouldn't like me very much, but I think you do."

He shook his head, gave a small laugh, laid down the napkin for the third or fourth time before meeting her clear, open gaze. He tried to fathom the look in her eyes, which was completely open and guileless, which he found extremely attractive.

She was simply different from any girl he had ever met.

"Yes," he said. "I do like you."

"I thought so. Good, I'm so glad. Now, since we have that out of the way, we can really enjoy the rest of the evening. Oh, and I also need to know, what are your thoughts on dating practices? Like, do you believe in the new way?"

Clearly taken aback, he questioned her with his raised eyebrows. "You know, the going thing is distant courtship, which means you never touch each other, not even hold hands, and certainly never, ever enter the girl's bedroom."

He stared at her, tried to comprehend her words.

"You don't have to answer right away. I just like to be upfront with everything. Ivan, my ex-boyfriend, was, well, let's just say very hands on, and that made me feel guilty. I hate feeling guilty. It's not fun. So, what do you say?"

He cleared his throat, took a drink, wiped his mouth.

"Well, let's just say I'm neither one of those." He felt the heat rise in his face.

"You're blushing. That's so sweet. Okay, so we understand each other. Thank you for being honest."

He laughed. "There is no alternative, is there? With you, I mean. No alternative to being honest."

"No, probably not. I hate beating around the bush. It's so much easier to just talk about things."

He sat back, folded his arms across his chest, amusement written all over his face, his eyes bright with interest.

"You are just the way I heard you were. And I am intrigued. Do you know how tiresome it is, dating girls who are never truly themselves?"

"Maybe I'm not either, and you'll marry me only to find I'm a real shrew, grouchy and discontented, hard to get along with. Marriage is like that, you know. You can never really tell what you're getting into. You just go ahead and jump off a cliff, hope for a soft landing."

She put her hands to her chin, rested her face on them, leaned forward and presented him with her wonderful gaze.

"But I think honesty is a good foundation, don't you?"

He was so lost in her eyes, he could only nod, then grinned a helpless lopsided grin.

"You know my mom is bipolar. She has a mental disorder, and I was afraid I'd have the same thing. I did have some of the symptoms, but so far I think I'm okay. I hope."

"What were her symptoms?" he asked, genuinely concerned.

"She was crazy as a bat there for a while. Lots of ups and downs, I guess, panic attacks. She's on medication now. Her dad, back when she was a child in New York, was a genuine piece of work, I guess, or so she says. Like, if we'd get married, there's a whole bunch of aunts and uncles that dress in the old way. But they're pretty nice to us."

He nodded again, speechless.

"What is your mother like?" she asked quickly.

"She's the best. She is a widow, you know. She's very patient and kind, stays busy, and probably spoils me. But we only have each other, so that's why."

"Does she know about us?"

"Yes, she does. She wants to meet you."

"Let's go tonight."

"Already?"

"If you think she'd like that? We could go there instead of the volleyball game."

They left the restaurant but decided against meeting his mother at this late hour, and instead drove around a while before deciding to go home to her place, where they spent another few hours with coffee and what remained of the bars her mom had made. She listened more, then, while he talked of losing his father, the hard times financially for his mother. He told her they lived humbly, nothing like the house she lived in.

"You know," Margaret replied, "I really love small houses. Less to clean."

She had a mysterious gift, that of making him feel as if he was capable of great things. She said how nice it was he took care of his mother, and that she looked forward to meeting his siblings.

Reluctantly, well after midnight, he said it was time to go. He felt awkward and unsure when she followed him to the door, and told her goodnight too quickly and then left, sat in his truck, breathing as hard as if he'd run a marathon. He drove home slowly, processing the whole evening.

Margaret climbed the stairs to her room, wondering why he hadn't asked her out for the following weekend. She'd probably said too much, scared him away. And when she turned out the light, all her insecurities came to haunt her. She often felt adrift at night, like a falling star without end. She wondered if that was a symptom of being bipolar.

Oh, calm yourself now, she thought, bringing her restless mind into subjection.

Unable to sleep, she turned her thoughts to God. What did it mean to trust Him with her life, her future? She had heard people talk about God like He was a close friend. What would that feel like?

"God, I'd like to know you better. Help?"

It was a simple prayer, but honest and heartfelt.

THE FOLLOWING MORNING, she asked her mother what it meant to be born again, which caught Mary completely off guard. She took a moment to gather her thoughts, and then tried to explain. She told her a little about her own experience of accepting Jesus's gift of salvation.

When she'd finished speaking, Margaret shrugged, said she didn't really understand. Then she asked if her mom had ever felt like a falling star, a meteor shooting through space, especially at night. "Is that part of bipolar disorder?" Margaret asked, watching her mother's expression for any clues.

"I can't say that I've felt that exactly," Mary answered cautiously. "For me, it was periods of feeling really happy and productive followed by periods of deep depression. And panic attacks, where I felt really nauseous and like the world was spinning and I couldn't escape. But I'm glad you told me about it. If it keeps up, we could talk to a doctor. I sure wish I had taken your dad's advice and gone to a doctor much sooner than I did."

At work, Margaret struggled to keep her energy up. She thought of Mike's blue eyes, the long brown hair that was thick and wavy, so different from the short haircuts everyone sported these days. She liked his name, Mike, a good common name. She thought of him as she chopped tomatoes and refilled the pickle container. She relived their evening and decided she hadn't said more than she should have. She was just being herself, and if he didn't like that, it was better to know now.

After checking her phone far too often, she turned it off, deciding she didn't want to be the kind of girl who was desperate to hear from a guy. He'd contact her if he wanted to, and she'd see his message eventually.

She got home ravenous and exhausted. Mary was removing a pan of lasagna from the oven, the table set, the smell of cheese and tomato sauce making Margaret swoon.

The supper was delicious, as always, with lively conversation across the table. There was fresh chocolate cake with peanut butter frosting for dessert, and cornstarch pudding with peaches, her father's favorite.

Logan wanted to go to Washington Zoo. He'd heard about it from a boy at school whose whole family had gone on a charter bus. It was free, and why couldn't they go?

"I'd much rather go riding, like Margaret and I did," Rebecca announced. "We could take four horses, and Mom and Dat could just stay in the house. Right, Dat?"

"Sounds like fun," Steve said, raising his eyebrows at Mary.

"Sure. We could do that. Maybe Margaret would enjoy taking her new boyfriend."

"He's not my boyfriend. We had one date." Eyes on her plate, she drew the tip of her finger around the rim.

"Another one coming up?" Steve asked casually.

"That's more information than you need to know, Dat. I have never in my life seen a family quite as nosy as this one."

"You don't need a boyfriend to go to the zoo," Logan interjected.

"I don't want to go to the zoo, and I certainly don't want to go trail riding by the river, ever again. You all can just go without me."

She got up and stomped out of the room, leaving her family with the sure knowledge that there was no second date planned.

THE WEEKEND CAME and went with no message or call from Mike. She went to church, went to the youth gathering and hymn singing, but her mind was occupied with him. Why would he chose to ignore her after that first date? She tried to let him go and move on. She was determined not to waste time on blaming herself. It had only been one date.

And then one afternoon at market, she got a text message. Her heart raced as she scanned the words. His mother had had a stroke and was in the hospital. He wasn't sure if she would survive. He was sorry for not reaching out sooner.

Tears pricked her eyelids. She was relieved to have heard from him, and also felt the weight of his concern for his mother. She wrote back immediately, telling him how sorry she was about his mom and asking if there was anything she could do. She tried to be patient again, but for a few days there was no answer. And then a text saying she had passed. She felt a jolt when he asked if she'd come to the viewing. "I'd like you with me, if you're willing."

Once home, she threw her purse on the table and slid into a kitchen chair. "Mom, Mike's mother died. He wants me to sit beside him at the viewing. What am I going to do? I can't wear that old black suit. I guarantee I was thirteen years old when you made it."

"Mike? Was his mother ill? Why does he want you there? I thought you'd only had one date." Mary was flustered, trying to grasp what Margaret was saying.

"Mom, I want to go. But my black suit is, well, not wearable."

Suddenly brisk, in charge, Mary went to the fabric cabinet, taking the DeWalt battery lamp for better lighting. Muttering to herself, she extracted two pieces of black fabric as Margaret peered over her shoulder.

"Which one?" Mary offered.

"Plain fabric is the style, so this one. But Mom, it's tomorrow afternoon."

"I can do it. You have a new covering. You need to wear decent shoes. And now, Margaret, don't roll your hair all the way up to the top of your head. It's a time of death, so show some respect, and I mean it. Surely he has married siblings."

"Four."

Quickly, the dishes were washed, the table wiped clean, and Mary spread the black fabric and began to cut with the trusted patterns, creating a cape, apron, and dress, with Margaret hovering over her. Her mother clucked and lamented, saying it was such a pity she never got to meet the woman, the poor lonely widow, then wiped furtive tears.

A driver was set for three o'clock, with Margaret dressed in her new black suit, her hair smoothed and polished.

"You look nice, Marge, but beauty is as beauty does." Mary spoke in a gruff, strangled voice, her words coming out all wrong. She had meant to say she was proud of her daughter, but that would be vain.

The viewing was at his brother Paul's place. When she was dropped off, she hesitated, unsure of whether to go into the house or the large building that seemed to house some sort of woodworking business. The day was overcast, chilly, her skirt flapping around her ankles. She scanned the comings and goings of friends and neighbors, not one of them recognizable. She gathered they were heading toward the house and joined them. As she stepped inside, she heard his voice and caught sight of him hurrying toward her, his face so familiar, looking so right in his pale blue shirt with black vest and trousers.

"How are you, Margaret?"

"I'm okay. You're the one who should be asked."

"I'm alright. It's been a grueling week. My mom didn't have to suffer, which is so merciful. She would have despised being helpless. I'm glad you're here. Do you mind sitting with us? I'll introduce you."

She nodded, steeled herself, shook hands with four couples, Ben and Marianne, Eli and Rachel, John and Anna, Amos and Lynn, plus a handful of nieces and nephews. It was all a blur, a mixture of strange faces, greetings, sorrow, and searching looks.

She hoped she'd pass inspection.

And then she saw Ivan Stoltzfus sitting with his mother, both as neat and good-looking as a mother and her son could be. She couldn't avoid them, so she shook hands, averted her eyes, and moved on.

Mike took her to see his mother in her coffin, so pale and waxen, as is normal for the deceased, but Margaret thought she looked at peace, and so youthful-looking in spite of a lonely widowhood.

She watched Mike's face, which showed no emotion except that his mouth twitched at the corner. Aware of the feelings he was holding back, she found a tear sliding down her own cheek and wiped it away quickly, then walked out behind him as he led her out on the porch and across the yard. They sat on a concrete bench beneath a bare tree, and he told her the story of finding her helpless, calling 911, and the ensuing days at the hospital.

"I find it hard to believe, really. I'm going to miss her so much."

He stopped, leaned forward, his elbows on his knees. His shoulders strained at his jacket and Margaret put a hand on his back, a move that sprung naturally from the compassion she felt in her heart.

"I'm so sorry, Mike."

He straightened, leaned toward her, allowed her to see the sadness in his eyes, his eyelids heavy with lack of sleep.

"Thank you, Margaret. I'm so happy you're here."

Her hand had fallen away from his back when he sat up, so she didn't really know what to do with it, the way it was stuck at an awkward angle, so she brought it out from behind him and clenched the opposite hand. He reached over and freed it, opened her fingers, and laced them with his own. They sat silently, listening to the wind play with the remaining brown leaves above them.

"It means a lot to me, and I appreciate it."

She said nothing, content to let him hold her hand.

"Maybe this is a strange time, but I guess grief has a way of making you realize the important things in life. Life is just so fragile, you never know when it might end, and I . . . I just don't want to waste any more time. So, will you be my girlfriend? You know, the real thing. I'm not saying we'll definitely get married or anything, but I'm not interested in a casual relationship. What do you think?"

"Yes."

She looked into his eyes, found the liquid sadness mixed with a budding joy, and laid her head on his shoulder.

Later, she sat beside him on a folding chair in the living room of the large stone house, his siblings and their spouses beside them. There was a long line of folks dressed in black, their somber faces showing respect for the sorrowing. There were handshakes and an occasional sob accompanied by hugs and heartfelt murmuring.

So many relatives cast curious glances at Margaret, thinking, my oh, such a pretty girl for Mike. Finally, he had asked someone. She was introduced to cousins, aunts and uncles, English friends and neighbors.

They were called to eat supper in the basement where long tables were spread and where ladies from the church district cooked, served, washed dishes, and put food away as it arrived—casseroles, ground beef, cakes, desserts, and canned goods. Margaret felt comfortable by Mike's side and was glad to be introduced, to eat the food the church women had prepared.

As the evening wore on, she became sleepy, the room heating up as hundreds of people moved through, some of them sitting on benches to visit. After everyone finally left, the family knelt as a brother read from the German prayer book, after which they were free to go. Margaret offered to call a driver, but Mike said he was looking forward to taking her home, so they walked to the end of the drive where his truck was parked and moved out into traffic.

For the first few miles, they were both quiet, until Margaret told him what was on her mind. She was remembering the times in Ivan Stoltzfus's car, and how she did not want to repeat those scenes. He told her he respected her a lot for that and promised to keep from doing those things.

"Well, I already blew the 'hands off' thing clear out of the water," she said bluntly.

He laughed, genuinely enjoying her honesty. "That was just a little bit of extended sympathy."

"Exactly. It was like comforting my brother."

"Wasn't it more than that?"

She smiled in the half light of the truck cab as they pulled up to her house. "Well, maybe."

"Okay, now you get out before I ruin this 'distant courtship' thing entirely."

"Certainly, I will. Goodnight, sir."

They both smiled for a long time afterward, caught up in the freshness of a brand-new budding love.

SHE WAS THERE for the funeral, but seated with the cousins on a wooden bench behind the older relatives. There was no singing, only preaching and the announcement of his mother's name and age, before the entire congregation moved past her coffin to view her for the final time, after which the family was left alone to mourn the loss of their mother.

Margaret stood with a cluster of relatives, knowing Mike was in one of the first carriages in the funeral procession, then was seated at one of the extended tables to eat dinner. It was a traditional meal of mashed potatoes, cold sliced roast beef and cheese, pepper slaw, applesauce, and gravy. A labor of love, the church district worked together to provide comfort and sustenance, cleaning, putting everything in order before the family departed.

Margaret spoke only briefly with Mike before boarding a van going in her direction, with the promise of seeing him on the weekend, creating a song in her heart for the remainder of the week.

Now that he'd asked her to be his girlfriend, the anxious waiting to hear from him would be over. She found herself thinking about the little house with the wide front porch, and how long he would live there by himself.

She was too young, everything was still new, but it was something to dream about.

CHAPTER 19

By the end of November, he'd taken her to see the house, and by Christmas he'd presented her with the gift of silverware in a wooden chest, plus the pitcher and tumblers she would use on her wedding table, a sort of pre-engagement gift, both traditional, both absolutely stunning.

She was thrilled, of course, but Mary's mouth was clamped shut like a vise, her eyebrows lowered with concern. She told Steve he was moving way too fast, and what good could ever come of it?

Steve patiently laid his newspaper aside and gave her his full attention, his eyes on her troubled ones before he cleared his throat.

"Mary, she's eighteen. I'm sure they'll wait another year. Many of our young women are married at nineteen."

"But not Margaret. She's so not ready for a husband. She knows what she wants, and she'll go to all lengths to get it. She doesn't give up. That's no way to enter a marriage. How will she ever submit the way a wife must?"

Steve sighed, picked up his paper.

"They aren't married yet, Mary."

Mary went off to bed in a huff, tired of hearing Steve take her daughter's part, always. They hardly knew Mike, but she knew he drove a truck and hadn't joined church yet at, what was he? Twenty-four, five? With his mother gone, who would push him into being Amish? Oh, she could see it now. Margaret with her hair cut short, driving a car. *Dear Lord, keep your hand over her, please.*

She lay awake long after Steve came to bed, imagining her oldest daughter going English. Her legs ached, her back was itchy, her mind ran into overdrive. She tried calming herself with deep breathing, but it didn't work. And so, she unloaded her heart to her Father in Heaven.

The following morning, groggy from lack of sleep, she steeled herself to have the necessary talk with Margaret. She got the boys off to school, then yelled up the stairs for Rebecca and Margaret. Even on their days off, she never allowed anyone to sleep past eight.

They stumbled into the kitchen, disheveled and sleepy, poured coffee, and sprawled on kitchen chairs.

"I guarantee, Mother, you are the only one who has this eight o'clock rule in her head. Marianne sleeps till noon on her day off."

"Good for her," Mary quipped.

Margaret opened a cabinet door to check on the type of coffee she was drinking. "I thought so. Why do you insist on buying Maxwell House coffee?"

Mary turned her back, chose to leave the question unanswered.

A few minutes in the kitchen and everything out of Margaret's mouth was negative. That did not bode well for marriage. Did Mike have any idea what he was getting into?

"When I'm married, I'll drink Starbucks."

Rebecca sipped her coffee, blinked, and smiled sweetly in her sister's direction. "Hope he has money."

Mary buttered a slice of whole wheat toast, cut it in half, and sat at the table with her girls, listening to the talk about Mike's job, the cute little house, what Margaret would do with the small yard.

"Well, I hope you're not planning to get married this fall."

"What?" Margaret leaned forward, defensiveness all over her face. "Why not?"

"You will barely be nineteen."

"Mom, I'm not waiting for two more years. I already asked Mike if he's joining church and whether he thinks we'll be married in the fall.

It's not up to you. Amish parents don't boss their grown kids around like that."

"You asked him what?" Rebecca asked, her eyes wide with alarm.

"What?"

"You did *not* ask your boyfriend that."

"Of course I did. I have every right to know."

"Margaret, listen," said Mary. "You must listen to me. I know it seems heartless, but you really do need a few years to mature, to grow spiritually and emotionally. Marriage is hard at times. You know that joining the church means giving up driving, cell phones, music, and neither of you have much practice giving things up. That's going to be a real stretch for you both, and it would be wise to give yourself some time to make those adjustments before throwing marriage challenges into the mix."

She was trying to speak with a level, compassionate tone, but when Margaret rolled her eyes, Mary lost it.

She leaned back, slapped her palms on the table, and pierced Margaret with a no-nonsense look. "I mean it, young lady. There will be no wedding in the fall."

Margaret eyed her mother in disbelief, absorbing the fact that she meant what she said, and that likely Steve would back her up. An impenetrable wall descended, and hopes were dashed. She would have to wait two long years before they could marry and move into that cute little house with the man of her dreams. None of this was fair, not remotely right. Why did her parents have to be so ridiculously strict?

She tried tears, threats, and silence, but her mother remained steadfast, like a boulder of considerable size.

She pouted, spending hours alone in her room, until one evening after the boys were in bed, both parents asked her to come sit with them in the living room. Rebecca sensed the advancing of the war's front line and disappeared up the stairs.

Together, her parents laid down a solid line of resistance. Eighteen was simply too young. No matter how close she was to nineteen, she was only eighteen, and all her wails about Mike being in his mid-twenties did not change that fact.

Steve interjected, trying to keep the peace. "He hasn't actually asked you to marry him yet. Maybe this whole argument is premature?"

"But I have my silverware and crystal pitcher set," Margaret stated defiantly, her green eyes snapping.

"Which is a good thing, the way he must be thinking of marriage, but it still doesn't increase your age."

"We talked about marriage," she snapped, then sat back and crossed her arms, pouting.

But there was no giving in, nothing to do but leave the room, walk heavily up the stairs, and slam the door to her room, giving herself the satisfaction of letting them both know she was upset.

Mary wanted to go upstairs, to reason with her, but Steve shook his head, said she'd get over it, and Mary let it go.

ANOTHER WEEKEND, ANOTHER date, a visit to his sister Lynn, and Margaret fell into Mike's family with ease, charming them all with her beauty, her warm personality, and her straightforward way of speaking, with Mike glowing with approval beside her.

She told him her parents' position in the timing of their marriage and then there was no more talk of marriage, no more dreaming of the little house, the years stretching ahead like an endless ribbon of roadway. It seemed like an eternity to wait until she was almost twenty-one, and by then Mike would be going on thirty, which seemed ancient.

Christmas came and went, but no clock appeared, the Amish version of an engagement ring. It could be a wall clock, a clock for the mantel, or a gorgeous, costly grandfather's clock—it didn't matter which, as long as it solidified their engagement.

She told him she was thrilled with the chair and the large rug for her room, her face a conflict of emotion.

"Something's wrong, Margaret," he said softly. "What is it?"

"Oh, nothing. I love it. They're both beautiful. Thank you for your gift. I sure don't deserve a recliner like this. It's too much." Before she thought, she blurted out, "A grandfather's clock would go well with it."

He looked at her, found her clear eyes on him, with no embarrassment evident.

"But I didn't think . . ." He swallowed, shook his head.

"Oh, don't worry. I didn't mean it's your fault or anything. I told you I'm not allowed to get married for two more years. And that little house is just going to sit there and become moldy and filled with mice."

"What? But I live there," he reminded her.

"You're hardly ever there."

He thought about this, then looked into her green, guileless eyes and knew. He just knew. Yes, she was stubborn, and wanted her own way. She was immature, headstrong, and sometimes rebellious. But she had no guile. She was not conniving, or mean, would never hurt a flea, had never heard her speak a vile word about anyone, was always truthful to a fault. No doubt their union would be imperfect, weren't they always? Marriage was not a "lived happily ever after" deal, no matter how many young hearts were smitten with the stardust of romance. Real life would come after, when the checkbook wouldn't balance, when carpeting was stained and there was no money to replace it, when the first wave of nausea hit after the pregnancy test, when he sold his truck and started driving a horse and buggy and had to call a driver to go to town. He had seen enough of his siblings' and friends' marriages to know that marriage wasn't all easy.

All this ran through his head, and plenty more. He loved her. He loved her to distraction. He was not worthy of her, would never be. He would give his life for her, of this he was certain.

"In the spring, we'll both join the church," he said evenly.

"But do we have to?" she asked. "It won't be fun dating without the truck. I can't imagine getting around in a horse and buggy."

His only reply was a smile, his blue eyes crinkling.

WINTER SET IN with a serious blizzard in January, one that kept Mike at home on a Saturday night, and Margaret at home with her family. Mike tried to concentrate on the book he was reading, which he thought was rather lame considering all the reviews it had garnered. He stoked the fire, swept up the sawdust from the chunks of dry oak, then went to the front porch to see if there was any possibility of going to her house. The cold air hit him like a smack in the face, the whole world grayish white, the only sound a soft swishing of falling, blowing snow and the brittle rattling of brown oak leaves desperately clinging to bare branches.

Hushed and still.

He felt the presence of God, the way he sometimes did. As if he was only a dot, a pinhead, in the vast order of things, and yet in all of that, he felt cherished, as if he mattered to Someone.

He was awed by the sheer force of nature, the wonder created by the driven flakes of snow, the houses and barns huddled and still, the rectangles of yellow light from neighboring homes.

He breathed deeply and turned his face to the sky as he marveled at the storm. He wanted to be with Margaret, but this time of being alone was perhaps what he needed, to reflect on how far their relationship had come.

He still didn't know what kept him from showing her his love in the usual way, but so far, they had not touched except for an occasional clasping of hands or a discreet touch on the shoulder. It wasn't any of his convictions, or any shyness, or fear of upsetting her—it just didn't happen.

But they talked. They had endless dialogue about every single thing in both of their lives.

He turned back and let himself in, closed the door firmly behind him, and went to the woodstove to rub his hands and shiver.

He looked around, noticed the old-fashioned wainscoting, the chipped green paint, the linoleum worn thin, black spots where sparks from the woodstove had melted the finish. And he remembered the one thing he could never share with Margaret. He thought he'd stuffed it away, closed the latch and never bothered to open it again, but it was there. In his mind's eye, he saw his father acting strangely, slurring his words, sometimes singing odd snatches of country music, and his mother's tight face. He shook his head, squeezed his eyes shut to rid himself of past haunts, the ghosts of a closet alcoholic, the patience and long-suffering of his saintly mother. She had tried so hard to protect her children from an unhealthy situation. And yet, it had not been entirely possible. The smell of it would never go away, that alcohol-laced breath as he wheezed into the house, already too drunk to care if he seemed arrogant, or bold, roughhousing with Mike, his youngest son, teasing the girls.

It was buried, dead and gone. He'd forgiven his father for his weakness, the clutching grip the alcohol had on him. Who knew what his father's own childhood had been like?

So many winding paths, so many years of Amish ancestors, and so much kept quiet. Who was to know the failures, the hurts, the hidden abuse?

Growing up, he had never imagined being Amish for the rest of his life, but he'd lived the English lifestyle for more than a decade now and it still didn't feel fulfilling. Shortly before he'd met Margaret, he'd told his mother he'd likely do what she wanted of him and join the church. Yes, he wanted to honor his mother's memory by following through, but it was more than that now when he imagined his future with Margaret, he saw them surrounded by the community of their ancestors, riding in the buggy to church, gathering with his siblings' families for holidays. When he tried to picture them raising children as an English family, he couldn't. It just didn't feel right.

He laid the book aside, unable to concentrate, moments of his childhood playing through his mind. He had been painfully aware of their circumstances, unable to build a shop or garage large enough to accommodate church services, so they would have to ask the neighbors to host them, every time. He'd hear the deacon announce in church, "Services will be held at Jacob Miller's for Abner Kings," an announcement that their kindly neighbor's benevolence would enable them to provide food and take their turn at hosting church services.

He'd load up the express wagon with pies and pickles, red beets and coffee, knowing there would be no lunchmeat, no delicious thin sliced ham or sweet bologna to go with the bread and cup cheese. He'd suffer through the dinner table, the boys searching for bologna or ham, snickering the word "poor." He had come to detest Amish church services, and eventually refused to go.

No, Margaret need not hear about this. Thank God he'd turned out stable, normal, a human being without being fettered to the past.

He blinked, listened to the wind as it hurled bits of frozen snow against the north window, hitting it with a sliding, pinging sound. He looked at the plaster walls, the cracks in the open stairway, the rounded arches for doorways, and thought it amazing Margaret wanted to live here at all.

He would speak to her parents, try to get them to agree to a wedding in November.

And he did just that, the following month, before Valentine's Day, when he planned on proposing, having the clock delivered to her house.

He surprised Margaret by asking to come in that Saturday night, surprised her even more when he shrugged out of his coat, and sat at the kitchen table as if he planned to stay. Margaret asked if he wanted coffee, and wasn't he worried about getting to Rueben's party on time?

He shook his head, which was when she noticed the pinched look around his mouth.

"Ask your parents to join us for a moment," he said quietly.

"Sure."

She beckoned to them from the kitchen, and both appeared, a bit disheveled from being nestled on recliners, eyelids heavy from reading sleepily. There was a muted yell from the basement, where Logan and Christopher were playing shuffleboard.

"Yessir. Good evening, Mike."

"Hello, Mike."

"Yes, good evening to both of you, too."

"Think it'll start to thaw here after a bit? I think my chaps have about had it with being off work for so long."

"Yeah, it's been a real winter."

There was an awkward space of silence, then Mike took a deep breath and began.

"I hear from Margaret you won't approve of our marriage in the fall, which is perfectly understandable."

Before he could continue, Mary snapped, "That's correct."

"I was hoping I could persuade you to see it another way."

Steve smiled slowly, broadly, which helped tremendously.

"Fire away," he said, inserting two fingers into his coffee cup handle, lifting it to his mouth, his eyes smiling over top of it.

"I'm not exactly a young man . . ."

"But Margaret is very young," Mary threw in.

He started over, and simply stated outright that he would like to have their consent to be married in the fall.

Margaret went pale and a hand went to her mouth.

"I know she's young, but she's also more mature than some."

Margaret's eyes shone.

"I know, Margaret, how unusual this proposal is, but I thought it best to have all of us together, and you and I will be alone later."

"She's too young, too stubborn." Mary would not yield.

"Thanks, Mom, for your vote of confidence," Margaret said quietly. Then Mike told them frankly all he saw in Margaret, and that no marriage was ever perfect, he was well aware of it. He said he wanted a clear yes or no, but was afraid he'd go ahead with it in November either way.

Margaret simply sat like a stone, her green eyes wide with wonder, filled with hope of her dream fulfilled so much sooner than expected.

Steve looked at Mary, who refused to meet his eyes, and a silence as thick as pudding settled over the room.

"Well," Steve said finally. "I guess it's up to Mom here."

"It's not up to me," Mary said hoarsely. "We said no, and we meant it. Still do. You're too young, Margaret."

"Almost nineteen, Mom."

"Exactly."

Margaret's lips trembled. "I grew up at the edge of the river the day I almost died. God saved my life and since then, things have been different. I'm ready to join the church."

At this, Mary burst into tears, left her chair, and went out of the room. Steve looked at Margaret and understood her. He breathed a soft sigh.

"Let's wait, give your mother a few minutes."

When Mary returned, her eyes were red-rimmed, her nose discolored, but her face was composed. Margaret saw the wrinkles lining her eyes, the soft sagging of her jowls, the lines on her forehead, and realized the aging taking place.

"Mom, I don't want to hurt your feelings, but . . . think back to when you wanted to get married. Imagine being told you weren't allowed."

"Obviously, you don't know how many times that happened."

"I'm sorry. Of course, I forgot. You told me all that."

"But, I don't know, Mike. Margaret. Perhaps . . ."

Her voice trailed off.

"Maybe you're a bit like your father, Mary," Steve said gently.

"I know," she said, nodding. "Time after time. I find myself letting ultra-conservative views crowd out common sense. And I have this awful need to control those around me. Maybe I don't even think you are too young. Maybe I just need to control how fast I'm going to lose you to Mike."

"It's not that you think I'm not fit for marriage?" Margaret asked, her voice quavering.

"*Ach* Margaret, of course you're fit. It's just that you're so willful, so much the way I used to be. But if this is what you want, and if you feel it's what God wants, then I suppose we can be ready to have a wedding in November."

"I haven't asked her yet," Mike said softly, and reached for her hand.

Steve and Mary looked at each other, remembering their own engagement.

Did time, or age, or circumstances matter when two people were in love? Of course they'd have trials, rough times, arguments, even moments of regret, but God willing, that would be balanced with the good times. When you were young and so in love, the future was brilliant.

THEY WENT UPSTAIRS for the first time and sat together on the small sofa. He complimented her tasteful room, then began to talk in that low tone, the one she loved to hear.

"Margaret, I know my house isn't much, and I don't have a lot of money to hire someone to renovate, but I'm hoping that together we can make it a home you'll love."

For once in her life, Margaret didn't have anything to say.

Slowly, he got off the sofa, down on one knee, and looked at her face until she met his eyes, those clear, pure green eyes he loved so much, and this is what he said.

"I know, Margaret, I'm not worthy of you, and never will be, but will you be my wife?"

And she said very soft and low, as sincere as she knew how to be, "Yes, Mike. I will."

His eyes filled with tears, and hers caught the emotion in his, before he got to his feet and reached down to draw her up and into his arms for the first time. He drew back and asked if she thought it okay to kiss her this one time. Just once, he said.

She nodded, and he touched her chin so lightly it was like a benediction. He stroked her cheek very gently, then lowered his mouth to hers. The room spun, righted itself, and still he could not set her free.

When they broke apart, both of their eyes were shining with the love awaiting them, the soft, beautiful bud of promise for a lifetime together.

"Oh, and I forgot. Here is your engagement gift." He drew a photograph from his shirt pocket, the picture of a grandfather's clock, in oak wood, with a golden pendulum, and weights.

"Oh, it's gorgeous!"

"You mean it?"

"Do I ever say things I don't mean?"

He laughed, with real joy. "No, you don't. That's the best thing about you. The one quality that sets you apart from everyone else."

CHAPTER 20

THEY WERE MARRIED ON THE TWENTY-FOURTH OF NOVEMBER, AND true to their word, had never kissed after the proposal but saved themselves for marriage, which proved to be a wholesome blessing in their lives.

Together, they worked on renovating the old house, restoring walls, removing two of them, taking up carpeting, restoring pine floors, often with Steve and Mary's help.

Life was everything they had anticipated, and more, as time moved into early summer. A garden brought them a newfound sense of accomplishment, coupled with digging around the house and planting flowers and shrubs.

Margaret reveled in all of it, even the dust and dirt created by the remodel, cheerfully sweeping after Mike and his sawing and pounding.

She told him shyly, so uncharacteristic of her, that they were going to be parents, and their happiness knew no bounds. It was in the heat of July that she endured a painful miscarriage and had to be rushed to Lancaster General by ambulance late at night. Bills piled up. Margaret grieved.

Alarmed one night when she awoke and his side of the bed was empty, she sat up, patted the mattress beside her, and felt her heart beat thick and heavy.

"Mike? Mike?"

There was no answer. The fan in the window kept up its quiet hum, but there was no other sound. She swung her legs to the side of the bed and padded softly through the house, calling his name, but he was nowhere to be found.

Taking down the yellow DeWalt battery lamp, she pushed open the screen door and started across the porch, casting the light into corners, then down the steps and across the yard.

She called again and again.

Where could he be? He would never leave the house without telling her.

He was such a good guy, the best husband, the light of her life, even now, in the midst of her sadness. Her grieving had been deep and hard, even as it was now, but she'd clung to Mike and his sturdy strength.

The odor of hay and sweet molasses horse feed, manure, and the scent of horses wafted through the open door of the barn. She called his name once, listened, then turned to leave, when she heard her name being called out, thickly, as if under water.

"Mike?"

"Over here."

In the corner, where bales of hay were delivered, she found him, his face swollen and blotchy, the smell of alcohol and sour vomit like a nightmare she could not escape by waking up.

"Mike!"

It was not a soft, gentle, loving sound, it was his name, called out in a terrible voice, brittle with anger.

"Get up!"

"I don't . . ."

"Get up!"

She drew back a bare foot and kicked him, hard.

"Have mercy, Mar'."

"I'm leaving. Get yourself cleaned up and get back to the house."

Her fury propelled her, and she had no more sleep that night, lying awake listening to him stumble about the house, breathing heavily, flopping on the couch.

In the morning, her fury sustained her, and when he appeared freshly showered, his face still bloated, shamefaced and apologetic, she launched straight into the prepared lecture. "What were you thinking?"

His mumbled reply about the baby and the bills was brushed aside.

"You think I didn't suffer? You think I'm not suffering now?" She had never felt so angry.

He acknowledged this, but said none of this was easy, and he didn't know how they would ever swing all these bills and keep remodeling the house. "And the baby . . ." he said, his voice drifting.

"Well, guess what, Mike? Life happens. We're married now, and with marriage comes responsibility, and disappointment, and stuff you have no control over. So grow up and get on with it."

"Marge, I can't believe this is you, talking to me like this."

"Well, believe it, because it's real. I have no time for someone using alcohol to escape their problems. It's cowardly, it's stupid, and there will be no tolerance from me."

"Forgive me. I don't know what came over me."

"Well, figure it out."

He could not believe this stony-faced, powerful woman to be his Margaret. *Dear God,* he thought, *what have I done?* A great black claw reached from some unknown depth and grasped his heart, followed by a terrible fear. Fear of becoming his father, fear of being unable to be the courageous man she had married.

"Margaret?"

A cool raising of her eyebrows, a cold stare from those green eyes.

"Hmm?"

"I never told you."

"What?"

"I didn't think it mattered, but maybe I was wrong. My father was a closet alcoholic till he died. I remember the times he drank, the smell, how he was strange and slow and scary at times. I thought the memories were gone, but I have to talk about it."

"Go ahead. Talk. But it's not your father's fault you chose to suck on that bottle of whatever it was."

"Please, Margaret. Hear me out."

"Mike, you are not your dad, and you cannot blame him for your bad decisions."

"But why not? It's in my DNA, in my lineage."

"What is?"

"The tendency toward addiction, using alcohol to get through tough times. Like bills and . . . the miscarriage, and our house being all torn apart."

"Hard things happen to everyone, Mike. What did that bishop, Jonas Stoltzfus, say on our wedding day? Trials will come, but together, with God, the triangle complete, we will be strong.

"Well, let me assure you, we will not be strong with alcohol in the mix. You can talk about your father till the sun goes down tonight, but at the end of the day, you're responsible for your own self. If you need help, then go talk to a counselor who knows more than I do. Now get out the door and go to work."

He did.

When he got home that night, he planned on meeting the old, loving Margaret, the one he fell in love with, but was bitterly disappointed to find her resolve as solid as a rock. She simply was not putting up with this, and he found his spirits sinking.

"Supper ready?" he trilled hopefully.

"Not tonight. Get it yourself."

He stood staring at her in disbelief. His sweet wife? How could she?

"But, darling, I . . ."

"Don't 'darling' me."

"But this is not the way a Christian woman should be. You know—"
He was cut off rapidly.

"And a Christian man should be allowed to drink himself silly?"

"Well, no."

"Well, I guess not. And if he does, he has it coming."

He dodged the rapid fire of her words, could not believe how soon the bliss of their newlywed stage had come to this, this awful precipice into which he had fallen. Surely he hadn't been able to help himself, as overwhelmed as he'd been.

"But, Margaret, listen. Please believe me when I say likely in my DNA there's that weakness, the trauma I endured as a child."

"If you want to carry that around like a pacifier, go right ahead, but don't expect me to feel sorry for you. If you care one bit about me or our marriage, you will own up to your stupid actions and decide right now it's never going to happen again. That's it. If you sulk around thinking you're destined to be an alcoholic like your dad, then that's exactly what you'll become."

So he moved in careful circles, trying to avoid his wife's frostiness, until he gave in and went to talk to a professional counselor once a week for six months. He came away from his final session with renewed hope, the strength to face tomorrow, and a deep gratitude to Margaret, who refused to show pity or enable him to be a self-absorbed coward.

Slowly, their world righted itself and old tenderness was restored. A visit from the young deacon, Jake Stoltzfus, brought the offer of alms to pay the hospital bill and the ride in the ambulance. Steve offered a substantial sum for the remodeling project, to be paid back without interest.

THE AIR WAS alive with the sound of Christmas carols as they drove through town.

"Margaret," Mike said suddenly, "do you think any young couple is fully prepared for marriage?"

"No way. They'd never get married."

"You sound a bit cynical."

"It's the truth. Remember? That's what you admired in me."

"Ouch, though. It hurts sometimes."

"It might have to."

"Do you love me less these days?"

She didn't answer for some time, the horse plodding steadily on the hard macadam through the cold winter night.

Finally she said, "Not less. No, definitely not that. Just different. Steady. More real. We've weathered a storm, now we know we need to stay strong, level, together, no matter what. It's better, in a way."

As they turned in their road, a few teams passed on the opposite side. They both lifted hands, waving.

Beneath the branches of the huge maple trees, the little house was as cute as ever, with fresh white siding and dark windows, a wide front door in polished oak, flanked on either side with boxwoods in concrete urns, a gift from Mrs. Roberts. So many useful, beautiful things had been given to them on their wedding day, which allowed her to be grateful a whole year later.

The black porch rockers were stored in the garage, the patio furniture and grill alongside, and now the winter winds had started to blow in earnest, and they truly loved the cozy house beneath the stately trees.

On the inside, walls had been removed to allow larger living space, and new kitchen cabinets in clean white installed, and how Margaret enjoyed the decorating, buying cheap bargain antiques and cleaning them up. Mike loved to accompany her on their excursions, sometimes taking her parents and the boys.

They built a new building, a sturdy shop to host church services, and Mike told her how they always took their turn hosting services at the neighbors, too poor to put up a shop, and how he hated those Sundays.

"That couldn't have been fun," Margaret said kindly. "And your mother must have been a saint." She paused. "I'm not a saint."

"But still, Marge, think about it. Which is best? Years ago, it was all about total submission. Absolute obedience to the husband's will. He was lord over his household."

"Yes."

"I mean, come on. Someone should have stood up to him. Made him get help. But back in the day, these things weren't known."

WHEN A BABY boy was born two years later, they named him Matthew. Matthew Ames. He was a husky baby with a thick shock of red hair and his father's blue eyes, and Margaret cried and cried with a severe case of the "baby blues," as Mary called it. Extremely nervous and undone by this screaming little mite, it was Mike who was courageous and bundled her off to the doctor for antidepressants. He walked the floor at night with the howling little chap that never fazed him.

And Margaret found a whole new respect for her husband, admitted her own weakness, truthful as ever, and let him deal with the bouts of discomfort in his tiny son.

"That's it. No more babies. I can't take it," she moaned one night from her pile of pillows on the recliner, trying yet again to nurse him to sleep.

"Soaked with milk, my back hurts, my head hurts, my neck is stiff as a board. I wasn't made to have babies," she groaned.

"Why don't we try formula?" Mike suggested, suppressing a yawn from the couch, where he sprawled in a pile of blankets.

"You have to be kidding me. I can hear the collective gasp all over Lancaster County. You don't give up breastfeeding."

"We do if that's what you need."

That evening he came home with a can of Similac. He sterilized bottles, water, mixed the powdered formula and introduced it, patiently working all evening, with Margaret retreating to the bedroom intermittently to cry and beseech God to help her. The antidepressants weren't working.

Mike got the baby boy to settle down about ten o'clock, and they both crept to bed and fell asleep. On a Saturday, there was no jangling alarm, so when a gray light shone through the Roman shades in the bedroom, Margaret was terribly confused, then instantly alarmed. Her baby! He had likely died an awful crib death.

She rushed to his crib to find him sleeping soundly, as he'd done all night.

They stood together, his arm around her shoulders, her head on his chest, smiling as they watched their child sleep.

"It's so amazing," she whispered.

"Sleeping or having a new baby?" he asked, bending to kiss the top of her head.

"I meant, it's amazing how a good night's sleep changes your perspective."

"And formula."

She nodded, slipped an arm about his waist, and squeezed.

"Thank you, Mike. You're a wonderful father. I could not have come through these first months without you."

"I know I'm good, Marge. I already know that," he teased.

"The only way I'll ever have another one is your promise to help the way you do now."

"You have my solemn vow."

AND HE DID. When Matthew was being potty-trained, she felt the familiar nausea return. Running after an active toddler while nauseated all day, every day, was miserable. With Rebecca's wedding coming up, it was enough to send her over the edge, she told Mike.

She always looked forward to his homecoming, when he would take Matt outside with the horses, leaving her to flop on the couch, close her eyes, and do nothing but let the waves of nausea roll over her.

Eventually, after a few months, the nausea lessened, and she was able to enjoy life more fully again.

They purchased a dog for Matt, a poodle mix of some sort, born with a hernia, so he was inexpensive. The puppy proved to be the best thing that ever happened to Matt, keeping him occupied for hours at a time.

And when Makayla was born, Margaret greeted her brown-haired, green-eyed daughter with courage and a newfound determination to do better, though the newborn phase was almost as overwhelming as it had been with Matt, except that the breastfeeding went more smoothly.

Mike was protective of her, truly caring, and for this she loved him, with a deeper love than ever before. On the weekends, he got up in the morning to care for the little ones while she slept in as long as she could.

They created a circle of friends within the church, a group of young parents with which to share joys and sorrows, times of conflict, marital struggles, troubles in the church, exchanging views and values with one another.

Mike became a song leader in church and went to practice singings a few nights a month, and so became incorporated into the community, keeping tradition alive. Twice a year at communion, they gave alms, remembering their first need being met so graciously, and the blessing it had proved to be.

When Mike became tired of barely making ends meet, he decided to start his own mason crew, learning the skills from Steve. They went to the bank, procured a loan, and took a few jobs Steve offered him, the whole thing turning Margaret into a nervous wreck.

Her mother, growing in faith as she grew in years, assured her Mike knew exactly what he was doing, and business would pick up in time.

"But in the meantime, there's no money," Margaret wailed.

"There will be, have faith. Faith in God to see you through. You can help by being frugal yourself. You can buy cheap stuff at the B.B. store in Quarryville. You don't need new dresses, or sneakers for the children. Make do for a few years."

"Did you ever have to live like that?"

"Of course. Most young couples do."

"Well, you surely don't now."

Mary watched Mike and Margaret grow together, and learned to keep her peace when she felt her daughter's voice too demanding, too strident, when Mike would be ordered to get his daughter, or take Matt to the bathroom, or bring her a lemonade.

But years roll on, she reasoned with patience, and time brings changes. There is no longer the same submission, the woman being much more a partner, her voice being heard. Even now, more so than when she was married, and her mother before her.

Ah, but there was a marked change from her own weary, beaten-down mother, her days marked by hard physical labor, a voice subdued, and finally, rest only in death. No, she would never wish her mother's life on any of her daughters or granddaughters.

She watched little Makayla in her swing, just as cute as a button, and prayed for her soul. Who knew what would become of her with the world and all it had to offer? Would she stay plain? Would she want the old values? Or would there be a time when she'd see her drive a car up to the porch, climb out as an English girl, dressed in jeans and a T-shirt, glad her grandmother loved her anyway?

Life is what it is, she mused. *Lord, give me strength to face the changes as they come.*

Margaret came over to sit beside her, and they pushed gently on the porch swing.

"You have tears in your eyes," Margaret said quietly.

"Do I? *Ach.*"

"What were you thinking?"

"Oh, stuff. Just stuff. About Makayla."

"What about her?"

"Oh, it's just that the years roll by so quickly and so many changes happen around us. How many generations will stay with the Amish? How many will abandon the faith?"

"Now you're spinning your famous yarns. Overthinking. Driving yourself batty."

"I know. But so many of our young people see no value in the way we dress, in driving a horse and buggy."

"True, Mom, absolutely. But rest assured, Mike and I will do our best. But who knows? Time brings changes, and God is the judge of every soul."

Mary took Margaret's hand and gazed off across the lawn, as stars gathered in the corner of her eyes.

"I know you will. And did I ever tell you how proud I am of who you've become? I appreciate you, Margaret."

A lone tear hung on Margaret's eyelashes, quivered, and dropped, leaving a trail down her cheek, completing the circle of love between a mother and her daughter for many years to come. As if Makayla knew she was a part of this circle, she waved her arms and legs, her mouth widening in a happy smile, creating mirrored smiles in her mother and grandmother.

THE END

About the Author

Linda Byler was raised in an Amish family and is an active member of the Amish church today. Growing up, Linda loved to read and write. In fact, she still does. Linda is well known within the Amish community as a columnist for a weekly Amish newspaper. She writes all her novels by hand in notebooks.

Linda is the author of several series of novels, all set among the Amish communities of North America: Lizzie Searches for Love, Sadie's Montana, Lancaster Burning, Hester's Hunt for Home, the Dakota Series, The Long Road Home, New Directions, Stepping Stones, and the Buggy Spoke Series for younger readers. Linda has also written several Christmas romances set among the Amish: *Mary's Christmas Goodbye*, *The Christmas Visitor*, *The Little Amish Matchmaker*, *Becky Meets Her Match*, *A Dog for Christmas*, *A Horse for Elsie*, *The More the Merrier*, *A Christmas Engagement*, and *Love Conquers All*. Linda has coauthored *Lizzie's Amish Cookbook: Favorite Recipes from Three Generations of Amish Cooks!*, *Amish Christmas Cookbook*, and *Amish Soups & Casseroles*.

OTHER BOOKS BY
LINDA BYLER

LIZZIE SEARCHES FOR LOVE SERIES

BOOK ONE

BOOK TWO

BOOK THREE

TRILOGY

COOKBOOK

SADIE'S MONTANA SERIES

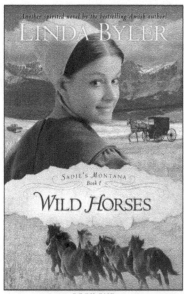

BOOK ONE

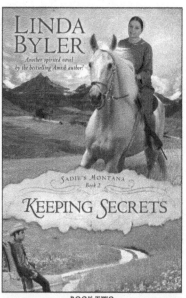

BOOK TWO

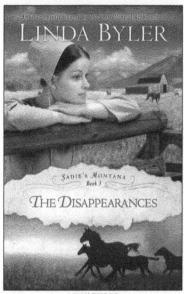

BOOK THREE

TRILOGY

LANCASTER BURNING SERIES

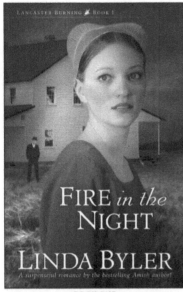

BOOK ONE

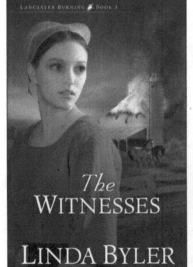

BOOK THREE

TRILOGY

HESTER'S HUNT FOR HOME SERIES

BOOK ONE

Which Way Home?

BOOK TWO

BOOK THREE

TRILOGY

The Dakota Series

BOOK ONE

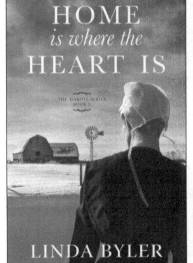

BOOK TWO

BOOK THREE

TRILOGY

LONG ROAD HOME SERIES

BOOK ONE

BOOK TWO

BOOK THREE

New Directions Series

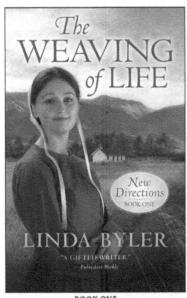

BOOK ONE

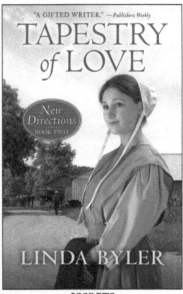

BOOK TWO

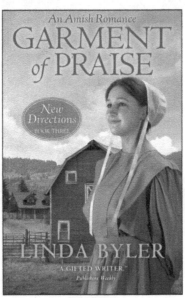

BOOK THREE

STEPPING STONES SERIES

BOOK ONE

BOOK TWO

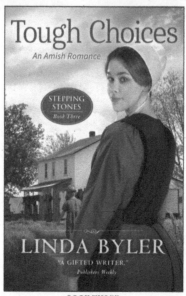

BOOK THREE

BUGGY SPOKE SERIES FOR YOUNG READERS

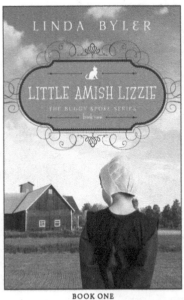

BOOK ONE

BOOK TWO

BOOK THREE

Christmas Novellas

THE CHRISTMAS VISITOR

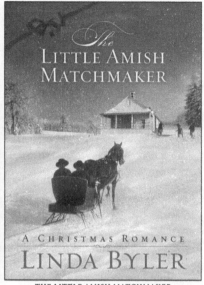

THE LITTLE AMISH MATCHMAKER

MARY'S CHRISTMAS GOODBYE

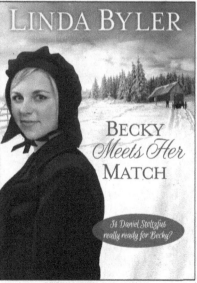

BECKY MEETS HER MATCH

A DOG FOR CHRISTMAS

THE MORE THE MERRIER

A HORSE FOR ELSIE

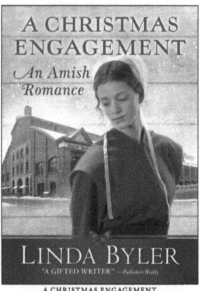

A CHRISTMAS ENGAGEMENT

CHRISTMAS EVERY DAY

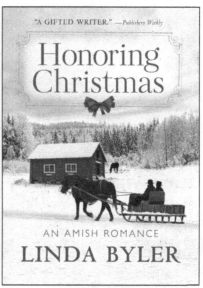

HONORING CHRISTMAS

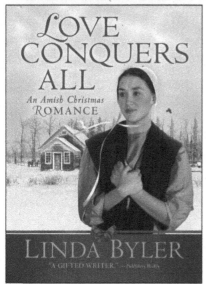

LOVE CONQUERS ALL

CHRISTMAS COLLECTIONS

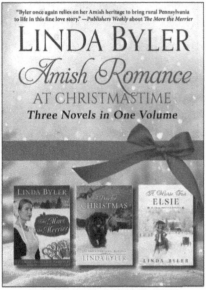

AMISH CHRISTMAS ROMANCE COLLECTION

AMISH ROMANCE AT CHRISTMASTIME

STANDALONE NOVELS

THE HEALING

A SECOND CHANCE

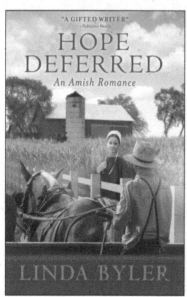

HOPE DEFERRED

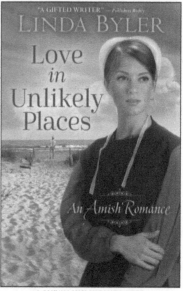

LOVE IN UNLIKELY PLACES